ANTIQUES SLAY BELLES

Also by Barbara Allan

Trash 'n' Treasures mysteries

ANTIQUES ROADKILL
ANTIQUES MAUL
ANTIQUES FLEE MARKET
ANTIQUES BIZARRE
ANTIQUES KNOCK-OFF
ANTIQUES DISPOSAL
ANTIQUES CHOP
ANTIQUES CON
ANTIQUES SLAY RIDE (e-book)
ANTIQUES FRUITCAKE (e-book)
ANTIQUES SWAP
ANTIQUES ST. NICKED (e-book)
ANTIQUES FATE
ANTIQUES FRAME
ANTIQUES WANTED
ANTIQUES HO-HO-HOMICIDES
ANTIQUES RAVIN'
ANTIQUES FIRE SALE
ANTIQUES CARRY ON *
ANTIQUES LIQUIDATION *
ANTIQUES FOE *

* *available from Severn House*

ANTIQUES SLAY BELLES

Barbara Allan

SEVERN
HOUSE

First world edition published in Great Britain and the USA in 2024
by Severn House, an imprint of Canongate Books Ltd,
14 High Street, Edinburgh EH1 1TE.

severnhouse.com

British Library Cataloguing-in-Publication Data
A CIP catalogue record for this title is available from the British Library.

ISBN-13: 978-1-4483-0964-1 (cased)
ISBN-13: 978-1-4483-0965-8 (e-book)

All Severn House titles are printed on acid-free paper.

Typeset by Palimpsest Book Production Ltd.,
Falkirk, Stirlingshire, Scotland.
Printed and bound in Great Britain by
TJ Books, Padstow, Cornwall.

Praise for the Trash 'n' Treasures mysteries

"A mystery that has it all: zany characters, antiquing tips, and recipes to brighten to your day"
Kirkus Reviews on *Antiques Foe*

"Framed by small-town life in Iowa, with interesting details on antiques, this fun cozy includes recipes and tips"
Booklist on *Antiques Foe*

"Allan delivers the cozy goods"
Publishers Weekly on *Antiques Liquidation*

"For readers of cozy mysteries who enjoy small-town living, humor with a side of murder, and cute canine companions"
Library Journal on *Antiques Liquidation*

"Amusing mystery chockablock with antiques lore"
Kirkus Reviews on *Antiques Liquidation*

"Allan consistently entertains"
Publishers Weekly on *Antiques Carry On*

"Delightfully quirky . . . For those fond of feel-good cozies, Allan delivers"
Publishers Weekly on *Antiques Fire Sale*

About the author

Barbara Allan is the joint pseudonym of husband-and-wife mystery writers, Barbara and Max Allan Collins. Barbara is an acclaimed short-story writer, and Max is a multi-award-winning *New York Times* bestselling novelist and Mystery Writers of America Grand Master. Their previous collaborations have included one son, several short story collections, and twenty novels. They live in Muscatine, Iowa – their Serenity-esque hometown – in a house filled with trash and treasures.

www.barbaraallan.com

For our grandson
SAM
in hopes he'll read (and enjoy)
this one day

Brandy's quote:

And in despair I bowed my head;
'There is no peace on earth,' I said;
'For hate is strong,
And mocks the song
Of peace on earth, good-will to men!'

'Christmas Bells'
Henry Wadsworth Longfellow

Mother's quote:

Childhood's joy-land.
Mystic merry Toyland.
Once you pass its borders,
You can ne'er return again

'Toyland'
Victor Herbert, Glen MacDonough

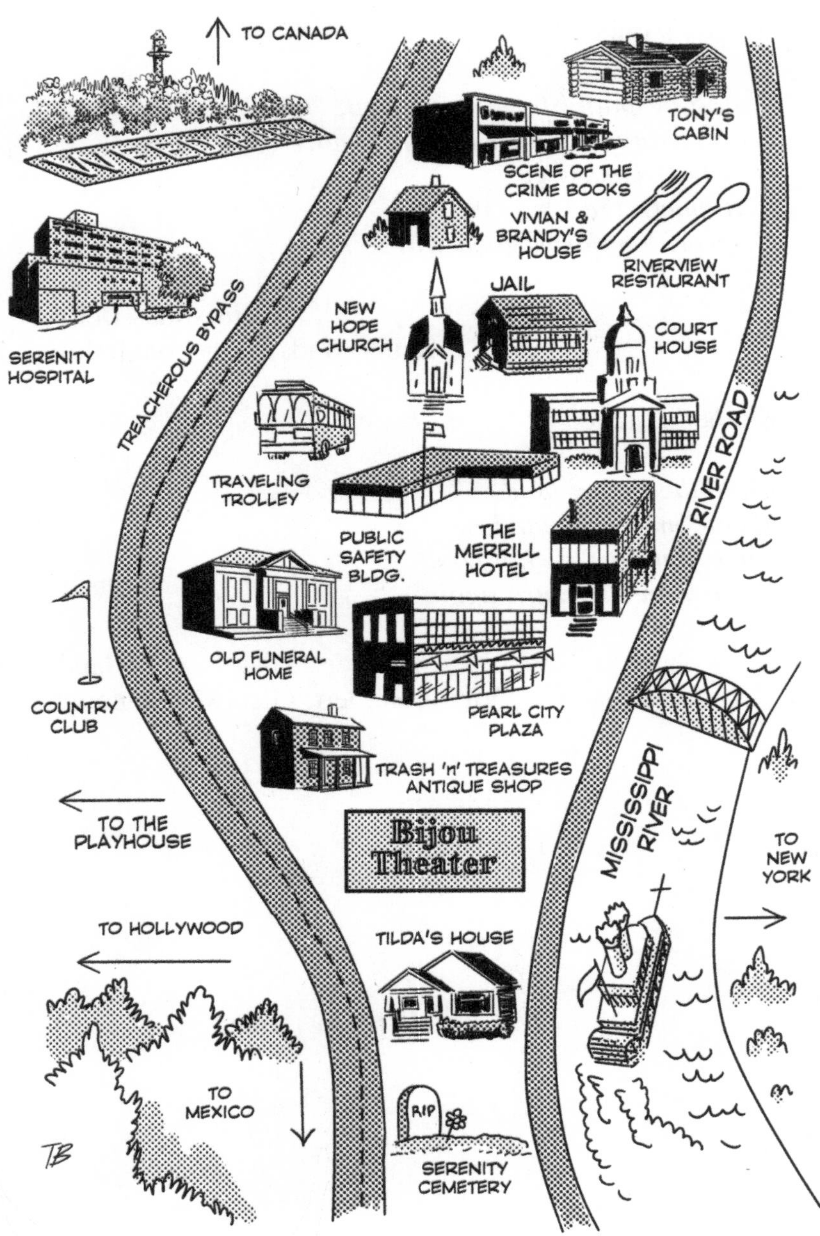

TO CANADA
TONY'S CABIN
SCENE OF THE CRIME BOOKS
VIVIAN & BRANDY'S HOUSE
RIVERVIEW RESTAURANT
SERENITY HOSPITAL
TREACHEROUS BYPASS
NEW HOPE CHURCH
JAIL
COURT HOUSE
RIVER ROAD
TRAVELING TROLLEY
PUBLIC SAFETY BLDG.
THE MERRILL HOTEL
OLD FUNERAL HOME
COUNTRY CLUB
PEARL CITY PLAZA
TRASH 'n' TREASURES ANTIQUE SHOP
TO THE PLAYHOUSE
Bijou Theater
MISSISSIPPI RIVER
TO NEW YORK
TO HOLLYWOOD
TILDA'S HOUSE
TO MEXICO
RIP
SERENITY CEMETERY
TB

ONE
Jingle Bell Shock

Five days before Christmas . . .

Christmas is a magical time in Serenity, our small Midwestern town nestled on the banks of the Mississippi River, Main Street strung with thousands of twinkling white lights, shop doorways framed by evergreen boughs.

Some decades ago, after an entire block of Victorian-era buildings adjacent to Main was demolished to make way for, you guessed it, a parking lot, irate citizens formed The Serenity Historical Preservation Society to prevent further destruction of its heritage. The organization spearheaded, successfully, the election of a slate of like-minded local politicians, and soon the city council seized the opportunity to increase tourism, adding faux old-fashioned lampposts to street corners, putting in cobblestone sidewalks, and installing wrought-iron benches where shoppers could take in a scenic vista enjoyed by such past residents as Samuel (Mark Twain) Clemens and Ellis Parker (*Pigs Is Pigs*) Butler.

At this time of year, store windows displayed a delightful assortment of holiday decorations, from nostalgic toys to the latest fad. Merchants vied to outdo each other in preparation of the stroll, where a Christmas red ledger could morph into End-of-the-Year black.

When the annual stroll first began, shop owners showcased their own wares as gift ideas; but after competition for the best display increased, proprietors began borrowing from personal collections. Such treasures included the dozens of open-mouthed Byers' Choice caroling dolls taking up residence at this pharmacy's glassed-in entryway, or the Lionel trains at that law-firm's front window, an elaborate, multilevel display, an engine with its cars and caboose zipping around and around, turning grown men into small boys.

This year, however, my favorite exhibit was at the Bijou, a one-screen art-house theater, whose display in the outside ticket booth showcased the puppets of Santa and Rudolph created for the 1964 Rankin/Bass stop-motion feature 'Rudolph the Red-Nosed Reindeer,' which over the decades became embedded in the psyche of millions of children everywhere. (Mother insisted on playing a DVD copy of the feature every Christmas, as if I were still five years old.)

But this snowy Saturday morning, Mother and I were recovering from the holiday stroll the night before – scads of shoppers doing not much actual shopping – hard at work in our antiques shop, Trash 'n' Treasures. We were preparing a presentation of holiday antiques at the country club's annual Christmas luncheon a few hours from now.

Who is Mother, exactly? Vivian Borne, age unknown but suspected mid-seventies, Danish stock, widowed, frequent local thespian, and sometime amateur sleuth. For three memorable months, she had also been the Serenity County sheriff before being forced to resign to avoid being thrown out of office for taking (what she calls) 'some minor liberties with the law.' In her defense, she did catch a killer during her brief reign.

Who am I, you ask? Sometimes I wonder myself, but my driver's license (Mother's was yanked after taking a cornfield shortcut) says Brandy Borne, thirty-three. I am a prodigal daughter, blonde by choice, blue-eyed by birth, who headed to her small-town home post-divorce (my unintentional doing, after a lapse of judgement with an old boyfriend at my ten-year class reunion caused an already crumbling marriage to topple).

The third member of our little troop was Sushi, my brown-and-white shih tzu, arguably the smartest animal in the house, and the only thing I brought home with me from the wreckage of my wedlock, believing it best my son Jake (then twelve, now fourteen) remain in Chicago with his well-off father (now remarried), though my offspring would come to Serenity to visit during holidays and the summer break.

Something else you should know about the Serenity Trio is that we were all medicated: Mother, Prolixin to manage bipolar disorder; me, Prozac to combat migraines (and Mother); and Sushi, insulin to curb diabetes.

Our shop was actually an entire if small house located at the end of Main, where the commercial area stopped and the residential section known as West Hill began its steady climb upward. Each home gained in stature and wealth as West Hill rose, till the top of the bluff where city founders, captains of industries in lumber, pearl button manufacturing, and banking had built their mansions. Like my marriage, some of these were crumbling; unlike my marriage, none had yet toppled.

As for the old two-story white clapboard house housing our shop, it was but a lowly shirttail relative to Serenity's rich past and present.

With the remaining proceeds from our short-lived reality cable show, on which we determined the value of previously unidentified antiques, Mother and I had bought the house that had been provided as a set by our now-cancelled show's producers. This we did for a song (any tune will do) due to a long-ago unsolved axe murder in the parlor, that of an elderly woman, causing subsequent owners to claim the property was haunted.

After moving in our stock, strange occurrences began: an antique rocker in the parlor would inexplicably start rocking, and upstairs doors would suddenly slam shut. Despite Mother obtaining a blessing on the property by Father O'Brien (we weren't Catholic but she took the movie *The Exorcist* as gospel), the haunting persisted . . . until we solved the long-ago, very cold case. After that, the rocker remained stationary, and the doors still. I like to think the woman finally found peace.

Anyway, this morning we the living were all a little short on peace. The stroll last night had gone well enough, although more free candy canes were given out than merchandise sold. And on this morning after, Mother was miffed because of where we were positioned in the country club's program; she was convinced that, since weren't members, we were being discriminated against. Sushi was sullen because she was staying at the shop, told sharply to 'Stay!' in her little bed as we wrapped up in warm coats. As for me, I was upset due to a misunderstanding I'd recently had with my fiancé, Tony Cassato, Serenity's chief of police, which had put our planned wedding on hold. Let's put it this way: I hoped he was *still* my fiancé.

(*Note to Severn House editor Olivia from Vivian:* Dear, don't you think *I* should take over the prose? Despite her Prozac popping, Brandy is bringing everybody down to her Sad Sack level! Crumbling mansions, axe murders, a wedding postponed – after all, *Ellery Queen Mystery Magazine* called our engaging books, 'One of the funniest cozy series going'; but so far I don't see anything the least bit amusing.)

(*Note to Vivian from Olivia:* Brandy is doing just fine, if suffering a touch of holiday malaise. Let's press on, shall we?)

(*Note to Olivia from Vivian:* Very well . . . if you think we can spare readers who might well return this book to the shelf at Barnes & Noble or BAM!, after sampling the first few pages while shopping. Or perhaps tossing it in box destined for Half-Price Books in exchange for what? Fifteen cents? . . . Hello?)

Mother, her chin high, was saying, 'Our presentation should come *before* the Secret Santa exchange, not after.'

Her large out-of-fashion glasses magnified those big light-blue eyes disconcertingly.

I shrugged. 'That's where the social director wanted us on the program. Not our call.'

She and I were facing each other toward the front of the shop, where I had been packing the antiques into boxes.

'All that rustling of wrapping paper,' she said, 'while I'm giving my performance. They might as well be booing me!'

'Stick around. You might get your wish.'

Her eyes flared behind the big lenses, below which her nostrils flared, too. 'If they do, I'll cut the presentation short! I really will!'

Which wouldn't bother me. After all, I was merely the magician's assistant, waiting for the right moment to hand Madam Houdini a top hat with a rabbit in it.

I said, 'Well, I'm surprised we were even invited after what you did last summer.'

Mother had 'borrowed' a golf cart at the club to chase a murderer around the grounds, tearing up a newly sodded course. Of course, in her time as an amateur sleuth, she had taken far worse liberties.

A regal eyebrow arched. 'I caught the killer, didn't I?'

She had indeed. And I must admit it had been amusing to watch, though I'd realized at the time (even if she didn't) that if we ever tried to join the club, we'd likely be black-balled. We were lucky just to be the invited free entertainment!

But Mother was on full-out pouting mode. Without asking me, she had rented costumes – Santa and an elf (you can guess which role I'd been cast in) – that she'd insisted we wear for the holiday stroll last night. Now she wanted to carry on this merry masquerade at the luncheon, but I managed to squelch this continuation of my Yuletide humiliation by pointing out there would already be someone there dressed as 'the man with all the toys,' passing out the Secret Santa gifts to the club women.

Mother harrumphed. 'I don't play second fiddle to *anyone*.'

'Is that right, Nero?'

Actually, she didn't fiddle at all, her instrument of choice being an old battered cornet on which she, from time to time, blatted out 'Boogie-woogie Bugle Boy (of Company B).' If somehow her musical leanings came up in conversation, and an intrigued party encouraged her, I would do my best to advise them otherwise.

'These sweaters will do just fine,' I said, mine being red and hers being green, 'and show those country club gals in their ugly Ex-muss sweaters how a couple of classy ladies celebrate a Holy day.'

The club was having an Ugly Christmas Sweater contest.

'We need to concentrate on sales,' I said, 'not show biz. Last night we gave out a lot of free candy and sold not a single pricey item. This crowd has money and we can use some of it.'

'So much for the Christmas spirit,' Mother grumbled.

'Get with the program and turn on your seasonal charm.'

Taping the last box shut, I said, 'I'll put these in the van and then we can go.'

I'd uttered two boo-boos in that sentence, as far as Sushi was concerned: the words 'car', and 'go.' And since I'd made it clear to her she'd be staying behind, this added insult to injury.

The little furball, who'd been standing nearby waiting for a reprieve, trotted behind the check-out counter to her leopard-print bed, where she curled up with her back to me.

If we were at home, I'd be worried about repercussions as Sushi had a vengeful side. These are some of my things that had been destroyed by her sharp little teeth: a vintage Juicy Couture rhinestone belt from when Pam and Gela owned the company; a pair of Kate Spade cork flats that said 'Pop' and 'Fizz' (just try to find those shoes anywhere, even on eBay – size 8); and most recently, a Japanese manga I'd been halfway through, *JoJo's Bizarre Adventure Part 5 Golden Wind*, book 7, shredding the exciting cliffhanger.

But Sushi had always been good about leaving the shop's merchandise alone, perhaps because nothing smelled of me, or intuiting (yes, she's that smart) that it wouldn't have the desired effect. I could, however, expect a tiny cigar somewhere when we returned in a few hours – right out in the open, making its statement.

While I loaded the boxes into the back of our van, which we kept parked behind the shop, Mother brought in our flying flags from their poles on the front porch (we each had one with our initials to indicate which of us was in residence) leaving Sushi's flag to warn burglars that a watchdog was present, even though she could be bribed with the smallest of biscuits.

Mother locked up the shop, joined me in the van, and I drove away amid snow flurries, heading to what we hoped would be a well-received and lucrative engagement.

The modern country club was located across what I referred to as the Treacherous By-pass, because the four-lane highway had few stop lights and no middle area for a driver to hole up after a misjudged attempted crossing. But after the mayor's wife – on her way from the club to a white sale at Ingram's

Department Store – got hit by a U-Haul, a traffic light suddenly appeared, as if by magic.

Soon, I was pulling into the club's driveway, then sliding our lowly second-hand Chevy Equinox van into the single remaining handicapped space a few yards from the portico, in a parking lot filled with BMWs, Audis, Cadillacs and Lincolns.

From the outside, the modern tan brick structure might be mistaken for a millionaire's mansion, its snow-dusted lawn beautifully landscaped, with drive-up front portico and, off to one side, an Olympic-size outdoor pool (covered for the season).

Right now Mother was hanging a disabled tag on the rear-view mirror, the placard an item she'd kept after her bunion surgery last year. She doesn't feel guilty about much, but she did affect a fake limp as she exited the van. Just in case we were noticed. (She did legitimately have trouble with gait post-surgery, and perhaps it was more her ham-acting gene kicking in than guilt.)

Double etched-glass doors took us into a vestibule where a pair of facing faux Louis XV chairs stood guard, and we passed through another set of similar doors into a greeting area whose focal point was a round cherry-wood table on which was displayed a large oriental vase filled with fresh flowers, greenery and sprigs of holly.

To the right, a carpeted hallway of geometric design led to an enclosed bar with a bored tuxedo-vested bartender, with the banquet room farther down, faint sounds of clattering dishes and chattering mouths signaling lunch was well in progress. We had not been invited to partake, which was another reason Mother was generally irritated today.

To our left was a corridor lined with various offices, and beyond that a staircase to the lower level and its more casual eating venue.

An officious-looking man in a conservative dark suit exited the first office, having spotted us through a window on to the greeting area. He'd looked at us with distaste, like someone who disliked zoos viewing animals through a windowed cage. He was a few inches taller than my five foot six, around forty, slender, with dark thinning hair and a pencil-thin mustache. His plastic name-tag read: Jared Eggler, social director.

Later Mother commented that the next time she staged the musical version of *Miracle on 34th Street*, he'd make the perfect person to want Kris Kringle institutionalized.

'Oh, *there* you are,' he said, as if we were late, which we weren't – we hadn't been invited to partake in the meal, remember. 'I thought you were going to set up *beforehand*.' His forehead was beaded with sweat.

If that *had* been the arrangement, Mother would have ignored it, not about to cool her heels waiting to go on. Not watching other people eat, she wouldn't.

She gave him a smile generally reserved for an anxious child. 'Well, we're here now, dear, but your presence is welcome. We can use someone to help bring the boxes in from our vehicle.'

With that La Diva Borne moved away and into the nearby cloakroom – I'd left my coat in the SUV to avoid the unavoidable search for it later among the hordes of others.

'Just find me a cart,' I told Jared, who was watching Mother hang up her coat; he wore an expression of puzzled indignation.

Five minutes later, I was wheeling the rest of the boxes down the hallway when Mother stepped out of the bar, nibbling on an orange slice.

I stopped. 'Anything in there for me?' My stomach was growling. Why hadn't we eaten something at the shop before leaving? Why hadn't the thoughtless rich thought to feed the humble gentry?

She handed me a cocktail napkin containing a cherry, strawberry, and a piece of pineapple, then took over the cart of boxes while I started popping the goodies into my mouth – cherry stem included – I was that hungry.

'That was thoughtful, Mother.'

'Well, I try.'

Not very often, she didn't.

As the cart entered the banquet room with me pushing it, Mother sneezed loudly. Mouths stopped talking, heads turned, all eyes focused our way. Which was her intention. The Grand Dame of entrances had arrived. She can fake a sneeze convincingly when she wants to.

In this instance, over the top was good.

Then, as quickly as the chatter and clatter halted, it resumed, as if a drum soloist had stopped to grab a breath and then returned to his bashing.

The large room spanned the length of the back of the building, large windows facing a picturesque golf course whose gently rolling hills surrounded by groves of pines and oaks might have been the subject of a Grant Wood painting. In the distance, a few children were taking advantage of the increasing snow, leaving snail trails with their sleds down the slopes. Soon they would be chased away by the groundskeeper, not out of meanness but due to the possibility of a lawsuit should someone get injured.

In one corner stood a large Christmas tree (fake) and I happened to know that beneath the skirt was a base on casters so it could be rolled out of storage every year, without dismantling the tree and lights, changing only the decorations.

(*Note to Olivia from Vivian:* Do you see my qualms? Snail trails and lawsuits? Christmas trees on casters? Brandy seems rather depressed over her break-up with Chief Cassato.)

(*Note to Vivian from Olivia:* Yes, I quite agree. Perhaps you should take over the narrative in Chapter Two.)

(*Note to Olivia from Vivian:* Problem solved!)

Adjacent to the faux tree was a long rectangular table covered with colorfully wrapped gifts of all shapes and sizes. It faced an audience of colorfully wrapped women of all shapes and sizes, seated around the dozen or so large round white-linen-clothed tables.

Never in my life have I seen such a hideous array of Christmas sweaters. While there were a few dissenters in the crowd (I just looked up dissenters on my computer dictionary to make sure it was the word I wanted, and it said, 'One who dissents,' thank you so much), most of these women went willingly to be sacrificed on the altar of fashion frivolity and questionable taste.

Back in the 1980s there had been some unquestionably

tasteful high-end designer holiday sweaters . . . but then every clothing manufacturer jumped on the bandwagon, eventually leading to the ugly-on-purpose Christmas sweater craze, which soon turned into a new tradition.

Next to a small podium was another rectangular table designated for our use in arranging the antiques we were here to discuss.

Among our array were: a vintage ceramic Christmas tree with a light in the base and colorful little plastic bulbs inserted into slots on the green pottery boughs.

A 1950s red-and-white Tom and Jerry punch bowl depicting a horse and carriage and six matching mugs.

A string of NOMA bubble-lights from the 1940s in its original box, nearly mint.

A rare ten-inch rubber-faced Santa doll made by Ruston Company.

An assortment of old hand-blown glass tree ornaments from Germany.

And several retired Department 56 Dickens' Village porcelain buildings, including 221B Baker Street with little figures of Sherlock and Watson, which Mother agreed to sell only because she already had that set. (She'd also bought the Hansom Cab accessory, but Sherlock didn't fit inside as I found out when breaking off his head. And no I hadn't switched him with the mint one we were selling, because Mother's bad eyes never noticed my super-glue fix.)

As we began setting up, waitresses were clearing away main course plates and passing out dessert, a dark mound of cake dripping with white icing and topped with a sprig of holly.

Thinking the confection might be a rich chocolate cake, my mouth began watering until Niagara fell as I heard a woman exclaim, 'Oooh, plum pudding, my favorite!'

I was not a fan of *any* dessert that contained slimy raisins (no such thing as un-slimy raisins), so Mother would occasionally make a plum pudding where I got to select the dried fruit used in the recipe.

Easy Plum Pudding

½ cup of butter (softened)
½ cup dark brown sugar
1 tbsp. molasses
2 eggs (room temperature)
1½ cups variety of dried fruits and nuts
1 tsp. ground spices mix (nutmeg, cardamom, cloves, ginger)
1 tsp. cinnamon powder
½ tsp. vanilla extract
zest of 1 orange
2 cups breadcrumbs (loosely packed)
2 tbsp. flour

Cream together the butter and brown sugar. Add the molasses and eggs, mixing well. Stir in the ground spices mix, cinnamon, vanilla, and orange zest. Add the breadcrumbs and flour, combining well, and finally fold in the dried fruit. The batter will be heavy and sticky.

Transfer the mixture into a liberally buttered pudding mold (we use one that has a capacity of 700 ml or holds approximately three cups), pressing down and smoothing the top. Cover with aluminum foil, allowing room for the top to expand. Place mold inside a roasting pan containing two inches of water, cover, and pop in the oven, preheated to 350 degrees Fahrenheit.

Bake for one hour or until a toothpick stuck in the middle of the mold comes out clean. (If you prefer to use a proper steamer on the stovetop, and have all the time in the world, be my guest . . . but you'll have to look up how to do that on the Internet.)

When the pudding is finished baking, let it cool completely before transferring to a Christmas plate (our holiday dishes are 'Christmastime' by Nikko, now discontinued,

> so we're always on the look-out to replace chipped ones). Top the pudding with a sprinkling of powdered sugar, or drip with thin icing. (One year we ignited it using hot brandy, and the tablecloth caught on fire. For weeks Mother called me Not So Hot Brandy.) Serves four to six people depending whether or not they like plum pudding. Store in a cool place for up to a week, or longer in the fridge, or even longer in the freezer.
>
> Substitutions for raisins: dried cranberries, chopped dates, apricots, or prunes.

The table directly in front of us was comprised of four members of Mother's Red-Hatted League mystery book club: Alice Hetzler, retired math teacher; Cora Van Camp, former court secretary; Frannie Phillips, part-time nurse; and Norma Crumley, socialite and world-class gossip. The other woman at the table, seated next to Norma, was Ellen Fridley, a widow Mother thought might make a nice addition to their small reading group, and was being given a try-out.

Norma, having recently stepped down from the position of country club social director (replaced by Jared Eggler), stood from her chair, and swept up to the podium. Thrice divorced, a Elizabeth Taylor wannabe (the older version), she was fond of make-up, beauty salons, jewelry, couture fashion, and tittle-tattle. And did I mention make-up?

Norma tapped the podium's microphone to ascertain whether it had been switched on, and it had, so she said, '*Ladies, ladies . . . may I have your attention!*'

The room quieted a little.

She tried again. '*Your full attention, please.*'

Mouths stopped moving, whether gabbing or chewing.

'*I have it on good authority,*' Norma continued in a louder voice, '*that Santa Claus has arrived safely in Serenity, has stabled his reindeer at Strawberry Farms, and is here among us now.*'

Many smiles and a smattering of applause.

As Norma gestured to the ballroom doorway, a red-costumed, white-fake-bearded figure stepped through.

'Cary Hudson,' Mother whispered in my ear.

I'd already pegged him as the thirty-something owner of the Bijou Theater, our revival movie house. Cary was perhaps too young to play Jolly Old St Nick, requiring a white wig and beard to fit the part; but his round face and ruddy cheeks and no need for padding made the bachelor a fine choice.

Mother went on, still sotto voce. 'His mother named her cute baby boy after her favorite movie star, Cary Grant, thinking "Rock" might be too . . . on the nose.' Vivian Borne was full of such trivialities. Among other things.

Behind Cary trooped a half-dozen waitresses wearing green elf caps, their roles having switched from kitchen servitude to workshop helpers. I had a thought I'd never had before: *Gee, I'm glad I didn't show up in my elf costume.*

The process of distributing the many Secret Santa gifts went surprisingly smoothly and efficiently, Cary calling out the name of each recipient, who in turn raised her hand, the waitresses delivering the packages.

Only once did I hear Mother sigh in consternation.

But she'd been right about the crinkling of wrapping paper, some ladies indecisive about what to do with it, others wadding the paper up into balls, creating even more noise.

It was at this moment Mother made a breach of programming etiquette. (Not the first time, just the first time *this* time.)

Norma had been standing on the other side of the podium, waiting to introduce us, when Mother decided to take matters literally into her own hands. She picked up a leather strap of large sleigh bells, which had been slotted as the first item of our show-and-tell, and shook them vigorously, startling everyone, forcing Norma to take the podium, but not before giving Mother a reproachful look.

'*Ladies*,' Norma said into the microphone, '*we will now have an informative program about holiday antiques by Serenity's very own Vivian and Brandy Borne of the Trash 'n' Treasures shop.*'

I could see (as could Mother) that Norma was holding a typed sheet containing far more words than that paltry introduction – *what about all the crimes we'd solved, and the books we'd written?* – but the woman stepped away from the podium, rejoining the other Red-Hatted League members clearly miffed by Mother's jumping the gun.

Mother appeared nonplussed by the slight. Perhaps she had realized that adding coin to our shop's coffers was more important than mere accolades. Actually, no 'perhaps' about it . . .

In a voice Mother reserved for the theater (rather high-hat with a faint British tinge) she began, sans microphone, 'Sleigh bells, which have become associated with Christmas, were first added to horses in the early nineteenth century as a symbol of wealth and status.'

Norma raised a hand.

'Please, dear, save your questions until the conclusion of our presentation,' Mother said, then continued: 'The bells also gave a warning to pedestrians of an approaching sleigh or carriage, much like the later bicycle bell.'

Again, Mother's friend tried to get her attention, this time waving both hands.

'Norma,' Mother rebuked rather sharply, 'there *will* be a question-and-answer period, after.' She again continued: 'In Pagan times, it was thought that jingling bells could ward off bad luck, diseases, and evil spirits.'

I grabbed Mother's arm. 'She doesn't want to ask a question! Norma's in trouble!'

Confirming my words, Norma flopped forward, face first, right smack into her plum pudding.

Brandy's Trash 'n' Treasures Tip

When deciding what holiday decorations to collect, purchase items based upon how they make you *feel*. Do nutcrackers, teddy bears, angels, or snow globes bring back warm childhood memories? Great. But! Keep in mind you are creating childhood memories for others, which is why Mother's creepy Christmas Annalee dolls that gave little Brandy nightmares are gathering dust in the attic.

TWO

It's Beginning to Look a Lot Like Murder

Vivian taking the reins of the narrative sleigh, and it can't be too soon following Brandy's Debbie Downer of a first chapter. Apologies for my darling daughter.

Firstly . . . (and isn't it irritating when people employ improper usage when continuing with 'second,' instead of the correct 'secondly'?) (what is the English language coming to?) I must contest Brandy's assertion that I was forced to resign as sheriff or else be impeached. The truth of the matter is that the city council offered me early retirement along with a severance package. And, since I was quite busy with local theatrical productions, plus running our antiques business, solving the occasional murder, and co-writing the true-crime books chronicling each case, well, it seemed the most prudent thing to do.

Secondly, to prevent Brandy from bouncing back in the next chapter with her rebuttal to my rebuttal (yawn!), I will concede that three months *is* a somewhat brief term to serve before retiring from public office, and confirm that my severance package *was* a bit paltry, consisting of a gently used Vespa scooter (which I am legally allowed to operate despite my revoked driver's license), plus an honorary sheriff's badge that doesn't really carry any authority, a fact of which the general populace is unaware, meaning when I flash my tin before their wide peepers, I usually receive answers to any questions I might have. Not always honest ones, but answers.

Now, while I have your attention, I will share an update on my on-going campaign to prevent people (mostly newscasters) from usurping the honorable word 'actor' to describe individuals who behave with questionable motives. Frankly, this effort is not going terribly well. So far I have recently heard, from various news sources, 'bad actors,' 'crisis actors,' 'bad-faith actors,' and 'fringe actors.' Recently, two more terms have been added: 'political actors,' and 'lone-wolf actors.' (My favorite of the actors who portrayed the Lone Wolf on screen, by the way, is Louis Hayward. That's what Google is for, kiddies!)

I cannot, however, complain about these new additions as there are indeed political actors. Mega movie star Clint Eastwood (the Good, not the Bad nor the Ugly!) was once the mayor of Carmel-by-the-Sea, while human action figure Arnold Schwarzenegger was for a time the governor of California. Shirley Temple – after diving from the deck of the Good Ship *Lollipop* into the stormy sea of adulthood – became a respected US ambassador to both Ghana and Czechoslovakia. And, of course, most notably, Ronald Reagan became the fortieth president of the United States (although some of his movies were, for instance *Bedtime for Bonzo*, impeachable offenses, though granted Ronnie was admittedly not yet in office and, anyway, the chimpanzee stole the show).

Where was I? Ah, yes – political actors.

Personally, my favorite showbiz politico is the late Jack Kelly, one-time mayor of Huntington Beach (located just south of Los Angeles), who essayed the role of Bart Maverick – the brother of Bret Maverick, who future movie-star James Garner limned in *Maverick*, the classic black-and-white TV western. Riverboat ring your bell! (If you watch only one episode of that 1950s–'60s series, make it 'Shady Deal at Sunny Acres,' which features many of the show's recurring characters in a yarn that's a humdinger of a stinger.)

And yet the 'lone-wolf actor' label remains a head-scratcher. It may not be a reference to the *Lone Wolf* film and early TV series. But it could just as easily be a reference to Lon Chaney Jr., the master of disguise, who played the ultimate werewolf! Or perhaps Michael Landon in the cult favorite *I Was a Teenage Werewolf*, made prior to him riding into the Wild West of *Bonanza* and *Little House on the Prairie*.

Of course, the label *could* be interpreted another way, as in Leonardo DiCaprio taking the title role in *The Wolf of Wall Street*. Are we talking about a predatory Lothario, or someone who defrauds wealthy investors, or both? Hard to say!

(*Note to Vivian from Olivia:* While I had, reluctantly, agreed to allow you an opportunity at the beginning of your chapters to refute anything Brandy writes in order to keep the bickering at bay, perhaps we should return to the woman with her face in the pudding. This 'political actor' discussion really is a needlessly discursive detour from the mystery at hand.)

(*Note to Olivia from Vivian:* A matter of opinion, but I will – in the spirit of hands across the waters – comply.)

(*Note to Vivian from Olivia:* Please do so.)

(*Note to Olivia from Vivian:* Righto!)

Now, back to our story.

Retired nurse and fellow Red-Hatted League member Frannie Phillips, seated on one side of Norma, was first to respond to the socialite's sudden collapse.

Frannie – slender, with short wiry gray hair and pointy chin (think actress Margaret Hamilton, albeit not in her Wicked Witch of the West *Wizard of Oz* regalia and unflattering green make-up) – gently leaned Norma back in the chair, checked for any throat obstruction, then lowered the unfortunate woman on to the floor, and began expertly administering chest compressions.

I had by this time positioned myself next to Frannie, cell phone in hand, having already called for the paramedics. After an endless minute with no response, the former nurse tried mouth-to-mouth resuscitation, but quickly pulled back.

My friend looked up at me, her frightened eyes adding emphasis to the sudden halting of resuscitation: was this something more than a heart attack? Had Frannie detected a whiff of almonds or garlic, telltale signs of cyanide or arsenic?

I bent to whisper. 'Poison?'

'. . . Possibly.'

'Is she . . .?' I asked.

'She's dead.'

'. . . *you've killed her*,' I breathed quietly.

'What?' Alarm widened Frannie's eyes.

'Not you, dear,' I said soothingly. 'It's what the Winkie Guard said of the Witch in *The Wizard of Oz*.'

You'd think a Margaret Hamilton lookalike would know that.

'That's very poor taste, Vivian,' Frannie said, frowning as she rose.

'It was.' I straightened as well. 'An unfortunate blurt. My apologies.'

Frannie's diagnosis of Norma's fatal medical condition had been loud enough to be overheard by those women at tables in close proximity, garnering gasps and murmurs that spread outward like the ripples from a rock dropped into a previously placid pond.

Brandy hadn't moved from behind our table of antiques, and as I returned to the podium I whispered, 'Call your friend the chief. Inform him of what you witnessed, and tell him I said that Norma appears to have been poisoned.'

'You've come to that conclusion awfully quickly, haven't you?'

I raised a forefinger. 'The telltale bouquet of bitter almonds, dear.'

Her expression of concern turned to distress. She nodded, then moved away, digging her cell phone from a pocket and heading toward the hallway for privacy.

I assumed the podium and its microphone. '*Ladies, please remain seated. The paramedics should arrive soon, and they undoubtedly will have some questions to ask.*'

Mentioning the impending arrival of police as well only heightened the group's anxiety – and speculation – as some women's fingers were already texting, spreading the news of Norma's death.

To buy time, and stop the jungle drums:

(*Note to Vivian from Olivia:* Is it proper in today's world to use 'jungle drums' even in a metaphorical sense? Admittedly various indigenous people on different continents did at one time use drums to communicate. But one does have to be so very cautious these days. I would suggest replacing the term with something less potentially offensive.)

(*Note to Olivia from Vivian:* Understood. I will avoid 'smoke signals' for obvious reasons, as well as 'Chinese whispers,' due to the already strained relationship between China and the US over those spy balloons . . . so I guess I'll reluctantly substitute the *trite*-and-true 'grapevine,' unless we are concerned that we might irk vineyard owners worldwide.)

(*Note to Vivian from Olivia:* Why do I now suspect you are being facetious?)

(*Note to Olivia from Vivian: Moi*? Perish the thought. But speaking of perishing, don't you think it's peculiar that people aren't the least bit offended by murder and mayhem, when the least tiny smidgen of snark 'triggers' them? And why use a word as inherently violent as 'trigger' when 'upset' has worked perfectly well for centuries? Although if they were upset by murder and mayhem, I guess I'd be out of business! Olivia? Are you still there?)

To buy time, and stop the news traveling through the grapevine, I singled out the wife of Pastor Tutor, seated at a table toward the back of the room.

'*Evelyn, dear,*' I spoke into the microphone, '*could you lead everyone in the Lord's Prayer?*'

The middle-aged woman with permed brown hair, having been called into service, stood, and in a loud voice asked everyone to bow their heads.

'Our Father who art in Heaven . . .' she began.

Voices joined in monotone-fashion, the conclusion of the prayer coinciding with the wail of a siren outside coming to an abrupt end – just as poor Norma's life had – the medical emergency vehicle having reached its destination.

Norma's destination was yet to be determined.

(A big shout-out to the MasterClass in dramatic writing offered online by David Mamet. And kudos to yours truly whose Lord's Prayer gambit worked perfectly!)

Moments later, with the room tamed into somber submission, two male paramedics in navy-color uniforms, carrying medical equipment cases, rushed into the ballroom without causing any more stir than turned heads.

'Over here!' Frannie called out, again on her knees next to the prone Norma.

As the pair approached, the former nurse got back up (I had not lowered myself completely, else I would have needed assistance), then quietly addressed the medics, sharing what I assumed was her deadly diagnosis.

(Not wishing to break the mood, I would like to direct writing students to my effective use above of alliteration. You're welcome!)

In the past, *I* had given these same men *my* diagnosis at the scene of a death that I suspected was a murder, only to receive a rebuke. But, obviously due to Frannie's professional standing, they listened attentively before proceeding through their usual routine.

After finding no pulse, however, and examining Norma's pupils and the inside of her mouth (where some white foam was visible), the paramedics exchanged looks and whispered remarks that indicated they had come to the same conclusion as Frannie.

A second siren could be heard, this one *not* ending abruptly, but rather like a clock alarm that had wound down, signaling a squad car had arrived.

(Effective use of metaphor, writing students!)

I moved from the podium to join Brandy where she had begun packing antiques into boxes on the table.

'Dear,' I said, 'do take your time.'

'Stall, you mean,' she said, giving me an incredulous look. 'To let you get your amateur sleuth juices flowing. Mother, I doubt anyone will feel like buying something now.'

'Well, there *are* only a few more shopping days until Christmas,' I reminded her.

'Moth . . . er . . .'

I touched her arm and said, sotto voce, 'I need to linger as long as possible.'

'Please,' she pleaded, 'don't get us involved.'

I pulled back. 'How can you ask that of me? Norma was my friend.'

Brandy opened her mouth to respond, and I could tell nothing was about to come out but recrimination; before that might occur, she closed her pretty trap again as Chief Tony Cassato strode in, his eyes locking with Brandy's for a moment, speaking in a language only they might comprehend, before he detoured toward the paramedics. (And no, I will not divulge the details of the rift currently between them; for that you will have to read *Antiques Foe*, which has gotten terrific reviews by the way.)

Approaching fifty, with graying temples, steel-gray eyes, a bulbous nose, and barrel chest, Brandy's on-again, now off-again fiancé was hardly my idea of a dreamboat (that would be the late, great Tyrone Power); but the man did have a certain charisma and an undeniable commanding presence.

Attired in his standard non-uniform of navy suitcoat over light blue shirt with navy striped tie, gray slacks, and brown Florsheim shoes, he apparently owned multiples of identical clothing, just as Charlie Brown's closet would have only yellow sweaters with black zigzags. (By-the-by, I'm distantly related to the creator of the comic-strip *Peanuts*, Charles Schulz, through an uncle of the half-sister of a third cousin, twice removed. But apparently that wasn't good enough for the cartoonist to send me a drawing in response to my polite letter pointing this out as I requested a freebie that never came.)

Following in the footsteps of the chief was Officer Shawntea Monroe, a recent addition to the force, with whom I was on relatively friendly terms due to our past history.

I will give you a brief rundown.

Some years back, I made a trek into Chicago with a few gal pals to see the Cubs play (or, as we hardcore fans call them, the 'Cubbies'). Afterward, we got turned around somehow upon leaving Wrigley Field, and our car suffered a flat tire in an apparently rough part of town known as Cabrini-Green. Shawntea, having just disembarked a smoke-belching bus, took pity on us fishies-out-of-water, and convinced her brother – who was a member of a possibly religious club with the unlikely name 'the Gangsta Disciples' – to change the tire. Before we drove away, I gave Shawntea my contact information and let her know that should she ever want to make a fresh start in Serenity, she should look me up. While my offer was sincere, I didn't expect the young woman to show up on my doorstep a week later, with three little adorable boys in tow.

I had managed to secure a day job for Shawntea, and encouraged her to complete her high-school GED in the evenings.

Eventually, she enrolled at Serenity Community College, and earned a degree in law enforcement.

Meanwhile, back to the murder scene . . .

The chief held a confab with the paramedics (a rather numb-looking Frannie having returned to her chair), after which the medics exited leaving their patient behind.

'Who's in charge here?' the chief asked loudly.

My mouth opened but Brandy squeezed my arm to shut what she sometimes unkindly refers to as my yap.

'I'm the club's social director,' Jared Eggler responded. Until now I hadn't noticed the slender man standing just inside the ballroom entrance. When had he arrived?

The chief waved Jared over.

'You have a list of the guests?' he asked. His manner was curt but not rude.

Jared nodded. 'With the exception of the Borne women, they're all members here.'

'I'll want a copy of names and addresses.'

'When?'

'Now would be good.'

Jared scurried off.

The medics returned with a gurney, which was wheeled over to the sprawled Norma, then lowered. Gently, her body was placed on to the stretcher, secured with straps, and covered with a white sheet. That our late friend had not been consigned (at least not yet) to an undignified body bag was a small blessing.

The silence was deafening but for a few squeaks as the gurney rolled toward the hallway, that is, until an arm embellished with a sparkling diamond bracelet, fingers adorned with gemstone rings, suddenly dropped below the sheet, eliciting a few horrified gasps at this grisly wave goodbye.

Norma always did have the last word.

'Ladies, thank you for your patience,' the chief said in an authoritative voice, stern but not unkind. 'Please leave in an orderly fashion.'

To the four women who had been seated with Norma – Frannie Phillips, Alice Hetzler, Cora Van Camp, and Ellen

Fridley – he said, 'I will need you ladies to remain . . . but do *not* touch anything on the table.'

Also refused early dismissal was a cluster of non-guests gathered near the kitchen doorway: the waitresses in their elf hats, a not-so-jolly-looking Cary Hudson holding his Santa hat, wig, and beard, and a male chef wearing a white apron who'd emerged from the kitchen to investigate the hubbub. His lack of holiday apparel made him seem the odd man out.

This employee group was assigned to Shawntea for questioning, the officer leading them off to a far corner, even as the dismissed guests continued to file out of the ballroom like a stunned herd of reindeer.

(Writing students pay heed to the thematic consistency!)

The chief's attention now turned my way, and I made a preemptive strike so as not to be removed.

'If you are wondering why we are still here,' I said, 'Brandy and I were closely positioned eyewitnesses. Also, we have to pack up our antiques.'

A few seconds ticked by before he replied, as if he'd mentally been riffling through a card file for something that might be said in public, but to no avail.

'All right, Vivian. You two can stay until you're finished gathering your wares.' He raised a finger. 'But no interruptions. Your presence at a crime scene is not called for.'

I splayed a hand on my chest. 'I completely understand! I wouldn't dream of interfering.'

He grunted. 'Your dreams are often my nightmares. One peep, Vivian, and you two can get your antiques later.'

I made a zip motion across my tight lips.

Planting himself behind Norma's empty chair, the chief removed a small recorder from a suitcoat pocket, placed it on the table, and began interviewing the four women with generally yes-or-no questions, designed to put them at ease. (I knew his technique well, having been on both sides of it myself many times.)

The chief asked, 'Did anything appear to be bothering Mrs Crumley this afternoon?'

The four women consulted each other with their eyes, before responding a unanimous 'no.'

'Then you would say she was acting normally?' the chief asked.

A unanimous 'yes.'

The questions became more specific. 'What was served for lunch?'

Of course, he could easily obtain the menu from the kitchen staff, but the object now was to get the women talking.

Alice – tall, thin, rather plain, reminding me of the actress Nancy Kulp, the banker's secretary on *Beverly Hillbillies* – spoke right up. 'A tossed salad, Chicken à la King with noodles, and plum pudding for dessert.'

The chief asked, 'How much of the salad and chicken dish did Mrs Crumley eat?'

Cora blurted, 'Oh, Norma gobbled it all up like she usually does. Well, did.'

The former court secretary – petite, with bird-like movements reminiscent of Elsa Lanchester's character in the 1935 flick *The Bride of Frankenstein* – had a tendency not to filter her words.

'And the plum pudding?' he asked. All eyes went to the decedent's partially eaten dessert with its unfortunate impression of a face having fallen into it.

'Norma didn't care for it,' Ellen replied. 'She said it wasn't "calorie-worthy."'

In her mid-sixties, the mystery book club recruit was plump and pleasant, partial to watching the Turner Classic Movies channel, and not terribly bright. But her ears heard everything.

The chief nodded almost imperceptibly. 'How long after the main course was the pudding served?'

'Perhaps ten minutes,' Frannie replied.

So the presumed arsenic had obviously not been administered in either the salad or Chicken à la King.

'What did Mrs Crumley have to drink?'

Alice replied, 'What the rest of us had – ice water, which was poured before we arrived, then coffee later.'

Cora countered, 'No, dear. I recall Norma putting a hand over her cup, declining the waitress's offer of coffee.'

Ellen interjected, 'Norma *did* have a cocktail from the bar, which she sipped throughout the meal.'

If so, the effects of the poison would likely have kicked in sooner. Drinks were apparently out as the deliverer of death.

Brandy whispered in my ear (one of them): 'Norma had a box of chocolates. But I don't see it on the table.'

I spoke up. 'Chief Cassato! If I might interrupt . . . I believe Norma received a box of chocolates as her Secret Santa gift.'

The chief's steely eyes nearly disappeared into slits as he regarded me much as a parent might a wayward child. Then those keen peepers widened as he scoured the table, came up short, and asked, 'Can anyone shed light on Mrs Borne's observation?'

Meekly, a hand rose, Ellen responding quietly. 'I . . . I was about to mention that.'

Was she? Or had I forced a killer out of hiding?

'Go on,' the chief said irritably, clearly annoyed by this vital omission.

Ellen shifted in her chair. 'Norma didn't get the chocolates as *her* gift, *I* did. But since my doctor recently told me I tested diabetic and would need medication if I failed to change my diet, I, well . . . traded presents with her.'

'Mrs Crumley's being?'

'Perfume.'

'Was the exchange your idea?'

'It was rather mutual,' Ellen replied. 'I'd opened my gift, then remarked I couldn't have sugar anymore. Norma unwrapped hers and said she was not about to wear the perfume because it was cheap – Red Door by Elizabeth Arden – and, well, that's my favorite scent, so we switched.'

Such a tactless remark was, unfortunately, not an unusual occurrence where the late Norma was concerned.

'Where's the chocolates box?' the chief asked.

Ellen's eyes went to some torn wrapping paper on the table. 'It might be under there.'

Hidden by happenstance, or concealed on purpose?

From a breast pocket, the chief removed a pen, with which he lifted the paper, exposing an open box, the bottom inserted inside the lid, containing perhaps a pound of chocolates in various shapes and types, nestled into brown paper liners, one of which was empty. A good trade indeed, unless it really had been spiked with arsenic.

Cora said, blunt as usual, 'Ellen covered up that chocolate box with the wrapping paper after Frannie and Vivian started talking about poison.'

Ellen flashed a dark look at her friend (perhaps I should say 'friend'), then said sheepishly, 'I wasn't trying to hide it . . . it's just that, well, *if* Norma *had* been poisoned, and *if* it was the chocolates . . .'

The chief finished the woman's sentence. 'You'd be suspected.'

Ellen nodded, gazing at the floor.

I filled the silence. 'Chief Cassato!'

The officer sighed and turned his gaze – actually a glower – on me.

I continued, unswayed by such negativity. 'If one assumes the exchange of gifts to be spontaneous, one must then arrive at the conclusion that *Ellen* was the intended victim.'

The chief's jaw flexed. 'Thank you, Vivian. That might never have occurred to me. How is the packing going?'

'Fine, fine. One must treat precious collectibles with care.'

I hoped he hadn't noticed that as Brandy loaded items into a carton, I would remove them when she turned away toward the next one.

Frannie came to my defense. 'Chief Cassato, Vivian is right! Ellen's life could very well be in danger.'

Rattled, Ellen all but cried out, 'Why would someone want to kill *me*?'

The chief deflected her question with his own. 'Mrs Fridley, do you live alone?'

Ellen nodded. 'I'm . . . I'm a widow.'

'Do you have any relatives locally, or in the area at least, that you might stay with?'

She shook her head. 'I have no children and the rest of my immediate family is deceased.'

Alice raised a hand as if this former teacher were a student. 'Ellen can stay with me.'

The chief's eyes went to the new potential murder victim. 'Is that acceptable, Mrs Fridley?'

The woman nodded. She turned to Alice. 'Thank you.'

'You'd do as much for me,' Alice said.

The Serenity forensics team – two men, one woman – were standing by, equipment bags in hand. Having been called in, they were awaiting instructions from their boss.

'I want to thank you ladies for your cooperation,' the chief said, again stern but not unpleasant, 'and ask that you not share any information that we spoke of. Please take *only* the items you arrived with.'

That meant their Secret Santa gifts were to be left behind.

As Frannie, Alice, Cora, and Ellen rose from their chairs and left, the forensics team clustered alertly around the chief.

'I need everything on this table analyzed,' he said. 'Glassware, dishes, utensils, gifts, discarded wrapping paper, and the box containing chocolates. Everything is to be cataloged for fingerprints. No exceptions. Any food is to be tested for poison – particularly the candy.'

While the specialists set about their work, the chief approached me.

'How are you doing, Vivian?' he asked, his brusque demeanor softening. 'I understand you and Mrs Crumley were close.'

'I'm all right,' I said, knowing what was really on his mind.

Which he immediately shared: 'I don't suppose you'll stay out of this?'

My theatrical training allowed me to produce a few tears. 'Norma *was* a close friend.'

I ignored Brandy, who was looking right at me, quietly disgusted. At least that's how I read it.

Please do not assume that I took Norma's death lightly – anything but. Or that I was a heartless wretch, regarding her death. But what purpose would mourning serve? How would it help the late Norma? I had mentally moved on to finding the killer.

But the chief didn't need to know that.

'Tony,' Brandy interjected, 'Norma did seem to be trying to communicate with Mother. Otherwise, why wouldn't she have turned to *Frannie*, a nurse?'

Eureka! The girl, who'd switched her allegiance from me to the chief since their engagement (however currently stalled) was now firmly back in my corner.

From the chief a heavy sigh came up, seeming to start at his toes.

Finally he said, 'All right. You two can investigate.' He added a caveat. 'As long as you're discreet. And if I tell you to back off, to exit a crime scene, you must promise to comply.'

I touched my bosom. 'When have I ever failed to display discretion?'

He smirked – a faint smirk but an undeniably identifiable one. 'Burning down the stadium at the county fairgrounds comes to mind.'

'Merely an accident,' I pooh-poohed.

Actually, I'd set fire to the old wooden structure on purpose, to attract attention after being cornered by a killer. Call it an extreme distress flare.

'And don't forget,' I continued, 'that was an accident that paved the way for the county's new state-of-the art stadium, even as justice was served. Win-win.'

The chief touched his forehead as if he had a migraine or perhaps was checking his temperature. 'Vivian . . . I'm not going to stand here and argue with you, or waste time with reasoning with the pair of you – I've got work to do. Just stay out of trouble.'

But somewhere within that brainy, balding lawman was an awareness that Brandy and I had helped solve every murder that had bedeviled him since he came to Serenity.

He turned and crossed the room to join Shawntea, who was still questioning her group. Brandy was watching him go, her expression unreadable . . . except by me.

Brandy and I fell silent on the return ride to the shop. In my mind, I was going over the events of the luncheon, solidifying details and, yes, already beginning to mentally form a suspect list. I don't know what my daughter was thinking about, but had a fair idea it was her estranged honeybunch.

After parking in the alley behind the shop, we left the boxes in the van and trooped inside through the back door, mindful of our step as Sushi was known to frequently leave a memento of her displeasure over having been left behind. The little doggie had behaved, however . . . at least as far as the mudroom, kitchen, and foyer were concerned.

We had barely hung up our coats on a rack, when Brandy turned to – or shall we say *on* – me.

'Mother, you just *can't* get us involved,' she wailed. 'You know Jake is coming the day after Christmas, and we promised Roger there'd be no amateur sleuthing while our son was here.'

In the past, Brandy had displayed little of my interest in murder investigation, apparently requiring some personal motive to join me in any of my inquiries. Take for instance the time Jake – then twelve – had been kidnapped by a killer for leverage, or the numerous instances when I'd been endangered or even attacked . . . or if anyone else she cared about had their life threatened.

As a matter of fact, after our first investigation (chronicled in *Antiques Roadkill*), when we collaborated on a book that we sold to an eager publisher, our then-editor assumed that Brandy was intended to be the lead sleuth in our cases. And I made the same assumption, but before long it became increasingly apparent my thirty-something child was not up to the job, and the books would be better served with Brandy in the role of a Watson, and me as Holmes (though we still quibbled about which was which, or is that who was who?).

I said, 'Dear, Jake's imminent arrival is exactly why we must work together to find this murderer as quickly as possible. He provides a ticking clock! Always good in a mystery.'

She frowned at me. 'But this is real life, not some mystery story. So if I agree to go along with you, you have to promise that unless the killer is in custody by the time Jake arrives, we – including *you* – will stop investigating!'

'Of course!' I said firmly. 'After all, I want my grandson here, too. And I want him safe, with not a whiff of peril.'

'That's a promise?'

'Then you're onboard?' I asked. (See how I deftly sidestepped her question and ducked a commitment?)

Brandy sighed. 'OK, I'm onboard the mystery train – wooo-wooo!'

One might think my choo-choo of choice would be the Orient Express due to my fondness for Agatha Christie mysteries, but really, it's the Atchison, Topeka and Santa Fe because I've always felt I was a Harvey girl in a former life. (Wasn't Judy Garland wonderful in that picture *The Harvey Girls*, especially during the hair-pulling scene with Angela Lansbury?)

Next stop: Murdertown.

Vivian's Trash 'n' Treasures Tip

Mass-marketed Christmas collectibles rarely retain their value. An exception is if someone damages an ornament in a series and has to scour the Internet for a replacement. Consider last year, when I dropped and shattered 'Alice the Goon,' one of six Popeye the Sailor ceramic characters made by King Features in 1987. I paid more for that Goon than the other less goony ones combined.

THREE

Jake is Coming to Town

Brandy back at the controls. To stick with Mother's train analogy, the Borne Express has indeed left the station, and will be gathering speed, so if you are having second thoughts, please consider your options. In continuing on to the destination you may 1) jump off now and hope for a soft landing, 2) head to the club car and keep the Mai Tais coming, or 3) sit back and enjoy the ride (or anyway endure it). In the case of options 2 and 3, however, keep in mind a runaway train is always a possibility.

Mother is correct about my reluctance at becoming ensnared in her cases because, unlike her, I find murder quite unpleasant. If my name was listed in the *Webster Dictionary*, it would read: Brandy Borne, (bran'dē börn) *n.* A reluctant amateur sleuth.

New readers (those who aren't getting sozzled in the club car) must try to grasp just how badly Mother had me at a disadvantage. I ask your patience in submitting for your approval (if this were a Mother chapter, we'd be getting Rod Serling's biography here) the following recap of the cliff-hanger from our last book, *Antiques Foe*.

A few weeks ago, I received an urgent phone call from my ex, Roger, worried about our son Jake's future and requesting a Zoom meeting that would include him, his wife Laura, myself and, at my insistence (but his reluctance), Mother.

At the arranged time, seated at our Duncan Phyfe table in the dining room, I logged into the site; Mother would be upstairs on her own computer sequestered in her Art Nouveau-decorated boudoir. Roger and Laura were already onscreen, side-by-side at a mahogany desk in the den of their upscale suburban home, files neatly stacked to one side, work from his investment firm in downtown Chicago.

My ex was looking older than mid-forties, more lines in his face now, brown hair thinning, graying at the sides and temples, but still quite handsome; he wore a blue sweater, the collar of a button-down pale yellow shirt showing.

Laura, a pediatrician in a hospital somewhere in the burbs, wore a crisp white blouse, her straight blonde hair shoulder-length, her pretty face strained with worry. She was a better match for Roger than I'd been, and we got along fine in the few times we'd met. Really, there was only one thing that bothered me about Laura, and it wasn't her fault: she looked a lot like me.

My blurry square on the screen paled in comparison with the crisp video of theirs. Not only did I look washed-out and tired, the candlesticks on the Mediterranean-style buffet table behind me made it seem like horns were growing out of my head, something I hadn't noticed till we were on the air.

And Devil Brandy was not the impression I wished to convey.

'Hello, Roger . . . Laura,' I said, adjusting my position, which only emphasized the impression that a horn was protruding from either side of my skull.

'Brandy,' the couple replied in lock-step, voices tight, smiles strained.

'Mother should be along shortly,' I said. 'Thank you for agreeing to allow me to include her.'

No surprise that La Diva Borne would keep an audience waiting. Dramatic entrances were among her many specialties, although sometimes that included knocking over scenery or tumbling into the orchestra pit, a hazard of her insistence to not wear her glasses on stage.

What the hey, any showstopping entrance eliciting from the audience gales of laughter or gasps of alarm is a plus, at least if the former production is a comedy and the latter a thriller.

Suddenly, like a pop-up ad, the grand dame of community theater made her on-camera appearance. Wrapped around her neck was a long multi-colored scarf worthy of Isadora Duncan (where was a vintage convertible when you needed one?), dressed up further by a plethora of pearl necklaces. A master of key lights, she had strategically placed a lamp behind her, taking years off her age (whatever that was).

Plowing ahead, I asked, 'What seems to be the trouble with Jake?'

Laura deferred to the boy's father, who responded, 'He's been suspended from school . . . and they won't have him back.'

Roger was referring to an expensive private high school, which I knew Jake abhorred. We'd heard all about the stuck-up girls and snooty boys from our down-to-earth son.

My ex went on, 'He had a fight with another boy, and since the school has a zero-tolerance policy in that regard, both students were expelled.'

Of course, knowing how our son felt about swimming in such entitled waters, I'd already guessed as much, and had come prepared.

'I have a proposal,' I said.

'And what would that be?' Roger asked, dubiously.

'That Jake transfer to Serenity High School for his second freshman semester.'

Roger's eyes widened. 'You mean . . . live with you and *Vivian*?'

Mother flinched at the emphasis on her name, but kept quiet, as I had previously insisted she do. ('Speak only if they, or I, directly address you!' 'I am but a spear carrier in this little drama.' I only hoped nobody got stabbed.)

Roger went on, 'Oh, no. *That's* never going to happen.'

Laura turned to him. 'Roger . . . let's hear Brandy out.'

'Thank you, Laura,' I said with a smile and a nod.

My ex sighed. To her he said, 'All right, fine . . . let's see what she has to say.' To me he said, 'I will endeavor to keep an open mind.'

I hoped that was the case.

I began, 'Serenity High is small compared to the school Jake has been attending . . . it's a highly rated institution – the teachers are excellent and work very hard for every student to succeed. Plus, there are lots of extracurricular activities Jake could get involved in – sports, chorus, drama. And he could work at our antiques store on weekends to earn some money.'

I could tell a certain party was champing at the bit and added, 'Isn't that right, Mother?'

Mother said, with all the charm she could muster (and she was cable of mustering some), 'The boy would be a big help backstage at the theater . . . perhaps even take on a part in an upcoming play.' She tried out a smile. 'It so happens I have an in with the director.'

Meaning herself, of course.

I went on, 'The arrangement could be a trial run to see how Jake does in this environment. If his grades are good, and he stays out of trouble, Jake could register here in the fall for his sophomore year . . . that is, if he *wants* to, and you are both willing. We would flip our current custody arrangement, clearing it with the court of course – Jake would be with you on breaks, including the long summer one.'

'And otherwise,' Roger said, a bit chilly, 'with you.'

Laura touched her husband's arm. 'Dear, I think Brandy may be on to something . . . what other option is there but some military school?'

Roger's expression melted – I could tell he didn't want that. He'd spent his own high school years that way and had looked back on those days with nothing positive to say.

After what seemed like forever, he said, 'All right, but before I agree to this so-called trial run, we first have to address the elephant in the room.'

The elephant on the Zoom, that is.

'I beg your pardon!' Mother said, straightening in her chair, any thought of restraint out the window. 'If you're referring to me, Roger, I take profound umbrage at that remark! Among other things, my weight is perfectly in sync with medical guidelines. And I happen to know my grandson has considerable fondness for me.'

Roger and Mother had never gotten along, one of the double-headed nails in our marital coffin.

He raised an appeasing hand. 'My apologies, Vivian. I should have phrased that differently. You are, of course, very well-preserved—'

'I take umbrage at *that* as well!'

He continued, 'But that is not the issue.'

Her eyes were so wide, the thick lenses of her glasses barely contained them. 'What *is*?'

Well, my attempt to control this conversation had lasted a good minute, anyway.

Showing admirable restraint, Roger quietly said, 'You've gotten Jake embroiled in several of your amateur-sleuthing escapades – even at times putting his life in danger.'

Before Mother could re-open her yap, I interjected, 'What if she promises not to do any such investigating while Jake is here. Murder inquiries, strictly off-limits.'

'Well . . . that would be a start,' Roger said, then addressed Mother directly. 'What about it, Vivian?'

'I *gladly* promise,' Mother replied. 'Jake's welfare is more important to me than anything else on this Little Blue Ball. And I guarantee that you won't get a single whiff of my involvement in any case coming from these quarters.'

Her last sentence was a little ambiguous, but Roger didn't seem to pick up on that. Mother hadn't *quite* agreed to avoid investigating a homicide, just that she wouldn't involve Jake.

Roger looked at Laura, who shrugged and offered a small smile. 'I feel it has to be your decision, dear. But I am not against it.'

I could see Roger was softening, so I turned over my ace in the hole. 'I'd like to point out that while Jake is here, Tony would be a big presence in the boy's life.'

At least I hoped as much, if the current Brandy/Tony disaffection could lose the 'dis.'

Laura touched Roger's arm. 'Darling, having the chief of police as a guiding force might go a long way toward easing any concerns you might have in this, uh, area.'

He nodded. 'Yes . . . yes, it would.' Then, 'If I get wind of anything going on in that "area," I will call Cassato, personally.'

'Of course,' I said, with a confidence I didn't fully feel.

'In that case, Brandy, I'll agree to your proposal.'

'Roger dear,' a beaming Mother said, just shy of sickeningly sweet, 'you won't regret your decision.'

'Let's hope I don't,' came his reply.

And now, back to our regularly scheduled chapter . . .

Having returned to our shop from the country club, I brought in the boxes of antiques from the van (a preoccupied Mother not helping), my huffing and puffing visible in the chill. Then I began unpacking them at the check-out counter, shaking my head a little as I did so.

The sale at the country club had been a bust, even from a sheer publicity standpoint a disaster. And now it was nearing four o'clock, with only an hour left before our Saturday closing. Plus, with the store regularly shuttered Sunday and Monday, the shopping days till Christmas that we counted on were dwindling.

I said, 'We could stay open the next few days. Or Monday, at least.'

Mother, her back to me as she replaced some items in the glass-enclosed curio cabinet near the foyer, replied, 'No, dear. We must sacrifice coin of realm for time in which to investigate. Keep in mind the ticking clock that is Jake's arrival!'

She was right.

I asked, 'What if we called Joe Lange in to run things?'

Joe was a friend from my community college days – a self-styled oddball – whom we sometimes employed to help out at the shop.

My partner in crime(solving) turned, displaying a furrow brow. 'You'd have to ask his mother how he's doing.'

Ever since returning home from a tour in Afghanistan, suffering from PTSD, Joe lived with the aging widowed Mrs Lange.

Mother went on, 'And I'm afraid without either of us here, with only *Joe's* flag flying, he might keep customers away.'

While good-natured and mild-mannered, Joe had a tendency to speak in barely penetrable military lingo that could be off-putting to some.

Joe ordering lunch at a restaurant: 'What is the ETA of a tenderloin?'

Waitress: 'Huh?'

Brandy: face hidden in embarrassment behind a hand.

I said, 'We *could* put your flag out along with his, even though you won't be here. Joe can say you just stepped out and should be back soon, and maybe they'll buy something while waiting around.'

Mother smiled, showing perfect white teeth, largely her own with just a few molar implants. 'Dear, you make me proud! Your suggested deception where Joe is concerned is delicious! Perhaps the apple does *not* fall far from the tree.'

'Don't get used to it,' I said with a smirk. 'We're in a time-crunch, that's all.'

Mother crossed to the coat tree. 'Then let's go home and start planning our strategy.'

We lived about five miles from the downtown on Elm Street, in a section of old homes built during the first part of the last century. Ours is white stucco, three-stories (including a large attic), with an enclosed front porch. It sports a sunroom wing and a stand-alone garage, whose door bulges thanks to Mother's accumulation of yard-sale junk within.

Spoiler alert: not long after I'd moved back home, the house blew up, when a murderer broke in during the night and turned on the gas fireplace. Fortunately, all three of us (Sushi included) made it out alive. Unfortunately, the garage with its junk also survived. Anyway, Mother insisted on rebuilding using the old architectural plans (kept somewhere in the aforementioned garage), saying that a modern-looking house would ruin the authentic integrity of the entire block. So, we dwelled in a disconcerting time machine of a brand-new old house.

End of spoiler alert.

Back as far as I can remember, Mother and I had eclectic tastes in decor, seeing the merits of style in every shifting decade. Therefore we decided to make each room represent a different era, which also allowed us to buy anything that struck our fancy and have someplace to put it.

Upstairs, Mother's bedroom – as mentioned earlier – is art nouveau; my bedroom, art deco; and the guest quarters, 1970s psychedelic (which ensures that visitors don't stay too long). Downstairs, the living room welcomes Victorian furniture and fixtures, while the dining area is neoclassical. The sunroom is filled with dusty old books and musical instruments (including a definitive collection of smelly, dented cornets), and is dominated by an old stand-up piano Mother rescued by the roadside that neither one of us can play (Sushi will walk across the keys now and then, when she's bored).

Usually, at Yuletide time, Mother placed our faux Christmas tree in the living room in front of the picture window, but this year she relegated it to a corner, avoiding the opening and closing of curtains, both drapes and sheers, so we wouldn't knock off the small antiques that liberally covered the boughs. Some past casualties had been: a Foley china blue floral tea cup (responsible party: Mother); a silver glass mercury Santa (responsible party: me); a hand-sewn and painted doll of a bejeweled Cleopatra by Gladys Boalt (responsible party: Sushi, who attacked it after the ornament fell on her head while she was sniffing at the gifts).

At the moment, we were all in the kitchen – an exhibition of 1950s splendor and ingenuity right out of a *Ladies' Home Journal* photo spread of that era – trying to decide on a quick dinner on which we all could agree (no vote for Sushi, neither the canine nor the Japanese cuisine).

Mother had come to the end of her rusk debacle, wherein she had meant to purchase, online, only *one* package of the round dried bread to try a new recipe, and instead ordered six *cases*. We had rusks for breakfast, lunch, and dinner until they were coming out our ears, nose, mouth, and (putting it delicately) elsewhere.

Sushi, at our feet on Linoleum that Mother had salvaged (on which was printed a braided rug), barked her impatience. Just because she didn't get a vote didn't mean she didn't have an opinion.

'Let's just have *smørrebrød*,' I suggested, using the Danish word rather than the American 'smorgasbord.'

'Satisfactory,' Mother replied, parroting Nero Wolfe.

The authentic Danish *smørrebrød* – which literally means spread or buttered bread – is not the generic, heavy American counterpart that tends to include breakfast, lunch, and dinner items. During Viking times, people would travel long distances to attend festivities such as weddings, christenings, and funerals, and the food they brought with them – breads, spreads, cheeses, fish, and game (served in a variety of combinations) – would feed a plenitude of guests. Thus was born the open-faced sandwich, and its smaller offspring, the 'snitter', also known as finger sandwiches.

While Mother selected cold items from our white 1950s refrigerator, I buttered four slices of wholegrain bread, removed the crusts, cut each into four pieces, and placed them on a jadeite vintage Fire King plate.

Meanwhile, Mother had arranged on a similar platter an assortment of thinly sliced toppings: hard-boiled eggs, tomatoes, onion, cucumber, bacon, roast beef, smoked salmon, ham, and chicken, along with a variety of cheeses. As a half-Dane, there were a few delicacies I didn't appreciate, such as smoked eel and lutefisk (seafood pickled in lye – no thank you).

And I had yet to warm to an old family meat spread recipe. Maybe you will.

Esther Jensen's Liver Pâté

2 pounds pork or calf's liver
1 medium-sized onion
1 pound pork fat
4 tbsp. butter
4 tbsp. flour
2 cups light cream
2 eggs, well beaten
2 tsp. anchovy paste
2 tsp. salt
1 tsp. pepper
½ teaspoon ground ginger

With the finest blade of the meat grinder, grind liver and onion twice. Grind pork fat twice. Set aside. Melt butter and stir in flour. Gradually stir in cream, and cook over low heat, stirring constantly, until thickened and smooth. Add ground pork fat and stir until fat has melted. Remove from heat. Add liver and all other ingredients and blend thoroughly. Spoon into 2-quart baking dish. Place in

> baking pan with hot water. Bake in 325 degrees Fahrenheit oven for 1½ to 2 hours, or until pâté tests clean. Cover with lid or aluminum foil if top is browning too quickly. Replenish water in baking pan if necessary. Cool before serving.

Or you could just buy the pâté at the grocery store.

Seated now at the Duncan Phyfe table, with Sushi at my feet waiting for handouts, we began the process of building our snitters.

Adhering to Nero Wolfe's dictum of never discussing a case during meals, Mother said, 'We should talk about refurnishing the guest room for Jake.'

Topping a piece of bread with egg and tomato, I replied, 'Maybe we should wait until he gets here. He may have some ideas.'

And anyway, if Mother reneged on her non-investigatory promise causing Roger to yank Jake back to Chicago, we'd have gone to a lot of trouble for nothing.

Mother said, 'Then let's make a priority of the overhaul of the dining room.'

Some time ago, while on a buying trip to a small Iowa town named Antiqua (known for its abundance of antiques shops), Mother had discovered a rare Heywood-Wakefield matching set of dining room furniture – table, six chairs, buffet, and hutch – produced mid-last century, entirely of yellow birch. Currently gathering cobwebs in the basement, the set would certainly be a nice change from the dark mahogany wood now in use.

This kind of banal conversation continued through the coffee and thawed petits fours (in keeping with the miniature sandwiches) until Mother's cell sounded on the table between us. (At my insistence, she had changed the ring-tone from the tune 'I Fought the Law' to that of an old-fashioned phone.)

The screen read name unavailable, calls I regularly ignore, but Vivian Borne will talk to anybody.

'Hello,' Mother said.

'*Vivian, it's Frannie.*'

Due to Mother's diminished hearing, the receiver volume

was set as high as possible, making me an eavesdropper whether I wanted to be or not.

A long silence. Mother frowned. 'How do I know it's really you?'

'*Because it is.*'

'Your name didn't appear in the caller ID as it usually would, and I don't recognize the number.'

'*That's because my cell phone died, and I'm using a private extension at the hospital in the morgue.*'

'How do I know you aren't AI?'

'*Who?*'

'Artificial Intelligence.'

'*Don't you recognize my voice?*'

'That could be easily faked by today's technology.'

'*Don't be ridiculous.*'

'If you want this conversation to continue, you'll have to answer a question from your past that only the real Frannie Phillips could know.'

A sigh. '*All right, what is it?*'

'When you were in nurse's training at Loyola, there was a certain married doctor . . .'

'*You know about* that?'

'A considerable number of people do.' Her eyes grew even bigger behind the magnifying lenses. 'Wait just one minute! If that many others know, then so could Artificial Intelligence.'

'*Vivian! I'm calling from the morgue. Do you want me to tell you what I found out from Norma's preliminary autopsy, or not?*'

Mother's anxious expression disappeared. 'I'll take the risk.'

'*The cause of death was listed as arsenic trioxide.*'

I leaned toward the phone in Mother's hand. 'Any results on the chocolates?'

'*The centers were filled with the white powder.*'

Mother said, 'Thank you, Frannie . . . if you *are* Frannie.'

An arched-eyebrow Mother ended the call.

(I will push the pause button to give you my assessment regarding authors . . . or publishers . . . using AI to write books. In our series that would be a problem, perhaps not in imitating me, but certainly Mother. If all her chapters from our eighteen books were fed into a computer, I think it would explode, thanks to the irrational nature of her thinking. Like in that old episode of *Star Trek*, 'The Ultimate Computer,' in which Captain Kirk tricks the machine into destroying itself by questioning its logic.)

Mother stood, pushed back her chair, and announced, 'To the incident room!' She might well have been talking about the Batcave, which I guess made me Robin. Better than Watson, maybe.

I gave Sushi one last smidgen of roast beef, then followed Mother into the sunroom/library/music room where she kept an ancient schoolhouse blackboard-on-wheels tucked behind the stand-up piano, on which to compile her suspect lists. (The board not the piano.)

Per usual, I took my place on the piano bench while she rolled out the board. From its lip, Mother picked up a piece of old-school white chalk (to use anything else would be sacrilegious) and began to write. When she was finished the board looked like this:

SUSPECTS IN THE MURDER OF
NORMA CRUMLEY

NAME	MOTIVE	OPPORTUNITY

Schoolmarm Borne turned to face her only pupil. 'Suggestions?'

'Well, naturally,' I said, 'you should include the person who drew Ellen's name and gave her the chocolates.'

'That goes without saying. Who else?'

'Ellen herself, of course.'

Mother frowned. 'How so?'

I shrugged. 'Agatha Christie's *The Mirror Crack'd from Side to Side.*'

My instructor's eyebrows climbed over the rims of her glasses. 'Ah! To throw suspicion off of herself, Ellen substituted her own gift with the box of poisoned candy, which she intended to give to Norma.'

I frowned. 'Frankly, though, I can't imagine Ellen doing that . . . she seems so nice.'

'Never let appearances fool you,' Mother replied, adding, 'You'd be surprised what people have hidden in their metaphorical closets.'

She had a shoe box on the top shelf of her literal one, filled with old love letters from various paramours. Pretty hot stuff!

As best student in this class of one, I had another question. 'Why did you want Ellen to join your book club? What I mean is, what did she have to offer?'

Mother put hands on hips. 'Dear, are you suggesting that I'm transactional?'

'Aren't you? For a mystery fan, a seat in Vivian Borne's Red-Hatted League must be a hot ticket.'

Mother beamed. 'Thank you!'

'Isn't that why you picked the others?'

She folded her arms and looked down at me. 'I challenge you to explain.'

I counted on my fingers. 'Frannie has access to medical information. Cora has legal connections. Alice is a wiz at statistics. And Norma was your conduit to the social network.' (By the way, while the Red-Hatted women had lots of discussions when they met, very little had to do with whatever mystery book they were reading.)

Mother's hands were on her hips now. She glared at me, an irritated Wonder Woman. (And what was Wonder Woman doing in the Batcave?) 'Your point being?'

'So?' I said. 'What was *Ellen's* function?'

Her sigh all but rattled the piano keys. 'Very well. Ever since Norma had been removed as the country club's social director—'

'She hadn't able to deliver the dirt,' I interjected.

Mother arched an eyebrow again, Spock-like this time. 'A crude way of putting it, but yes.'

'And Ellen *can*?' I asked skeptically. 'She's so quiet nobody notices her.'

Mother smiled. 'Rather like Miss Marple, silently sipping

her tea, overhearing conversations. As the Big Bad Wolf said of his ears, "All the better to hear you with."'

'Perhaps there's your motive. Ellen overheard something she shouldn't have.'

'A distinct possibility,' Mother agreed. 'But, getting back to Norma. People were beginning to realize anything they shared with her would likely wind up on social media.'

'Then you were going to *replace* Norma with Ellen in the group?'

'No, of course not. I'm not *that* transactional. Once you're in, you're in.'

'In other words, Norma still had *some* use to you.'

'Dear, sarcasm is not appreciated nor is it helpful.'

'Sorry,' I said. 'But let me ask you – how does someone get added to your group? Is it your decision alone?'

'No. We all have a vote and the outcome must be unanimous. And that vote was to be held at our next meeting.'

I mulled that a moment. Then: 'How did the others feel about Ellen joining?'

Mother hesitated. 'Frannie, Alice, and Cora all wanted her in.'

'But Norma didn't,' I concluded, based on the exclusion of her name.

'I can't say that for sure,' Mother admitted. 'But yes, I suspected Norma would keep Ellen out.'

'Why? Was there bad blood between the two?'

'Not that I'm aware of,' Mother said, adding with a shrug, 'But you know how Norma is. Was.'

I do. Did. She was an upper-middle-class snob who looked down on women like Ellen, who had neither money nor status.

Mother went on, 'Also, sometimes people just don't cotton to each other. At any rate, being barred from any group is not generally motive enough for murder.'

Depends on how badly someone wants something.

'Maybe we're coming at this the wrong way,' I said.

Teacher folded her arms. 'I'm listening.'

'Would you say Norma was well-liked?'

'Not particularly. And she did seem to have more than her share of enemies.'

Including Mother at one time.

I said, 'What if one of those enemies anticipated Ellen would trade gifts with Norma?'

Mother frowned. 'That would be risky. Murderers generally want their targets well-defined and perfectly positioned.'

'Generally, yes. But not necessarily.'

'. . . Proceed.'

I shifted on the bench. 'Well, Secret Santa gift exchanges have been around for a long time, but have evolved from yesteryear when you drew a slip of paper with a name from a bowl, to today, using computer applications.'

Mother once told me about an old Danish tradition called *Juklapp* where a disguised giver would knock on someone's door, throw a present inside when it opens, then run away.

I went on, 'More information now goes into the exchange with these computer programs – like what kind of gift the person would like to receive.'

'I'm beginning to catch on,' Mother replied. 'Let's say the killer knew what gift both Ellen and Norma had requested. Naturally, Ellen, having been diagnosed with diabetes, wouldn't have listed a box of chocolates. And Norma, who prided herself on expensive finery, wouldn't have asked for cheap perfume – but she did love sweets, which was no secret.' Mother paused, a finger to her lips. 'Of course we're making the assumption that the killer knew Ellen was diabetic, which, I guess, isn't that far-fetched.'

I said, 'So the stage was set, and all the murderer needed was for the two women to act naturally.'

Mother gazed at me. 'I like your theatrical metaphor, to which I will add my own: this time the play will close after one performance.'

'And it'll be curtains for the killer.'

'Dear, I don't enjoy being upstaged.'

As often as I've helped Mother during her plays, I still get confused over upstage and downstage.

'Where do we go from here?' I asked.

'To see the one person who would know for certain who gave the gifts to Ellen and Norma, and what they had requested.'

Mother paused dramatically.

'The person in charge of the exchange,' she said. 'Jared Eggler.'

Brandy's Trash 'n' Treasures Tip

Do not despair if you have an incomplete set of some Christmas collectibles – say, ceramic Popeye the Sailor figurines made in 1987 by King Features. There's always someone with butter-fingers looking for a replacement.

(*Note to Brandy from Olivia:* I do think that was a bit unkind, and not terribly informative. Shall we try again?)

Brandy's Trash 'n' Treasures Tip

Vintage Christmas decorations remain popular; they are available, affordable, fun to collect and can be found anywhere from high-end antiques stores to lowly yard sales. But the best place to start looking is in your grandparents' attic or parents' basement. I'm sure you can have anything you want if you offer to sweep and clean.

FOUR
It's a Harsh-Mellow World

Shortly after seven, Mother and I left the house, stepping out into a blustery night. Snow was swirling in the wind, but not new flakes, rather what had fallen earlier being blown around.

When Sushi accompanied us to the entryway as we'd gotten our coats, I'd anticipated the usual hissy fit that occurred whenever she understood she wasn't going along. But when the front door opened letting in a blast of frigid air, she turned tail and disappeared back into the warmth of the living room. As I said earlier, she is the smartest animal in the Borne homestead.

The streets were desolate in this sandstorm of snow, and I drove slowly, visibility at near white-out conditions. Mother, next to me, said, 'I recall mention of a private Christmas party scheduled at the country club tonight, so Jared should still be there.'

Good lord! Had it only been six hours since Norma Crumley died face-down in her plum pudding?

The Borne matriarch continued rather sternly, 'Now, you let me handle him.'

Wind jostled the van. 'Yes, Mother.'

A gloved hand reached over and patted my knee. 'Good girl.'

Why did I always seem to be reduced to a child around her?

Upon arrival at the club, I was surprised to see the parking lot nearly full, despite the inclement weather. But never underestimate the lure of a free high-priced dinner to rich people. Maybe not paying is why a lot of them are rich.

Again, I found a handicapped spot, Mother dutifully displaying her disabled tag. (Regarding signs posted threatening a fine of several hundred dollars for not having the proper authority – unless those spots are on public streets patrolled by police, or at malls employing parking lot security, who exactly is going to enforce the fine? Not a restaurant owner; not a grocery store manager; not a librarian. This rhetorical question is not meant to encourage ignoring such warnings.)

And if Mother's post-bunion surgery was one of the lesser appropriate uses for occupying such a parking place, I was nonetheless grateful in this blizzard for quick access to the club entrance, and hopped out of the van, not waiting for Mother – every woman for herself in below-zero weather.

In the reception area a sign on an easel said WELCOME SERENITY BANK EMPLOYEES, and I wondered if my recent exorbitant overdraft charge went toward paying for this party. If so, I should get a free meal.

From down the hall, loud voices and laughter burbled from the ballroom like champagne bubbles, the tragedy occurring at an earlier celebration apparently having no effect on the current merrymaking. Or perhaps word of the Christmas party gone wrong was not generally known as yet.

Mother joined me in the entryway, brushing snow from her hair and coat. 'Any sign of Jared?'

'No.' I nodded toward the window of his office. 'The blinds are closed.'

'There's light peeking from behind them, so we'll try there first.'

After we'd deposited our winter wraps in the cloakroom, I followed her lead.

The door was shut, but not locked, and Mother barged in without knocking, startling the man seated behind his desk in his nicely appointed, relatively spacious office.

The social director, who'd undoubtedly had a rough day, was looking a little worse for wear, his face gaunt, the same suit he'd worn at the luncheon wrinkled, his tie loosened like an unambitious noose.

'Vivian,' Jared said with just a hint of irritation but with eyes unhappy with surprise. 'What are you doing here?'

Translation: Your non-member pass on to the premises had expired.

I apparently did not exist, my presence not rating a glance much less a greeting, however rude.

'I need to ask you some questions,' Mother said, coming toward the desk.

He frowned. 'Can't it wait? I'm short-handed for this party because one of my waitresses didn't show up.'

'I'm afraid it *cannot* wait,' Mother replied. 'It's regarding the death of Norma Crumley . . . Might I sit? Thank you.'

She took a visitor's chair, holding her purse in her lap with both hands. I stood beside her like a wordless supporting actor in one of her plays.

Jared sighed. 'I've already answered questions from the police, so I don't know what else I could tell you. Not that it's any of your business.'

Mother's eyebrows rose above her glasses frames. 'We have the blessing of Chief Cassato to conduct our usual ex-officio investigation. Or are you unaware that we have a certain well-established amateur standing in that regard, my daughter and I.'

His only response to that was to close his eyes as if hoping when he opened them, we'd be gone. He opened them. We weren't.

The social director's gaze wandered to papers in front of him. 'While it's certainly unfortunate Mrs Crumley had a heart attack, these things do happen.'

'True enough,' Mother replied. '*If* she'd had a heart attack.'

He looked up sharply. 'What are you saying?'

'Norma was murdered, sir. Poisoned with arsenic.'

Jared sat forward. 'Well, that's horrible. Simply terrible.' He frowned. 'Chief Cassato said nothing of this to me earlier.'

'The cause of death had not been established yet. Now it has. And I've been given authority by the chief himself to assist with the investigation, due to my stellar experience as a former sheriff.'

She dug in her purse for her badge, which she displayed from a distance, holding her thumb over the word 'Honorary'.

The man was new in town, hired out-of-state to replace Norma as social director after Mother's brief sheriff reign had abruptly ended; so he wouldn't necessarily challenge the word 'stellar.'

Jared asked anxiously, 'Was the poison in the food she was served? Or a drink from our bar?'

'Mr Eggler,' Mother said officiously, 'I am the one asking the questions here. What I require are answers.' She paused. 'And need I say that this conversation is confidential? Your discretion in this matter is vital to the solving of the case.'

Jared nodded. Sitting forward, suddenly eager to help. 'Of course. What do you need to know from me?'

I had to give Mother credit; she knew how to make people feel simultaneously important and insignificant.

She said, 'Let's start with the application you used for the Secret Santa drawing.'

Jared drew the laptop computer on his desk closer to him, his fingers as ready as a virtuoso pianist. 'Let me bring it up . . .'

Mother rose and we went around the desk to look over his shoulders, one on either side of him.

With a few clicks of his mouse, the screen filled with the logo GIFTED, surrounded by dancing presents with shapely legs, as in that unintentionally campy 1950s Old Gold Cigarettes commercial I'd seen at a revival of early TV advertising at the Bijou Theater.

'Through this application,' Jared was saying, 'a group email is sent to all female members, inviting them to participate, with a posted cut-off date for doing so. If a woman wants to join in, she clicks on a link, and fills out a form, then receives a confirmation notice.'

I asked, 'What information is on the form?'

He looked at me for the first time, his expression indicating he felt so minor a player having lines was surprising.

'The person's name, of course,' he said. 'Their home address, and a place to list what sort of gift they might like.' He paused. 'Many of the women's suggestions are general, but others can be specific, for example, such and such a book.'

Mother asked, 'Are the women allowed to pick the person they want to gift?'

Jared swiveled to her. 'No. The names are randomly selected by the app, and emailed out after the deadline.'

'Let's say,' Mother said, 'I received Brandy's name.'

'Who is Brandy?'

'I am Brandy,' I said. 'Vivian's daughter.'

He swiveled to me. 'Oh. Sorry.'

Not as sorry as I was, at times.

Mother prompted, 'If I were a member, and had received Brandy's name, would the form *she* filled out be emailed to me?'

He swiveled back to her. 'It would. That's how the exchange works.'

'Good. Then I would like to see Ellen Fridley's filled-out form.'

He frowned. 'I would think you'd ask to see Norma Crumley's.'

'We'll get to that. Could you bring it up on your screen?'

'Certainly.' His fingers danced on the keyboard.

We leaned in on either side of our reluctant host and viewed his monitor.

On her form, Ellen had suggested only one item: a special holiday edition box of candy from the local shop, Les Chocolats.

Mother said, 'When did she fill out this form? The date, dear.'

'Ahh . . .' Jared squinted at the screen. 'The day the invitation was sent to all the women . . . December first.'

I knew what Mother was thinking: we needed to find out when Ellen had been diagnosed with diabetes – before or after she'd completed the form.

'Who drew her name?' Mother asked.

He pointed to the screen. 'It's there, highlighted in the bottom corner. Sheila White.'

Mother took that information in, then said, 'Now show me Norma's form, please.'

Jared did so. The deceased had listed several specific items, all expensive perfumes: Chanel (*Coco Mademoiselle*), Versace (*Crystal Noir*), and Dolce & Gabbana (*The Only One*).

Yet the person who had received Norma's name, Mildred Zybarth, had instead given the socialite the less costly Elizabeth Arden (*Red Door*).

The social director leaned back in his chair. 'Now – if that's all, Mrs Borne, I have things to do.'

She put a hand on his shoulder, as if to hold him down. 'Just a few more inquiries, dear. Who was in charge of implementing this application?'

'I was, of course.'

'And can someone change their suggestions once the form has been submitted?'

'Possibly,' Jared replied, starting to sound a little testy now. 'If that person contacted me. In that case, I would pass along the new information to whomever had drawn that name.'

'And *did* anyone contact you? Ellen perhaps? Or this other woman – Sheila White? Perhaps Mildred Zybarth?'

'No.'

I added a question. 'Was there a dollar limit set on the gifts?'

'There was not. This exchange predates my taking over the social director role, but my understanding is that fifty dollars was the top limit and twenty the least one might spend. But that was just sort of . . . understood. Not a rule or even a guideline.'

Norma's perfume requests were way above the unofficial budgetary restraint.

Mother said, as if to herself, 'So it was up to the giver what she wanted to spend.'

'Yes, and now you'll have to forgive me,' Jared said, hiking his volume some, 'but I've got to call that waitress and find out why she hasn't shown up.'

As he reached for the desk phone, and we came around his desk on our way to the door, Mother said, 'Thank you for your time, Mr Eggler. And please keep our conversation . . .'

'Yes, yes, confidential.'

At the office door, Mother had her hand on the knob when behind us Jared asked the receiver, 'Is Megan there?' Then: 'Oh, dear! What seems to be the matter?'

Mother's hand froze around the knob and her attention went back to Jared. Mine too.

The social director's voice softened. 'Well, of course . . . I hope she'll be all right. You'll let me know? When you can, of course.'

The receiver returned to its cradle.

Mother turned. 'Problem?'

His eyes remained on the desk phone. 'That was Megan's husband. He's just called for an ambulance. She collapsed after . . . after eating some chocolate.'

Mother yanked the door open and all but pushed me out.

She was moving faster than someone with a handicapped placard really should. I could barely keep up.

'We have to get to the ER before the paramedics do!' she said excitedly.

'Why? You don't think . . .?'

'Yes, that girl has been poisoned, too!' Then, like the hero in an action movie, she said, 'Now, go, go, go!'

At Serenity Hospital, I parked in a special section reserved for relatives of ER patients; enough other cars were there to tell me it was not a slow night. Otherwise, all was quiet in the drop-off area.

'Good,' Mother said, 'we've beaten the ambulance here!'

I let the van idle to keep the heat going. 'What do you hope to accomplish?'

'I have a plan.'

Very often Mother had no plan, making up the scenario as she went along. So this could be encouraging news. Or not, as some of her cunning plans have landed us in Ye Olde Slammer for thirty days.

So I had to ask: 'And your plan is?'

Mother leaned toward me, conspiratorially, whispering, as if someone were in the backseat who she didn't want eavesdropping: 'You're to sit in the waiting room, and try to get whatever information you can from Megan's husband.'

'How?'

She twisted toward me. 'Dear, use your imagination! The plot is thickening, and you have a winning personality.'

Did I?

I said, 'You think this waitress was poisoned, too, because she saw something at the luncheon?'

'A distinct possibility.'

'But we can't *know* that.'

'Not if you don't do a little recon, we can't.'

I nodded; she had a point.

'All right,' I said, 'I'll see what I can find out . . . *if* you tell me what you'll be up to.'

'That's on a "need to know" basis only, dear.'

'Mother! What I need to know is that I won't be behind bars as an accomplice to a crime when Jake arrives.'

'We're wasting time, Brandy. The ambulance will be here any minute.'

No use talking. The train's brief pause at the station was over and we were heading down the track already. Next stop Serenity jail?

I shut off the engine, and we got out, breath smoking in the icy air. Toot toot!

At the emergency room entrance, double glass doors sensed our approach and opened, another set within doing the same.

Straight ahead, a distraught couple with a crying baby was being checked in by a nurse at the counter, which gave us cover.

Mother gestured toward a door straight ahead that identified itself as access into the waiting room. Before I passed through, I looked back, but Mother had disappeared. Which was almost as disconcerting as her appearing again might prove.

A voice over the intercom announced, 'ETA one minute . . . priority two.'

Which was the estimated time of arrival not of a tenderloin, rather an ambulance, and the condition, of the patient. Priority two meant Megan was alive but in need of emergency care, more favorable than priority one: unresponsive. But hardly encouraging.

The waiting room was rather small by ER standards, the hospital sorely in need of expansion. On various holidays, after our state legalized purchase and use of commercial-grade fireworks by the general public, people would spill out into the corridors, waiting for word about their loved ones' blown-off fingers and toes, and assorted mangled arms, legs, and faces. Fortunately New Year's was almost two weeks away. But the ER was doing land office business, anyway.

I found a seat, putting another chair between myself and a woman with tear-streaked cheeks, pajamas peeking from beneath an open coat. Across from me was a man in a plaid shirt and dark jeans, face etched with worry, bouncing one leg nervously. And there were others, whose lives were suddenly altered at this moment in time, lost in their own thoughts, and prayers.

The door swished open and Megan's husband – I assumed – entered, his frightened eyes quickly scanning the room. I made a helpful gesture toward the chair next to me, and he slowly came forward, and sat.

In his early twenties, ruggedly good-looking with sandy-colored hair, his face and hands retaining the tan from long summer hours of outside labor, he had on a light denim jacket over gray sweatshirt and pants, speaking of a rushed departure with no thought of the freezing weather.

'I want to be with her,' he whispered, not necessarily to me.

I whispered back, 'I know. But we'd only be in the way.'

It was a somewhat dishonest way to indicate we were in the same boat.

'Why are you here?' he asked, which I took as wanting to talk.

'My mother.' Well, wasn't I? 'And you?'

We were speaking in low voices now.

'My wife, Megan. Do you know her?'

'No.'

He held out a calloused hand. 'Peter Harris.'

Avoiding providing my name, I asked, 'What happened?'

Perhaps that may have been a little too direct, since he seemed to stiffen.

So I offered, 'My mother suddenly got terrible stomach cramps and started throwing up.' Which I knew were symptoms of ingesting arsenic but not enough to kill immediately.

'That's exactly what happened to Megan! Maybe it's something that's going around?'

I shrugged. 'Could be. But it happened pretty quickly after my mother ate some meat.'

Peter turned in the chair toward me. 'Same with Megan, only it was some chocolate.'

'A dessert?' I asked. 'Or . . . a candy bar?'

'No. A box of chocolates.' He paused. 'She came home from work with it this afternoon.'

'How many pieces did she have before getting sick?' I asked, adding for cover, 'Might be your wife's allergic.'

He shook his head. 'Megan has chocolate all the time. And she only ate one – and not even a whole piece!'

Which explained the priority two code.

Trying to sound interested but casual about it, I said, 'You say she came home with the candy . . . did she tell you where she'd gotten it?'

'No. I do know from the box it came from that expensive candy shop downtown.'

Les Chocolats.

Peter went on, 'I just assumed it was a Christmas gift her boss gave all the employees where she worked.'

'Les Chocolats is pretty expensive,' I said. 'I doubt the country club would be that generous to its wait-staff.'

Peter twisted toward me for a better look. 'Hold on . . . you said you didn't know Megan, and I didn't tell you where she worked or what she did . . .' He studied me. 'Wait a minute . . . I *know* you. You're that girl who goes around poking into murder cases with her mother.' His voice was rising. 'Do all these questions have something to do with that lady who died at the country club today?'

Eyes were staring at us.

I touched his arm, and said softly, 'Please. I'm just trying to help.'

His expression was half-glare, half-hurt.

Waiting until the other occupants had retreated back into their thoughts, I whispered, 'I don't know if there's a connection between Megan and what happened to Norma Crumley – that's the woman who died – but Norma also got sick after having some of the same kind of chocolates. They were laced with arsenic.'

He went pale. 'How much of those chocolates did the Crumley woman eat?'

'One piece. And the fact that Megan had only a bite of one gives her a better chance. Where's the candy now?'

'At home, on the coffee table in the living room.'

'You need to make sure the police get that . . . and any paper it was wrapped in.'

I could tell the conversation was making him more upset, and I didn't know what else to ask, so we lapsed into silence. At least he hadn't gotten furious with me; he seemed to be able to tell I meant well.

The door to the ER opened, and a female nurse entered wearing blue scrubs, and matching surgical hat, face obscured by a white mask.

Everyone leaned forward in their chairs, hoping the nurse had come with good news for them, even as they braced for bad.

The nurse slowly scanned the room, then walked over to a woman seated next to a chair she'd put her red coat on.

'Mr Harris?' she asked the woman.

Now, sometimes I can mistake a woman for a man and vice versa, so I didn't think much of this.

Peter got to his feet. 'Over here!'

The nurse approached him. 'You're Megan's husband?'

'Yes.' His voice cracked with emotion.

'Congratulations! Your wife is doing fine!'

As if Megan just had a baby.

For one horrifying moment, I thought the nurse was Mother. But it couldn't be – this nurse wasn't wearing big glasses, and I *was* exhausted.

Peter buried his face in his hands and sobbed, his shoulders shaking with relief.

Then the nurse went out a door leading to the lobby, bumping into the door frame as she did, just as a white-smocked doctor entered the waiting room from the ER.

'Mr Harris?' he asked, echoing the just departed nurse.

I pointed to Peter, whose head came up with his rugged face a blank white sheet waiting to be painted either happy or sad.

The doctor approached, his name-tag identifying him as CHEN.

Dr Chen said, 'Your wife is in a recovery room right now.'

'Will she be OK?' Peter asked, wiping tears from his relieved face.

'Yes.'

'What was the matter with her?'

The doctor hedged. 'We won't know for sure until test results come back.'

'Can I see her?' Peter asked.

'Just for a moment.'

I tugged on Peter's sleeve and he glanced at me.

'Can Brandy come, too?' he asked. 'Ah . . . she's my wife's sister.'

Dr Chen looked right at me. But I had zero history with this physician, and he didn't seem the type to read cozies.

Chen nodded. 'All right. But please let her rest. She's been through quite an ordeal.'

As had the doctor, judging by the moisture on his brow.

Chen frowned. 'By the way . . . did a nurse come through here?'

Peter nodded. 'She left through the lobby.'

'Thank you.'

'Anything wrong?' I asked.

'No . . . no,' Chen said. 'Just wanted to speak to her.' The frown disappeared. 'I'll show you where to go.'

Better than being told *where* to go.

Megan was in a recovery room down a hallway from the ER, with only enough space for a hospital bed and one chair.

She lay on top of the sheets, a pillow provided for her head. Face pale, brown hair matted, the young woman in casual wear might have been dead but for the rise and fall of her chest.

Now I remembered her from the luncheon – more robust, of course – pretty, pleasant, efficient at her job. And someone had nearly taken all of that away. Forever.

Peter pulled the chair closer to the bed.

'Megan?' he said softly. 'Megan honey . . .'

Her eyes opened slowly, then her arms reached out for him. 'Peter . . .'

'Don't try to sit up,' he said. 'You're going to be fine.'

She murmured, 'I was *so* sick . . .'

I stepped forward. 'Megan, forgive me interrupting. But, uh, do you know who I am?'

She raised her head a little, eyes trying to focus on me. 'You . . . you were at the luncheon today, giving the program.'

'Yes. Could I ask you a few questions?'

Megan nodded, head lowering to the pillow. Peter gave me a look that said to make it quick. And gentle.

'Where did you get those chocolates?'

'Is *that* . . . that what made me ill?'

'Possibly,' I said.

Her voice was soft, scratchy, but the young woman was alert enough. 'After the luncheon, I was putting some garbage bags in the trash container outside, and saw a small wrapped box on top.'

'Megan, you didn't!' Peter said.

Her head turned toward him. 'I thought the box had gotten thrown away by mistake. So I took it out.' She paused. 'There was no name, so I opened it, saw the box had all its chocolates in it . . . and figured finders keepers.'

'Completely understandable,' I said. 'I'd have done the same.'

Peter was shaking his head.

Megan raised herself up on her elbows. 'Hey, don't be so quick to judge! When you saw the candy, you wanted some, too.'

Color was returning to her cheeks.

Quietly defensive, Peter said, 'Well, I wouldn't have wanted any if you'd told me you got it out of the garbage.'

'It was right on top!' She waved a hand. 'It's like that five-second rule when you drop food on the floor. Well, that box wouldn't really be garbage till some other garbage got put on top of *it*.'

Life was returning to normal for the young married couple.

Changing the subject, I asked Megan how much chocolate she had eaten.

'Just a bite of one,' she said.

Just as Peter had said.

She continued, 'Then I started having terrible stomach cramps and had trouble breathing.'

The door to the recovery room opened. Filling the frame was Tony, his eyes registering surprise upon seeing me.

Most certainly he'd been notified by Dr Chen as to the reason for Megan's sudden illness.

His eyes narrowed. 'Where's Vivian?'

Mother suddenly appeared behind him and made him jump a little. 'Did someone invoke my name?'

I managed not to smile.

Tony turned to face her.

'Chief Cassato,' Mother said pleasantly, 'and what brings you here?'

'I might ask you the same,' he snapped.

'You might *tomorrow*, dear,' she responded. 'We've all had such a long day, and Brandy has one of her sick headaches . . . isn't that right, darling girl?'

Actually, I did. And it was standing right there by Tony.

Tony's jaw flexed. 'All right. But we *will* talk . . . first thing tomorrow.'

Mother saluted. 'By dawn's early light!'

We made a quick exit.

On the ride home, with the van's heater desperately trying to ward off the cold, I relayed my conversation with Megan in her recovery room.

Mother was silent for a few moments. Then, 'If there were two poisoned boxes of chocolates, for whom was the other intended – certainly not Megan who got it by happenstance – and why did it end up in the trash?'

I asked, 'What if there were more than just two?'

'I'm sure Tony is already checking out the other gifts,' she replied.

'By the way, where did you disappear to?'

'Not now, dear. I'm knackered.'

And that was that.

Inside our warm house, she headed straight for staircase, along the way dropping her purse, and coat, then kicking off her shoes, leaving a trail like someone divesting herself of unnecessary apparel while lost in a blistering hot desert.

I picked up her things, and put them in the foyer, along with my own coat and purse.

Then I followed her upstairs, but to my own bedroom.

Sushi was already a lump beneath the covers. At some point, she'd crawl out, needing fresh air, but that hadn't happened yet.

I didn't brush my teeth, I didn't remove my clothes. I just flopped on top of the blankets.

Sometime later, on my way to the bathroom, I paused by Mother's room.

I could hear her behind the closed door, sobbing, the sound muffed as if she were crying into her pillow.

So Mother did feel something for nasty ol' Norma, after all.

Sushi was at my feet, looking up at me. I opened the door quietly, and she trotted in to comfort her other mistress.

Brandy's Trash 'n' Treasures Tip

Vintage decorations add a special touch to any Yuletide tree, but make sure when using old lights that their cords and/or wires are not frayed. One year our string of 1940s Noma lights did more than just glow – they set our live tree aflame. Oh Tannenbaum!

FIVE

Makin' a List

Darling reader, there is much to explain and Vivian Borne (*moi*) is back to do the 'splain'!

After instructing Brandy to question Megan's husband in the ER waiting room, I proceeded down a corridor that led to a supply closet where medical uniforms were kept, a handy fact I'd learned some time ago. There, I selected a set of blue scrubs, matching cap, surgical gloves, and mask, my idea being to stroll along seeming busy, up and down the emergency-room triage area, its cubicles separated by curtains, and be on hand to gather information on Megan's condition once she arrived via ambulance.

I had just begun my recon along the exam cubicles when Megan was wheeled hurriedly in by the same paramedics who had responded earlier to Norma's collapse at the country club.

To say it was a busy night was an understatement. All three beds were in use: on one lay an elderly man, a male doctor trying to revive him with a defibrillator; another was temporary home to a teenaged boy whose leg was mangled, most likely in a car accident, attended to by a second male physician; the last bed was occupied by a female in the process of giving birth, perhaps having misjudged the timing of her contractions, assisted by a distaff staff member.

A third doctor – looking impossibly young (think Doogie Howser, only Asian) – rushed to consult with the pair of medics on Megan's condition, which was apparently grave judging by their expressions. (By the by, ABC network shouldn't have canceled that unique sitcom after only four seasons. What a delightful show!)

The Asian physician turned, caught sight of me, and shouted, '*You! Nurse!*'

Now, dear reader, being pulled into this kind of activity was not something I had anticipated! However, I had followed the soap opera *General Hospital* since its inception in 1963, and also was a big fan of medical series, not only *Doogie Howser* but also *ER*, *Chicago Med*, *Code Blue*, and *Trauma: Life in the ER*, and had picked up more than my share of technical terms and therapeutic procedures. But then, I'd also thought I could learn to fly a plane by watching Penny at the controls in the 1950s TV show *Sky King*, which had proved a miscalculation. Still, that being said, wasn't I an actress, always ready for a challenging role? Didn't hospitals revolve around theaters?

Anyway, they can't sue you for malpractice when you aren't really a medical practitioner, can they?

I hurried toward the doctor who'd summoned me, whose name tag read CHEN. Handsome young fellow, but so young – I'm not sure I would trust my medical care to someone so inexperienced. Even *I* knew Doogie Howser was make-believe.

'The husband told the medics that she'd eaten some chocolate and immediately became ill,' the doctor told me. 'We have a case of acute allergic reaction.'

'With all due respect,' I replied, 'this appears to be arsenic trioxide poisoning.'

I pointed to the semi-conscious woman on the gurney.

'Note the red swollen skin . . . the evidence of vomiting on her clothes . . . the labored breathing . . .' I opened Megan's mouth, bent and sniffed. '. . . and the odor of garlic – hardly an ingredient typically found in a chocolate confection. These are the same symptoms Norma Crumley displayed earlier today after *she'd* eaten some chocolates at a country club luncheon.'

The medico frowned. 'I wasn't on duty then, but I heard about that.'

I continued: 'This woman was a waitress at the event, and perhaps received a box of similarly tampered-with chocolates, but put off eating any until later.'

'Recommendation?' he asked.

'Chelation therapy,' I answered.

I didn't know what that was exactly, but some actor playing

a doctor on *Chicago Med* had used those words in a similar situation of arsenic poisoning.

Chen nodded. 'All right . . . get ready to administer Dimercapto and Propanesulfonate.'

What and what?

Luckily, I wasn't asked to *prepare* the concoction – which turned out to be an antidote – only administer it through the IV the paramedics had attached to Megan's hand in route, which was well within my medical skill set (thank you, George Clooney!).

With the chelation completed, Chen monitored Megan's breathing, the semi-conscious patient stirring, while I kept track of her vital signs, which were improving with every passing minute: blood pressure and pulse returning to near normal.

Against the backdrop of a newborn crying, I asked, 'Doctor, can you do without me? I had been on my way to help in the ICU.'

'Yes,' Chen said, 'it appears everything is under control. Thank you . . . ah . . .?' His eyes were looking for an ID I didn't possess.

'Nurse Betty,' I replied.

I don't know why that came out; I'd never seen the movie of that name about a woman who'd impersonated a nurse and saved someone's life by remembering some procedure she'd seen on a TV show. Just one of those unexplainable things that emerge from the workings of the human mind.

Chen was saying, 'Nurse, it's due to your quick diagnosis that this woman is alive.'

'Tush-tush, now,' I said. 'I can't take all of the credit – it was a team effort. But until the police find out who's out there putting arsenic in chocolates, you'd better inform the staff, and of course the chief of police, that there's been another victim.'

'Quite right.'

'Goodbye, doctor. It's been a pleasure working with you.'

'And you.'

On the way out, I tossed my surgical gloves in a collector. I glanced along the row of cubicles. The elderly man was sitting up; the teenager had been taken to surgery; and the woman was cradling a beautiful baby. It made me proud to be a pretend nurse.

And while it rightfully should be Chen who informed Megan's husband of the prognosis of his wife, I couldn't help crowing a little. But before entering the waiting room, I removed my glasses, since Brandy might recognize me even in cap and mask.

I am admittedly, without my cheaters, as blind as a bat (apologies once again, David Mamet – but sometimes a cliché is called for). Brandy was still wearing her red sweater from earlier in the day, a scarlet blur that would help me locate her. And, if she'd followed my instructions, she should be seated next to Megan's husband.

What I hadn't taken into consideration was that all sorts of people came into the waiting room in all sorts of clothing, and with this being the holiday season, there just might be a lot of festive red.

So it took me a moment to realize I was about to congratulate someone seated next to a chair with a red coat thrown over it. Whether this individual was a man or woman, I couldn't say – but my odds were good. Fifty-fifty!

'Mr Harris?' I asked.

Someone called out, 'Over here!'

Oops.

Still, I rebounded well, locating him by his voice, giving the husband the good news.

Then I left through a door to the lobby, circled around to the ER via a back hall, returned to the supply closet, and got dressed in my own clothes. Clark Kent had nothing on me.

I knew Megan would be in one of several recovery rooms, toward one of which I was walking when I heard Chief Cassato mention my name.

That should catch you up nicely.

You're welcome!

On Sunday morning, a little before eight (my idea of early rising), Brandy pulled our van into the visitors' parking lot alongside the police station. There would be but a skeleton staff on hand, as crime and mischief in Serenity often seem to take advantage of the proverbial day of rest.

We had brought Sushi along because if, upon our return, the little darling got so much as a *whiff* of the chief's dog Rocky – the love of her life, a charismatic mixed breed with a black circle around one eye – our mascot might suspect betrayal by either Brandy or myself (or both!), in which case who knows what mischief the little rascal might serve up. The day of rest means nothing to a pooch!

The police station was situated at the edge of downtown, buttressed by the fire department on one side, and the county jail on the other, all modern facilities. (When I was sheriff, my office was in the latter. Good times!) Across the street stood the courthouse, a giant tiered wedding cake of white limestone built in the mid-eighteen hundreds that certain citizens with no regard for historical architecture (in this case Grecian Revival) insist on trying to get torn down.

Not on Vivian Borne's watch!

(Just a word about exclamation marks. Some writing teachers are of the opinion that exclamation marks should be used sparingly if at all. This advice is contrary to the Borne Ultimatum, which is that expressive writing should be every scribe's goal. That is why I say – use as many exclamation marks as you like!)

Anyhoo, the wheels of justice run smoothly in Serenity. A perp can be booked at the police station, remanded to the county jail, and arraigned at the courthouse, all within a distance of a few hundred feet – one-stop shopping! Or actually, one-stop incarceration.

We exited the vehicle, Brandy holding Sushi, and walked around to the front of the building through a little brick plaza with several stone benches and small shade trees whose snow-coated bare limbs sparkled in the sunshine. Here at the PD, it was beginning to look a lot like Christmas!

The waiting area of the station, though, had zero Yuletide touches, offering visitors four uncomfortable mismatched chairs (none occupied at the moment), an irritating humming soda machine, and a neglected banana tree plant whose limbs stretched like the arms of a begging ragamuffin toward a window providing the only light, save for a buzzing ceiling fixture that occasionally blinked on and off.

(Another note for aspiring writers: lengthy sentences are good. They pull you in. And keep you there.)

This depressing decor seemed designed to encourage short visits, as if to remind the public that the department wasn't wasting taxpayers' money.

While Brandy took a chair closest to the plant, I marched up to the Plexiglas window behind which a young woman in civilian attire worked diligently at a computer, neglecting her role as receptionist in favor of managerial duties . . . or maybe she knew it 'twas I. Her employment dated post-my tenure as sheriff, but word did get around.

Formerly this had been where a uniformed dispatcher sat – usually a woman – where I used to saunter up to the window, engage said dispatcher in conversation with the intent of gaining inside information by discovering her weakness, then assimilate that knowledge by way of an autographed photo of a favorite movie or pop star (that these were forgeries by yours truly has never been proven). Or perhaps offer her a part in my next play (a walk-on).

During my rather short stint as sheriff, however, I had kept a campaign promise to combine the separate dispatch stations of the sheriff, police and fire departments into one state-of-the-art command center on the basement level, believing my career in law enforcement would go on for a good long while (not just a month or so).

Now, having resumed my civilian status, I regretted fulfilling that promise as my ex-sheriff 'perks' did not include access to that very command center! As they say, no good deed goes unpunished.

'Vivian Borne to see Chief Cassato,' I told the young woman, whose name-tag identified her as Dawn.

Without taking her eyes off the screen, Dawn replied dismissively, 'I'll let him know.'

I expected her to reach for a phone, but she kept right on working.

'We'll just wait here, then,' I said.

She said nothing. Just went right on typing.

So. We were expected to sit and cool our heels.

I returned to the chairs, taking one on the other side of the banana tree from where Brandy sat. Sushi was on the floor, tail in the air as she inspected the base of the plant, looking for any signs of tiny bananas. (The last time she was here, the little scamp had pulled some off.)

Brandy was in the process of performing our police station waiting-room ritual of watering the plant with a bottle she'd filled at home. I removed some cuticle scissors from my tote, and began to trim off brown pieces from the leaves. The banana tree would have died if it weren't for our regular visits – some voluntary, others not.

Dawn called out, 'The chief will see you now.'

Which was sooner than I'd expected. I hadn't even caught her reaching for the phone!

We put our gardening gear away. Brandy scooped up Sushi, and we headed to a steel door that led to the station's inner sanctum. After a buzzer sounded, we passed through and proceeded down a tan-walled, beige-tiled corridor, the tedium of which was broken by a series of photos of police chiefs of bygone days, their stern expressions including eyes that seemed to follow us suspiciously. Bet they were fun at a party!

One photo had been giving me the fits, always hanging crooked, no matter how many times I'd straightened it. But the chewing gum I'd applied as a spur-of-the-moment adhesive to its framed back during my last trip down memory lane did seem to be holding. Small victories!

We passed two interview rooms (not in use); two detective offices (also empty); and one bathroom whose symbol over recent years had evolved from a man, to a man and woman, to a man and a woman plus a half-man/half-woman, to the current sign scrawled in permanent ink: anyone.

And yet I'd bet good money it was a woman who cleaned it.

The chief's office was on the left at the end of the hall, across from the break room, a position allowing him to keep tabs on anyone lingering in there past their allowed time.

I made a fist and gave the chief's closed door the Paul Drake treatment. What's that you ask? For those who aren't familiar with the *Perry Mason* TV series (not the recent HBO one depicting the lawyer as a flawed sad sack, which must have author Erle Stanley Gardner gyrating in his grave) (or possibly churning in his urn), Paul Drake is the private eye hired to investigate things Perry himself couldn't be bothered with in sixty minutes with commercials.

Anyway, Paul would always use a special knock on Perry's private door: the old 'Shave and a haircut, two bits.' But minus the two bits. TV Budgets were limited in the 1950s.

'Enter!' came a terse response.

To first-time guests – which were neither myself, Brandy nor Sushi – Tony Cassato's office might seem strictly utilitarian, providing few clues about the man himself, befuddling even Sherlock Holmes. No mementoes, no award plaques, no photos, not even of his current 'squeeze' Brandy nor the grown daughter from a failed marriage.

In fact, that the chief had retained the same decor as the man he'd replaced, from carpet to furniture to the duck prints on a wall, was actually quite revealing. It said Serenity's Top Cop thought he might have to vacate the position at a moment's notice, so why bother redecorating? (Which turned out to be the case only a year into his stint – see *Antiques Con.*)

Seated behind the desk, the chief looked somewhat weary, though his usual attire was crisp and neat. The granite face, however, was unreadable . . . so this interview could go any which way (but loose).

The chief gestured to the two chairs in front of his desk, and I sat first, then Brandy. Sushi had already wiggled out of her mistresses's arms to disappear behind the desk and sniff their host's slacks, finding a familiar canine aphrodisiac – evidence of her beloved Rocky.

'What were you doing in the ER last night?' he asked, steely eyes taking me in and then Brandy and back again.

Before I'd had a chance to gather my thoughts and reply, Brandy said, 'We were at the country club in Mr Eggar's office, learning about how their gift exchange app worked. We were on our way out when he called Megan Harris to find out why she hadn't shown up for work, and was told by her husband, Peter, that his wife had just became violently ill after eating some chocolate.'

Quite concise. Just the facts, ma'am (man)! I couldn't have done better, although admittedly adding a little color would have painted a more fulsome picture.

I sat forward, smiled and added, 'Naturally, we thought there might be a connection to the candy Norma had eaten, and we went to the hospital to find out.'

'Naturally,' Tony said.

With just a little edge to her voice, Brandy said, 'It turned out there was.'

The chief leaned back in his chair. 'Fortunately, a nurse named Betty was on hand to correctly diagnose arsenic poisoning. Oddly, no nurse with that name is on staff.'

Oh, dear. So this is why we'd been called into the principal's office at such an early morning hour.

'Yes, wasn't it,' I said. 'Quite fortunate.'

He rocked a little in the chair. 'Dr Chen says that perhaps he got the name wrong. But no one at the hospital seems to know who the nurse was, or if she even worked there.'

I summoned a smile. 'Just some random do-gooder, apparently, who saved the day, or anyway evening, then rode off like the Lone Ranger.'

I could feel heat coming off Tonto, that is, Brandy. I hadn't told the girl I was Betty, so as to not make her an accessory-after-the-fact in impersonating a nurse.

The chief's gaze moved slowly from my face to Brandy's and back again, like a figure in a Glockenspiel clock. 'Did either of you see this woman?'

I splayed a hand across my chest. 'Nurse Betty? I certainly didn't.'

A vein throbbed in the chief's forehead. 'Vivian, where did you go once you arrived at the hospital?'

I shifted in my chair, which was as uncomfortable as the ones in the lobby. 'Since the emergency room was quite busy,' I said, 'and the ambulance hadn't yet arrived with Mrs Harris, I went to find another doctor to whom I might express my concerns, and, well, I simply lost my bearings. You know how those corridors are . . . quite the Catacombs!'

'Uh-huh.'

The chief didn't seem to be buying what I was selling.

Then, to my surprise, Brandy said, 'Tony, if you're implying *Mother* was masquerading as this "Nurse Betty," that's impossible. I *did* see this woman. She came into the waiting room where I'd been sitting next to Peter Harris, and told him his wife was going to recover. True, the nurse was wearing a cap, and mask, but she *didn't* have on glasses . . . and Mother can't take two steps without hers.'

Whether the chief believed Brandy, or just didn't want to widen the gulf between them, I couldn't say.

He sat forward. 'All right, let's move on. Brandy, did you learn anything from Mrs Harris in the recovery room? I didn't have a chance to question her before she was taken to the ICU for observation.'

Brandy told him where Megan said she'd found the chocolates, and that she'd taken only a bite before becoming sick.

'The box should still be at their home,' Brandy concluded. 'I told Peter you'd be wanting it and any wrapping paper, too, and not to touch it.'

He nodded. 'Anything else? . . . Vivian?'

'Not that I can think of,' I said, then turned to Brandy. 'How about you, dear?'

'No.'

The chief rose, looking down on us.

'If either of you should run into this Betty,' he said sternly, looking right at me, 'please inform her that not only did she break the law by impersonating a nurse, but there could have been any number of lawsuits brought against her. What she did was dangerous, reckless, and criminal.'

'I quite agree,' I said, and stood. 'Come dear, we've taken up enough of the chief's valuable time.'

Brandy picked up Sushi.

'It's a good thing everything turned out all right!' I said. 'At least this "Nurse Betty" knew what she was doing!'

Now I can't be sure, due to my earwax build-up, but after we left and I closed the door, I heard something thump against it on the other side.

There's no point in rehashing the lashing I received from Brandy on the drive home, regarding my impersonation. And anyway, I wasn't really listening. My mind was compiling a list of possible suspects. I did hear her conclude her diatribe with, 'And forget making any lame excuses or explanations, because I'm not speaking to you!'

Inside, I hung up my coat, then went directly into the library/music/incident room, where I began writing furiously on the board, adding names under the appropriate columns.

When I'd completed this task, I returned the chalk to the board's lip.

Behind me, Brandy said, 'You forgot one.'

I turned.

She was sitting on the piano bench eating peanut butter with a spoon straight from the jar.

'I thought you weren't speaking to me,' I said.

She shrugged. 'Changed my mind.'

'Very well. Who did I leave off?'

'Megan Harris.'

'Dear, she was merely collateral damage.'

'Not necessarily.'

'Explain.'

Brandy sucked peanut butter from the spoon. 'Megan could have poisoned the box of chocolates that she claimed to have found, just to take suspicion off herself. Eating the smallest bite, enough to require a brief hospital stay.'

'Ah!' I exclaimed. 'A bold – if somewhat risky – move, considering how sick that made her.'

Brandy gestured with the spoon. 'Or she could have been the original poisoner, the actual murderer. As one of the elves at the country club, she had the opportunity to swap the box Sheila White had given Ellen. And, again, nibbled the choc to make her less of a suspect.'

I picked up the chalk (not choc) and was adding Megan to the board, when someone else occurred to me.

I included one final name.

When I finished writing it, Brandy frowned. 'Yvette Fontaine?'

'That's right. The owner of Les Chocolats, who hand-makes the candy.'

Brandy then slowly nodded. 'She'd be in a perfect position

to add arsenic to any box of chocolates – assuming she knew who they were for.'

'I think this makes a fine start,' I said, and stepped back from the board.

SUSPECTS IN THE MURDER OF NORMA CRUMLEY

(in alphabetical order)

NAME	MOTIVE	OPPORTUNITY
JARED EGGLER (created gift list)	?	YES
YVETTE FONTAINE (made chocolates)	?	YES
ELLEN FRIDLEY (traded gifts with Norma)	?	YES
MEGAN HARRIS (helped pass out gifts)	?	YES
CARY HUDSON (oversaw gifts table)	?	YES
SHEILA WHITE (drew Ellen's name)	?	YES
MILDRED ZYBARTH (drew Norma's name)	?	?

Now, I know what some readers might be thinking – that I purposely left the killer off the list just to fool you. Not true! I detest crime writers who do not play fair. I still haven't forgiven dear Agatha for the identity of the killer in *The Murder of Roger Ackroyd* – the narrator who kept that information from the reader! (Perhaps I should have preceded this with a Spoiler Alert. But the book was published in 1926 and mystery fans have had plenty of time to read it.)

Anyway, rest assured, our murderer will be on *my* list; but keep in mind, it is a work-in-progress. Stay tuned!

Brandy was saying, 'It's only mid-morning, and we have the whole day ahead. Who should we question first?'

'Let us go see . . .' I paused for dramatic effect. '. . . Sheila White.'

The effect was lost on my daughter, sucking more peanut butter. 'I don't know her. Would she be at home?'

I thought for a moment. 'No. Sheila would be where she always is on a Sunday morning.'

St Mary's Church, middle section, midway down.

Vivian's Trash 'n' Treasures Tip

Decorating your Christmas tree with small antiques – such as silver spoons, china teacups, and red plastic cookie cutters – is a great way to showcase collections. Unless, of course, you then hang the tree by its trunk from the ceiling and it comes crashing down.

SIX

The Bells of St Mary's

A little before eleven, we left home for St Mary's Church, where Mother was confident we would find Sheila White attending mass.

Built around the turn of the last century, St Mary's was a gloomy, gothic limestone structure sitting high on a hill in the center of town. As a child, I'd heard members of other congregations complain (not exactly in a sense of good Christian fellowship) that St Mary's on its perch above Serenity was 'lording itself over all the other lowly churches.' Maybe so, but being on high ground in a Mississippi River town during spring flooding season might have been behind the long-ago decision to build there.

As I steered our van up a steep winding drive to the rear of the church, the enormous bell in its tower had just struck the last bong of the eleventh hour. Sometimes, if the wind was blowing in the right direction, the faint ringing could be heard all the way to our house, which I considered a pleasant treat. But those who lived near St Mary's might well have a different description of the hourly toll.

The cement parking lot was full and I, per Mother's request, invented a spot close to the walkway leading around to the front. I hung the disabled placard to justify this liberty. About the only people who ever climbed the two-hundred-plus steps from the street level were high-school jocks in training, Sylvester 'Rocky' Stallone wannabees.

During my childhood, Mother and I didn't belong to any one churchly persuasion; but you could say we'd attended most of the options, at one time or another – the churches in Serenity, anyway: Presbyterian, Methodist, Episcopalian, Baptist, Lutheran, Catholic, Jehovah's Witness, Mormon . . . we even went to synagogue. While Mother said she believed in God in heaven, she spent years shopping, looking for just the right earthly fit.

For me, I didn't mind the church-hopping, because the variety of services never got boring, which was a common complaint from other kids, condemned to weekly bouts of the same old unison chants and dreary hymns whose meaning was lost by becoming rote. We always signed in as 'visitor,' Mother putting what she could (or what she considered fair exchange for an hour of 'enlightenment and entertainment') in the collection plate. Everyone was always so nice to us because we were potential converts.

But, after all those years of religion-searching, we had finally settled on the aptly named New Hope Church, or as I dubbed it, the Church of Common Sense and Mild Scolding. The (also aptly named) pastor, John Tutor, had been a minister of another local church, but when told by the national church-type powers-that-be he was being transferred to another state, Tutor balked. After his holy superiors insisted, he left the sect, formed New Hope, and took half the congregation with him. Others then joined, churchgoers from all over town who had become dissatisfied with their present holy houses for a variety of reasons, which made an interesting mix of tolerant, nonjudgmental folks.

For example, you'd never hear someone say self-righteously to Mother and me when we showed up at New Hope, after being lax in attending, 'Well, we haven't seen *you* for a while.' My only concern with our church is how much Pastor Tutor (wife Evelyn led the prayer for Norma at the country club) had become synonymous with New Hope, and knowing no other Mr and Mrs Pastor could ever take their place.

Meanwhile, back at St Mary's . . .

Mother and I followed the walkway around to the front, our feet crunching on the pillar's worth of rock salt that had been spread to prevent slips and falls, and ducked inside the small marble vestibule. More doors led to an octagon-shaped narthex – a large lobby area – where a stooped-over man with spectacles, holding church programs, handed one to Mother, tossing in at no charge a disapproving stare as late-comers.

Not the beaming expression we'd get at the door when we rolled into New Hope a little late.

Mother took the folded sheet as presented to her, but I declined one – we weren't staying, Mother just making an investigatory pit stop. She marched forward, and I followed her as far as the baptistry, where she dipped her fingers in some holy water, then crossed herself right to left instead of left to right (she knew the drill – sort of), and continued on alone into the main church sanctuary.

At the moment, the congregation was seated, the service having proceeded to the first scripture reading – or maybe the second – by an assigned lector in suit and tie who stood in the ambo (pulpit to you non-Catholics) (or seasoned church-hoppers).

Mother continued down the center aisle, bending one knee unnecessarily at each pew she passed. (She never did get all the rituals quite right.) Spotting Sheila, my fearless leader entered the already packed pew, bulldozing her way toward the woman, along her path eliciting whispered cries of 'Ouch!' 'Watch where you're stepping!' and causing necks in forward pews to crane at this ungodly racket.

Seemingly unfazed, Mother forced a place for herself next to Sheila, whose face, unfortunately, I couldn't see.

Now you might be thinking, *Oh, poor Brandy, having to put up with Vivian's embarrassing behavior.* Not so. I derive some perverse satisfaction from watching others having to deal with her actions. Welcome to my world.

Mother had been seated for just a short while – perhaps thirty seconds – when she stood abruptly, then repeated the painful process, heads swiveling once again at the outcries, a backward replay of our entrance.

Needless to say, she and I made a swift departure from the church. And lest you think I am being hard on the good churchgoers of St Mary's, we had from time to time (upon arriving late for a service) been similarly impatiently met by worshipers at nearly every house of worship in town. Except at New Hope.

I didn't speak until we were back inside the van. 'You didn't talk to Sheila very long.'

'No. Just long enough to find out that she had traded Secret Santa names with Lydia Kincaid.'

Lydia was the owner of a women's clothing boutique, The Perfect Closet, where I had finally found a brand of jeans that fit me, a Bible-worthy miracle.

I asked, 'Did Sheila say *why* they traded?'

'We'll have to find that out from Lydia.' Mother pointed ahead. 'Engage.'

She'd been watching *Star Trek: The Next Generation* lately.

I started the van.

Normally, the stores downtown were closed on Sundays, but this being the final weekend before Christmas, merchants wanted to wring every December dollar out of shoppers.

The Perfect Closet was located in Pearl City Plaza – so named because Serenity had once been known as the pearl button capital of the world (or at least the USA) due to its many factories built along the banks of the Mississippi, making use of the abundance of mussel shells reaped from the river. Then along came plastic, making possible cheaper buttons, and later, the criminal ramifications of the wholesale harvest of mussels, which had become an endangered species. Even today, you can walk along the riverbanks and pick up one of the old discarded shells with holes punched out of it, looking like it was shot with bullets, a reminder that humans can ruin anything for money.

The Plaza wasn't really a plaza, per se, but a reference to the last block of Main Street, where Victorian-age brick buildings restored to their former grandeur were now occupied by upscale bistros, fancy cocktail lounges, specialty coffee shops, antiques stores, and women's boutiques, including my favorite, The Perfect Closet. (Tattoo parlors, pawn shops, and biker bars had been relegated to the other end of Main. I had no favorites among those.)

I found a parking place and we disembarked, then entered the boutique through an etched-glass door, an old-fashioned bell overhead announcing our presence.

The shop had its original tin ceiling, red-brick walls, and wood flooring – all beautifully refurbished. The merchandise catered to both working women and women of leisure who wanted to be stylish without breaking the bank. I would call the clothes trendy, meaning a customer would wear them for a year or two, then be back for the current look-of-the-moment. Which, of course, kept the merchant doing brisk business.

Lydia Kincaid was behind a glassed-paned counter, attempting to coax a roll of tape into the cash register's dispenser.

Somewhere in her fifties, Lydia was curvy with auburn hair cut in a short bob, attractive but chasing youth through too much make-up. Her attire reflected the merchandise, almost as if she were a walking mannequin. I sometimes wondered if the woman arrived every morning in a bathrobe before opening the store, and picked out an outfit from the racks.

'I'll be with you in a moment,' Lydia said, pleasant but distracted. Then, 'Oh! Hello Vivian . . . Brandy.'

'Let me help you with that, dear,' Mother replied, going around the counter.

'It's my arthritis,' the owner complained. 'I'm afraid I'll have to upgrade to a touch-screen with e-mail receipts.'

By the time Lydia finished speaking, Mother – despite her own challenges with arthritis – had already snapped the roll into place and threaded it.

Lydia sighed and smiled. 'Thank you, Vivian. You must have had some experience with an old cash register such as this.'

Mother had – thanks to serving a three-month probation for breaking and entering by working the check-out at a Salvation Army store. (My penance had been volunteering at Heart of Hearts, a refuge for battered women located in the old YMCA building. My specialties: cleaning bathrooms and mopping floors.)

Lydia was asking, 'Is there anything I can help you find?'

Little did the shopkeeper know what Mother's act of kindness might cost her. Vivian Borne always had an agenda, hidden or otherwise.

'As a matter of fact, dear,' Mother said, while returning to the customer side of the counter, 'it's not finery I'm after, but information.'

'Oh?' Suddenly Lydia was – as most folks around Serenity would be when Vivian Borne started asking questions – guarded and slightly less friendly.

'You weren't at the club yesterday when Norma was taken from us.' Mother made it sound like cherubs had swooped down and lifted the woman away.

Lydia shook her head, arcs of auburn hair swinging. 'No. I'd planned on attending, but had to drive to Des Moines Friday night to check on my mother, who's taken a fall.'

'Oh, my,' Mother said, feigning concern. 'I hope she's all right.'

'Yes, just some bad bruises. But I stayed through Saturday just to be sure and got back late last night.'

'Thank goodness she didn't break a hip, which can be rather brittle at *her* age,' Mother replied – as if she herself weren't a candidate.

Lydia continued, 'Unfortunately, I had to close the shop Saturday, since Sheila was attending the luncheon and wasn't available to help me out, as she often does. So I lost a lot of Christmas season revenue.'

Mother narrowed her eyes, always a bit disturbing due to the magnification of her thick lenses. 'I understand you exchanged Secret Santa names with Sheila, who had drawn Ellen Fridley.' She paused for a possible denial, and when none came, continued, 'Whose idea was that?'

'Sheila's,' Lydia replied, then frowned. Defensively, and a bit puzzled, she asked, 'Is there some reason why we shouldn't have traded names?'

As if Mother was the Secret Santa police.

'No, no, not at all,' Mother replied and summoned a phony sincere smile. She leaned across the counter. 'Confidentially, I'm helping out the police in their investigation of Norma's death. Former sheriff, you know.'

Lydia did know. Everybody in town did.

'There's nothing much to it,' Lydia said with a shrug. 'Sheila came in the shop one day, shortly after the names were emailed, and asked if I would swap with her.'

'Did she say why?'

'No. And I didn't ask. It was more like a "do me a favor" kind of thing, and Sheila is a good customer. As I think you know, she helps me out here in the store, sometimes.'

Mother nodded. 'So you said. Whose name did *you* have?'

'Evelyn Tutor.'

Our pastor's wife.

'So,' Mother pressed, 'you didn't mind trading?'

'Not at all. In fact, I would have rather drawn *anyone* but Evelyn.'

'And why is that, dear? Evelyn is such a sweetheart.'

Lydia sighed. 'For her gift, Evelyn requested a cash donation to her church. And, well, that rather took the fun out of the exchange for me. I don't go to New Hope, for one thing – I'm not currently active in *any* church. And just writing a check takes all the joy out of it. Secret Santa is just as much about *giving* as receiving.'

'I quite understand,' Mother responded sympathetically. 'The idea is to gift something a person wanted that represented an indulgence they might not spring on for themselves.'

'Exactly,' Lydia said. 'And what Ellen wanted was a box of chocolates.' She laughed lightly. 'Now, that's right up my alley. And on my hips, if I'm not careful.'

With chocolates like that, you could wind up with worse results than a few calories might bring.

Mother cocked her head, much as Sushi would have. 'You didn't mind that the chocolates were expensive?'

Another shrug. 'Not at all. Ellen's a regular customer, plus I always try to do business at other downtown stores, like Les Chocolats.'

Spoken like a true quid-pro-quo merchant.

I asked, 'Since you weren't at the club for the exchange, how did the chocolates get to Ellen?'

Lydia seemed to notice my presence for the first time; that happens a lot when I'm accompanying Mother on the prowl. 'I called Les Chocolats before I left town – I had ordered a box last week but not picked it up yet – and asked them to deliver the gift to the club with Ellen's name on it.' She paused. 'Why all these questions about the chocolates?'

The bell above the shop's door tinkled, and a middle-aged man in topcoat entered along with a gust of icy air.

'I'm looking for something for my wife,' he said, gazing around, somewhat befuddled, having wandered into this female domain.

Lydia turned her attention to him. 'I'd be happy to help you . . .'

And that's what is called being saved by the bell.

Back behind the wheel of the van, I asked, 'Should Sheila White be taken off the suspect list, since she traded Ellen's name with Lydia's?'

Mother was frowning in thought. 'No. Sheila still knew what gift Ellen had asked for, and could have substituted a poisoned box sometime during the luncheon with the one Les Chocolats had delivered.'

'Well, then should Lydia be *added* to the list?'

'Not unless she wasn't really out of town on the day of the luncheon. Or we find evidence that she drove back from Des Moines, earlier than Saturday night. And perhaps drove back to build her alibi.'

'That would be a three-hour drive. Six, round trip.'

Mother's smile was withering. 'Your math skills are excellent, dear.'

'Just trying to help,' I said. 'Where to now?'

Then her smile turned wicked. 'I feel like having a chocolate truffle – hold the arsenic.'

I felt like having a hot meatloaf sandwich covered in mashed potatoes and gravy, and I was willing to risk the arsenic. It was lunchtime! But I remained a good little Watson and started the engine.

As for the owner of Les Chocolats, Yvette Fontaine was someone I didn't know at all well. Yvette had arrived in Serenity by herself a few years ago, from New York, with a penchant for mentioning her parents had been born in Paris with lineage dating back (she would say, only half-jokingly) to French nobility who managed to avoid getting their heads cut off. Another of her romantic throwaway tales was that she had taken a cross-country trip with her folks as a teenager, and when they'd stopped in Serenity for the afternoon, she fell in love with the *petite ville*.

Mother and I could have easily walked to Les Chocolats at the other end of the Plaza, and actually really should have, since empty parking places were getting scarce due to procrastinating shoppers taking advantage of these rare downtown Sunday-before-Christmas hours.

But Mother's post-bunion-surgery tootsies were acting up, so I called on my Indian guide Yellow Feather (bestowed to me by our late aunt Olive, whose ashes now resided on a shelf in our library, encased in a large glass paperweight) to find me a nearby place. Promptly a spot up the block appeared.

(To read about how Aunt Olive's paperweight got mistakenly sold in one of Mother's garage sales, and wound up in the torpedo tube of the USS *Ling* docked in Hackensack New Jersey, go to www.BarbaraAllan.com and click on 'Read the missing chapter,' located on the image of the cover of *Antiques Con*. If it's a hundred years from now, and the Internet has been replaced by a chip in your head, you're on your own.)

Compared even to the rest of Pearl City Plaza, Les Chocolats was a small shop, a virtual bonbon boutique, which only added to its mystique and exclusivity. It wasn't uncommon to see people queued up outside in all kinds of weather, or seated on the two elaborately scrolled white wrought-iron benches buttressing the entrance, paying sweet-tooth penance.

Within the shop, everything was Parisian, or anyway your idea of Parisian if the closest you'd been to France was watching *An American in Paris* on Turner Classic Movies (and what was more French than Gene Kelly dancing?). Here in the midst of Serenity, Iowa, were framed wall replicas of paintings by Toulouse-Lautrec to a front window curtain made of chintz with the shop's fleur-de-lys imprint to a shelf display of chocolate Eiffel Towers, Arc de Triomphes, and even edible guillotines. A little ice-cream-shop-type table provided two chairs for significant others to occupy while their partners couldn't make up his/her/their minds on what exquisite confection to buy for inconspicuous consumption at home.

Reality or illusion, who cares! This was as close to Gay Paree as most people in Serenity were liable to get.

But the shop's real showcase (or showcases, as there were several squeezed in) were the luscious-looking house-made chocolates arranged on trays on shelves behind gleaming glass.

Yvette Fontaine was darn near as luscious-looking as her sweet-smelling wares, with a figure that seemed untouched by such trivialities as calories. Just take in those long black tresses, that porcelain complexion, the dark-lashed blue-green eyes, petite straight nose, and wide ruby-red lips, the latter being (at least as far as I could tell) her only make-up. She was a vision in a white cashmere sweater, white wool slacks, with black ballet slippers and a single strand of pearls. *Magnifique!*

At the moment, Yvette stood between two display cases, handing a white sack bearing her shop's fleur-de-lys to a high school boy wearing a purple and gold letter-jacket; most likely purchasing a present for his girlfriend.

'*Au revoir!*' the hostess said.

The boy blushed, and practically fled, nearly knocking me over in the process. Possibly he was shy around so lovely a physical embodiment of the fairer sex as Yvette, or maybe embarrassed because really he was on his way to his wheels to sit within and stuff himself silly. Either way, who could blame him?

Mother approached the shop owner. 'My dear, you look absolutely ravishing.'

'*Merci beaucoup* . . . ah, Mrs Borne, is it not?'

'Please call me Vivian.'

Yvette smiled, showing teeth as white as the embossed wallpaper. 'Very well . . . Vivian. What may I offer you?'

OK, now our hostess was starting to irritate me. It was her ancestors who had fled to the USA during the French Revolution, somehow avoiding getting a much-too-close shave. What was with the French accent from some transplanted New Yorker?

'A pound of truffles,' Mother said. 'Any kind as long as they're dark chocolate. I understand that's good for you.'

Dark chocolate: Mother's idea of health food.

Our hostess said, 'Would this be a gift?'

'No. Just for me,' Mother said, adding deadpan, 'I'll eat them here.'

The woman's smile froze.

'That's a joke, dear,' Mother said in a Foghorn Leghorn accent that seemed to mystify Yvette.

See? I just love watching this kind of exchange.

Yvette forced a little laugh. 'Oh, of course.' Then, 'But you might be surprised how much of what I sell never makes it out the door.'

She had dropped any pretense of French words, although I could still detect the slightest accent, as if she had spoken the language as a small child before her family came to America, where perhaps French had been spoken at home. That would make her, what? Going on three hundred?

Yvette retreated behind her glass cases, from one of which she began filling a signature white box embossed with the shop's name. Mother started up a casual conversation.

'Your special holiday edition certainly is popular. I don't suppose you have any of those left?'

'No. I sold out weeks ago. It's a limited edition or else I'd prepare one for you now. Wouldn't be fair to those who ordered ahead.'

Mother sighed. 'That's what I get for waiting until the last minute. Well, perhaps next year.' A pause. 'Do you send out a pre-order form to your customers?'

Yvette paused in her task. 'I don't.'

'You really should.'

Where was Mother going with this?

'That would be difficult,' Yvette replied, 'because I don't keep a customer database.'

Ah. That was where.

'Why is that, dear?' Mother asked.

'Since I offer a ten percent discount for paying with cash,' Yvette explained, 'the majority of people prefer to come in personally.'

In recent years, many smaller merchants have gone the cash discount route, to avoid overtly passing on built-in credit card fees to the customer. But usually it was only five percent.

Mother said, 'I see. Do you have a delivery charge?'

'I'm not able to offer deliveries,' Yvette responded. 'You see, there's only me here in the shop.'

'A one-woman operation!'

'Yes.'

At least she didn't say *oui*.

I asked, 'How do you find time to make the chocolates?'

Yvette's smile was a tad patronizing. 'Oh, I employ a few

confectioners to do that at a small factory in the Quad Cities. But they work from my recipes, and I visually inspect each and taste-test every batch to make sure they're up to my high standards.'

Mother was frowning. 'Then I must have misunderstood Lydia Kincaid.'

The blue-green eyes went to her. '*Excusez-moi?*' The facade had returned.

'We just dropped by Lydia's clothing store, and she said you delivered a box of your special holiday edition to the country club for Ellen Fridley . . . before the luncheon yesterday?'

Yvette nodded stiffly. 'That was just a favor. I dropped it off after work Friday evening on my way home.'

'How kind of you,' Mother said, again faux-sincere.

The woman went on, 'Lydia and I both belong to the Downtown Merchants Association and often try to help each other out if we can. We women merchants must stick together.'

Mother and I hadn't joined the association, as Vivian Borne doesn't do well in any organization where everyone has a vote.

I cleared my throat and tugged Mother's sleeve. A line of customers had started forming behind us, which within this little shop could get oppressive in a hurry.

Yvette closed the box of truffles, secured it with a gold elastic ribbon, then used a hand-held gadget to figure out the bill, which came to $42.80 charged, or $38.52, cash. (The special edition boxes had gone for a whopping $65.00 each.)

Of course, *moi* got stuck with the bill because I carried cash. Had I known I'd be paying the freight, I'd have insisted on including some pecan dainties (AKA turtles).

We returned to the van where I began stuffing my mouth with chocolate, much as I imagined that boy in the letter-jacket had.

'*Chomp . . . chomp . . . chomp?*' I asked.

'Dear, do swallow before you speak.'

I did. Delicious. 'Where to now?'

'Pearl City Art Gallery.'

What was that about? But I didn't ask. Ours is but to do and . . . eat chocolate.

The art gallery, which specialized in the work of popular Midwestern artisans, was one of several businesses located in an old funeral home on First Street, running parallel to Main. The building was a box-shaped, two-story, gray stucco affair, with gray-and-white striped awnings, and once had been a rather grand place to be taken, before the last stop at the graveyard – or some relative's shelf like Aunt Olive.

The gallery was in the first viewing parlor to the left as we came in the door. The other three parlors were occupied by an upscale antiques store, a picture framing business, and a jewelry shop. A man who repaired clocks had once occupied the 'Preparation Room' in the rear of the building, where he blithely used the old embalming tables as work benches. People either dropping off clocks or picking them up would avert their gaze away from the ancient embalming paraphernalia – like black rubber hoses and tools – that were affixed to the walls, much like a country-style restaurant might display small antique farm implements. Needless to say, he went out of business, and no one has moved in there since.

The parlor Mother and I entered was filled with sunshine, compliments of the tall front windows, which cheered up the room, along with expensive fixtures, floral carpeting, and everything else one might expect to find in a nice art gallery.

There was a lot to look at, but not too much, giving each item its space – be it paintings on the walls, bronze sculptures on columns, or pottery on pedestals, with plenty of room for customers to walk around without bumping into one another. The only thing that hinted at the parlor's former purpose were small wall alcoves here and there, once used to display funeral floral arrangements and now displaying various sculptures.

The owner of the gallery, Mildred Zybarth, approached us with an undertaker's smile. Around sixty, she wore a tan tweed jacket and matching knee-length shirt, nylons (I have never owned a pair!) and sensible beige patent-leather pumps.

She was the kind of lady who went to the beauty parlor once a week for a wash and curl, apparently comfortable with the gray invading her brown hair, much like a homeowner content to allow weeds to take over a lawn as long as they're trimmed back. Her facial features added up to what was once described as 'handsome,' a nice way of saying not really attractive but well shy of unattractive. She was a woman who made the most of what she had, and I had to admire that.

'Vivian . . . Brandy,' Mildred said, her smile blossoming a bit. 'How nice of you to drop by.'

We knew her through a business deal. From time to time Mother and I attended auctions of the contents of storage lockers whose renters have become delinquent in their payments. Usually, this is what we Midwesterners call buying a pig in a poke, since most of the stuff proves to be worthless.

But now and then there's treasure among the trash, like an original oil painting by Margaret Keane of a 'big-eyed' girl wearing a flowered hat. Knowing we could get more for the painting in an art gallery setting, we consigned the piece with Mildred, not only drawing national attention to her store, but – even after giving Mildred her commission – netting us more cash than we might have received through places like Heritage auction house in Texas, avoiding packaging and shipping fees if nothing else.

Now back to our story.

'Lovely to see you,' Mildred said, hands folded before her.

Mother said, 'And it's nice to *be* seen.'

'Isn't it, though,' the woman replied with a chuckle. 'We're none of us getting any younger.'

Speak for yourself, I thought, at least where Mother is concerned.

What followed was to be expected between two antique women (ambiguity intentional): details of hip replacements, bunions, bad eye-sight, herniated discs, fractured vertebrae, shoulder bursitis, elbow bursitis, knee bursitis . . . pretty much all of the sitises.

I wandered over to a small but elegant desk fashioned in the Louis XIV style, paired with an equally posh armchair.

On top of some opened mail was a letter from the Downtown Merchants Association.

Out of sheer boredom, I read it.

Dear DMA members,

Greets! We hope you are all enjoying a prosperous holiday season.

It's hard to believe that spring flooding will soon be upon us in just a few months. And you know what that means! Now is the time to put in your order for rodent control, so please fill out the enclosed form and drop it off at the mayor's office.

In further news . . . blah, blah, blah.

Here's the thing. New York City has cockroaches; Las Vegas has scorpions; Albuquerque has rattlesnakes; and, during spring flooding season, Serenity has river rats.

These furry brown creatures can weigh up to twenty pounds, and have a length of three feet with their rat-like tails. And when they get driven from their underground homes on to the banks of the Mississippi, they take refuge in the dark, damp basements of our downtown Victorian buildings.

Just the thought of the creatures made me shiver.

Since it seemed the medical gabfest was winding down, I returned to Mother's side where Mildred was asking, 'Are you here to offer me another consignment on some new find?'

'No, dear. I merely want to ask you something.'

'Oh?' Mildred's eyes narrowed. 'I'll bet you're investigating Norma's death!'

Mother didn't bother answering, instead asking, 'Why did you give Norma an inexpensive perfume rather than one of the posh brands she requested?'

The question took the woman by surprise. 'How did you know I had Norma's name?'

'Dear! I never divulge my sources.'

That was the *one* thing she didn't divulge. And her age.

Mildred considered whether or not to answer. Then, 'I thought those perfumes were too expensive.'

'It's as simple as that?'

'Well, no. But the reason is rather unkind.'

As unkind as murder?

'Please,' Mother said, 'be frank.'

'I . . . I wanted to see the expression on that woman's face when she unwrapped it.'

'Why?' Mother asked.

'Why do you think?' Mildred frowned. 'Because I didn't care for Norma or her snooty ways . . . Vivian, you're not suggesting *I* caused Norma to have that heart attack? Just because of my gift?'

'No, of course not,' Mother said reassuringly. 'But were you aware that Red Door was Ellen Fridley's preferred perfume? Or that she was recently diagnosed as diabetic?'

'What? I barely know Ellen.' Mildred's eyes narrowed further in suspicion. 'Why these questions? You don't suspect me of inadvertently . . .' Her voice dropped to a barely audible whisper. '. . . killing Norma.'

Not inadvertently, I thought.

Mother shrugged. 'Not at all, dear. I was merely curious about tying up a few little loose ends in the affair.'

Despite the sunshine streaming in through the windows, the room suddenly felt chilly.

'Well, Vivian,' Mildred replied, stiffly. Hurt. Offended. 'You know what happened to the cat.'

Was that a veiled threat?

'Now if you'll excuse me,' Mildred said crisply. And went over to assist two young men who'd entered the gallery.

Out on the sidewalk, I asked, 'Well? What did you make of her?'

Mother was walking just fine now. Striding even. 'Not liking someone isn't a motive for murder, Brandy. But the reason behind that animosity just might be . . . By the way, what cat was she talking about exactly?'

Brandy's Trash 'n' Treasures Tip

According to research, the first nativity scene was displayed by St Francis of Assisi in the year 1223, when he used real animals and people to depict the birth of Christ. The most desirable (and valuable) sets are made in Italy by Fontanini, originals selling for thousands of dollars, depending of course upon when they were produced. Our nativity scene (not Fontanini), includes the Baby Jesus, Mother Mary, Father

Joseph, the Three Wise Men, an angel, a shepherd, sheep and lamb, and ox and donkey. As a child, I thought that cast could be improved upon by adding the dancing California Raisins I'd gotten courtesy of McDonald's Happy Meals. Was I wrong?

SEVEN

Do You Hear What I Hear?

The Sunday matinee had just concluded at the Bijou, a single-screen second-run theater located on a side street off Main. (Mostly older) folks were exiting through the art deco double doors, clutching coat collars around their chins, or trying to tame an unruly scarf unraveling in the wind.

Mother and I paused to look up at the vintage marque overhang where black letters on a white background read: **MERRY CHRISTMAS**! Glassed-in one-sheet posters announcing the current attractions were on either side of the entrance, one depicting Jimmy Stewart lifting Iowa girl Donna Reed in the air, both actors starring in the 1946 classic, *It's a Wonderful Life*; the other was a montage of various children's holiday features and cartoons with a caption:

SPECIAL FREE
SATURDAY MORNING SHOWING
FOR THE KIDDIES!

And in smaller letters: **Drop them off while you shop**. The Stewart/Reed poster looked to be a slightly weathered authentic one, while the other was a crisp photoshopped compilation.

We walked by the central enclosed ticket booth whose counter displayed the Santa and Rudolph puppets I mentioned previously, as if the Man with All the Toys might be a mini-ticket-taker assisted by his diminutive reindeer. (An accompanying card told the curious that these figures had been created by Japanese puppet maker Ichiro Komuro for the enduring 1964 stop-motion feature.)

Once inside, Mother paused to take a deep breath.

'Ahhh . . . there's no smell quite like that of an old theater,' she said, pronouncing the last word, 'thee-a-tah.'

If you relished the aroma of popcorn mixed with spilled Coke and musty carpeting, that is.

Very little about the interior had changed since the building's construction during the Great Depression of the 1930s when – as the Palace Theater – demand for cheap escapism meant that even the smallest town could support multiple movie houses. Such was the charm of the Bijou, despite the occasional broken seat in the darkened auditorium or that seemingly eternally out-of-order restroom stall in the Ladies.'

Still, this must have been what it was actually like back in the day to see James Stewart and Donna Reed up on the silver screen when the beloved Frank Capra film was first released, the couple jitterbugging while blissfully unaware they were about to tumble into their high school swimming pool, as the dance floor covering retracted thanks to a prankster who seemed strangely familiar (as well he should – it was a teenage Carl 'Alfalfa' Switzer, a graduate from *The Little Rascals*).

A certain shopworn elegance remained in the old movie house. From the lobby's high-domed ceiling hung a large chandelier whose tear-shaped crystals had once sparkled brightly, but had dimmed over the decades. The faded gold-flocked wallpaper looked to be original, as was the well-worn carpeting, an art-deco design in burgundy, black, and gold.

To our right, the concessions stand had also survived, its ancient popcorn machine still popping away in eternal enthusiasm. The long chrome and glass counter retained its twentieth-century futuristic look, stocked only with old-fashioned candies that had managed to survive into another era – Goo Goo Clusters, Raisinets, and Mallo Cups among them. I've been known to see any number of flicks that Mother and I already had at home on DVD or Blu-ray, just to be able to buy an Abba-Zaba bar. (No, you couldn't just walk in off the street and buy one without purchasing a ticket, too. I tried.)

Behind the concessions counter, a teenage Goth girl with short, spiky black hair, and more pierced earrings than a pirate, her job to dispense tickets along with goodies – was tending to a female theatergoer who was doing what I always did: buying another candy bar on the way out to take home.

Straight ahead were doors to the main floor seating while

a staircase on the right led up to a balcony area – the so-called Smooching Section, as it was known back in the day – now closed off, perhaps by the health department.

Though the place had undergone some restoration, the age of the structure and its demanding interior had made maintaining the Bijou a constant chore for its film-loving proprietor (and Serenity's favorite Santa).

To our left was an old wooden door that said manager in faded black stencil, which was where Mother was heading.

For once, she knocked before entering.

'Come in,' came Cary's rather high-pitched voice.

Mother went in first and I of course dutifully followed. If only I'd stopped for a bag of popcorn from which to toss handfuls in the air above her like flower petals as she made her grand entrance.

Not that there was far to go. The room was more like a large closet than an office, or perhaps it seemed that way due to the plethora of old movie memorabilia, the walls chock-a-block with framed posters and lobby cards from vintage films, 1950s era mostly.

Cary Hudson sat behind a small desk – like a student in a cramped dorm room at a small sad college – that had barely enough space for his laptop, a compact printer, and lamp. The plump king of the Bijou kingdom wore a dark three-piece suit whose vest buttons were straining a little over a white shirt, the conservative nature of his clothing offset by his colorful Looney Tunes tie arrayed with various Warner Brothers cartoon characters. The Tasmanian devil seemed in a particularly good mood.

Leaning against the wall behind Cary was a vintage life-size faded-color standee of the Creature from the Black Lagoon, reptilian arms held high as if about to strike, his long curled fingernails needing a trim (the Creature, not Cary). Last fall, it had been displayed in the lobby along with classic standees of Frankenstein's monster, Dracula, the Wolfman, and the Mummy, inviting one and all to the annual Halloween Extravaganza, a twenty-four-hour, back-to-back showing of old horror faves. Nerds of all ages could be found in the Bijou's squeaky seats well into the night, while college students from the area in full costume descended in the evening and remaining till dawn, their presence accompanied by the occasional whiff of doobie smoke, an infraction ignored by a manager welcoming the business.

Serenity was fortunate to have someone like Cary, whose love of old movies kept many celebrated but obscure older films alive – ones you couldn't see on cable TV or have access to – for various generations of Serenity movie lovers. One evening every month, the Bijou devoted its screen to silent movies, the antique cellulose nitrate film reels winding through the old theater's projectors while a lady who played the organ at the Baptist church accompanied the feature on a synthesized keyboard.

And, for a die-hard coterie of *The Rocky Horror Picture Show* fans from the nearby Quad Cities, there was a monthly midnight presentation. Once I attended to see what all the fuss was about, which appeared to be a hardy handful of fully costumed attendees lining the front of the stage and singing along. Soon I learned this was just the start, as I got pelted with dry toast, toilet paper, playing cards, and went home early, soaked by water pistols with rice in my hair, muttering, 'Damnit, Janet!'

'Mrs Borne . . . Brandy,' Cary said, beaming at us proudly. 'How did you like seeing Jimmy Stewart up on the big silver screen? Quite a different experience than seeing it at home, isn't it?'

Home was where we had *It's a Wonderful Life* in 4-K, actually a preferable experience, in my opinion. The main attraction could be paused for bathroom breaks, if nothing else. And the snacks, while less nostalgic in nature, were cheaper.

'Call me Vivian, please,' Mother replied. 'And we didn't attend today's matinee.'

'Oh, well,' he replied, disappointed if still cheerful, 'if you missed it there's another showing at seven.'

To counter Mother's curtness, I said, 'We'll try to catch a showing before Christmas. The movie is one of our favorites.'

He nodded. 'Who could disagree? . . . What is it I can do for you good ladies?'

Since there was no place to sit, Mother moved right up to

the edge of the desk. Cary looked up quizzically at her. The Creature from the Black Lagoon glared directly at her. 'It's about the luncheon yesterday.'

'Dreadful,' Cary said with a frown and a wag of the head. 'Simply dreadful. I wish I hadn't been there – and I nearly wasn't.'

'Oh?' Mother said. 'Why is that?'

He leaned back in the chair, jostling the Creature who fell forward a touch, its hands comically grabbing at him.

While I stifled a smile, Mother prompted the Bijou manager, 'You were about to say?'

Cary half-turned in his chair to push the standee back in place. 'I'd had that children's event in the morning, which was supposed to end at noon, but it went long because of some technical problems.' He paused. 'Anyway, I arrived at the club late, and then had to suit up in my Santa costume in the men's room, and barely made it to the gift table in time to pass them out.'

'Then you weren't present when the presents were dropped off?'

'No.' Cary sat forward, folding his hands, his pudgy face troubled. 'Mrs Borne . . . er . . . Vivian, I'm aware of the murder cases you and Brandy have solved, so I'll put my cards on the table right away.'

Those would be the ones swept up after the midnight showing of *Rocky Horror*.

He continued, 'Personally, I don't think Norma Crumley had a heart attack.'

'No?'

'No.' He leaned forward, almost whispering, as if keeping this from the Creature. 'I think she may have been poisoned.'

'And why is that?' Mother asked.

'I was standing close enough to see the convulsions just before she fell forward on to the table, which to me isn't typical of a heart attack. While I'm no doctor, I have had, as someone dealing with the public, CPR training . . . and grabbing your throat and making choking sounds seems more like some food that didn't go down right. Anyway, that's what I thought at first. But then, when that other lady who was helping

Mrs Crumley didn't lean her forward and perform the Heimlich maneuver . . . well, maybe I've seen too many crime movies, but that led me to think poor Mrs Crumley been poisoned.'

'Very astute, dear,' Mother said.

He leaned back in his chair bumping the Creature. 'Then I'm right?'

'Yes. But Norma may not have been the intended victim.'

He frowned. 'Oh?'

Briefly, Mother explained that it was Ellen Fridley who had received the deadly box of special holiday chocolates, having switched gifts with Norma due to Ellen's recent diagnosis of diabetes.

Cary's frown deepened. 'Do you know what the poison was?'

'Arsenic trioxide.'

A hand came up to cover his mouth. 'Good Lord!'

'Yes. Quite an unpleasant way to die.'

'How well I know,' he said. 'I've seen how quickly . . . and indeed unpleasantly . . . it can kill rats.' Suddenly his face turned pale, even the ruddy cheeks. 'Mrs Borne, I *have* arsenic trioxide! Right here at the Bijou! I use it in the spring when the river floods and the rats invade our basement.'

'Oh dear.'

He gestured with open hands. 'It's provided by the Merchants Association to *all* downtown businesses.'

'Perhaps you can tell me,' Mother said, leaning a hand on his desk, 'why the association became involved in dispensing such a lethal form of pesticide.'

Cary nodded, color returning to his face. 'It's because the type of rodent poison available at hardware stores isn't designed to kill these large river rats. I would go down into the basement and see one in agony, and have to use a hammer or shovel to . . .' He shivered. 'It was horrible, simply horrible. Once, one of those poor half-dead creatures crawled up into the lobby causing a crowd at concessions to scatter.'

Suddenly I wasn't in the mood for an Abba-Zaba bar.

Mother asked, 'How does the association acquire arsenic trioxide?'

'Through the mayor's office. They submit orders to the city Maintenance Department.'

I asked, 'Hasn't the use of arsenic trioxide been banned due to environmental concerns?'

Cary looked at me, possibly surprised I had the ability to speak. 'Not entirely. But I do think that day is coming.'

Which could motivate merchants to stockpile the poison.

Mother asked, 'Did you happen to buy one of the Les Chocolats special holiday boxes of chocolates?'

Despite her casual spin, he had to know what she was after.

'I've never been in that store,' Cary said flatly. 'If I get an urge for candy, I have a concession stand teeming with the stuff.'

That came off a little indignant, considering he'd been plump enough to play Santa.

The Goth girl stuck her head in the door, giving me a better look at her oversized black sweater, red-and-tan plaid skirt, lace tights, and floral combat boots.

'Mr Hudson,' she said. 'Sorry to interrupt, but I'm going home for supper. Be back at six.'

'Thank you, Alexis.'

She disappeared.

Cary stood. 'I've got some sweeping up to do before the next show, ladies, but my door is open any time.'

We thanked him and headed to the door (which wasn't much of a trip).

But before we'd gone out, Mother paused to ask, Columbo style, 'One more question.'

'Yes?'

'Was a gift left unclaimed after the exchange?'

The theater owner squinted in thought. 'I *do* remember one present not being claimed, but can't recall who it was for. You'll have to ask Jared Eggler.'

He seemed about to say more but stopped himself.

'Something else?' Mother asked.

'Yes, but I'm uncomfortable mentioning it, because it might seem to point to someone. And I certainly don't want to make a false accusation, and cause trouble for anyone.'

Including himself.

Rather sweetly, Mother said, 'What you say stays between the two of us, dear.'

The three of us, but who's counting?

When Cary's eyes went to me, Mother said ridiculously, 'Do not worry about Brandy. She is my confidential secretary.'

First I'm Watson to her Sherlock, now I'm Della Street to her Perry Mason.

The movie manager sighed, apparently hating to get into this. 'When I was passing out presents, I handed Ellen Fridley's to one of the waitresses – I think her name was Megan – and she gave it to another waitress, saying, "You do it. I hate that . . . that B-word."'

Mother paused, drinking that information in. Then she said, 'Thank you, dear. You've been most helpful.'

As I backed up to leave, my foot knocked over some film canisters stacked on the floor.

'Sorry,' I said, stooping to straighten the tins.

Cary came around the desk. 'My fault for putting them there.'

'Anything interesting?' Mother asked, referring to the canisters.

'Certainly is,' he responded with boyish enthusiasm, as he looked up from restacking them, the unpleasantness of poison having passed. 'I just purchased a silent from 1926 called *Risky Business*.'

I doubted this one starred Tom Cruise and Rebecca De Mornay.

'Ah . . .' Mother said. 'Starring Vera Reynolds with Zasu Pitts and directed by Alan Hale . . . You'll want to keep that away from flames, of course.'

'Oh my, yes,' Cary responded. 'I have a special fireproof room in the basement for cellulose film.'

Tucked away in our van, after getting the heater going, I said, 'Alan Hale, Vera Reynolds and Zasu Pitts? How can you know *that*, and not your cell phone number?'

'Because I never call myself.'

Ask a stupid question, get a stupid answer.

In any case, she was using her cell now, scrolling through her contact list, then tapping on a number. Shortly, I heard Jared Eggler's voice, Mother putting him on speaker.

'What is it now, Vivian? I'm busy preparing for an evening event.' The club's social director did sound harried.

'Tell me – was there any malice between Megan Harris and Ellen Fridley?'

A sigh came across the line. 'I don't give out that kind of information, Mrs Borne. I do not traffic in gossip.'

'Neither do I, Mr Eggler,' Mother said sternly. And ridiculously. 'I hope you're not trying to impede my investigation. I doubt Chief Cassato would appreciate that.'

Oh brother.

Jared came right back with, 'No! Of course not.'

'Well?'

He sighed again. 'Ellen wanted me to . . . to fire Megan.'

Mother frowned at the phone. 'Why?'

'Because, according to her, Megan had a criminal record.'

'Was this common knowledge when the young woman was hired?'

'It was not. But it didn't matter to me, one way or another, because Megan was one of the club's best waitresses.'

I leaned toward the phone, speaking up. 'Jared, this is Brandy . . . Did you have the authority as social director to fire her?'

'Well, I'm in charge of the wait staff. So, yes, that would fall well within my purview.'

Mother asked, 'How does the club deal with gophers?'

'With what?'

'Those furry little creatures that can tear up a course.'

Hadn't Jared ever seen *Caddyshack*?

'Oh,' he said. 'The groundskeeper puts toxic bait in any holes that turn up on the fairway.'

Mother asked, 'Arsenic trioxide, by any chance?'

'I wouldn't know about such things,' Jared said irritably, his patience clearly running out. 'You'll have to ask the groundskeeper.'

Mother didn't let up. 'What happened to the gift that was left over from the exchange?'

'Now what are you talking about?' he snapped.

'The present for Lydia Kincaid.'

'Oh . . . that. It's right here on my desk for her to pick up.'

'Would it be shaped like a box of candy?'

'Yes.'

'Open it.'

'That's really not appropriate.'

'*Not* opening it would be inappropriate.'

Paper ripped.

'Well?' Mother asked, impatiently.

'It's a book . . . *Destiny, the Authorized Biography of Christian Dior*.'

'Oh,' Mother said flatly. 'Never mind.'

She ended the call.

'Dead-end on that front,' Mother said, adding, 'It would seem Lydia has greater aspirations than ready-to-wear.'

I nodded. 'So she's not suspect-list-worthy?'

'No.'

'But now we have a motive for Megan.'

'We do indeed.' She put on a blatantly phony look of concern. 'Let's go see how the poor girl is doing, shall we?'

I shook my head. 'I'm not going anywhere until I get something to eat. And that *doesn't* include more chocolate.'

My stomach was already queasy from having too much.

'I am a tad peckish, myself,' Mother admitted. 'But we have to make it fast.'

Across the street from the Bijou was a little place called Capone's that served, among other yummy sandwiches, the best Chicago hot dog this side of the Windy City. And that's exactly what I had, with all the dragged-through-the-garden toppings. Mother ordered the Maxwell Street Polish sausage smothered in mustard and grilled onions, and we shared an order of fries while seated at a table for two while the movie *Scarface* staring Paul Muni played on a wall-mounted flat-screen.

Most of the tables were taken by other patrons of fine cuisine, some of whom I recognized as having coming out of the Bijou after the matinee. The eatery's owner, a burly bearded man in a black sweatshirt with a Capone's logo, was milling among them, inquiring as to their satisfaction.

When he came over to us, Mother asked, 'How's business, Nick?'

'Not bad, Vivian,' he said. We'd been customers long enough to be on a first-name basis.

Nick went on, 'In fact, I ran out of hot dogs and fries after the kiddie show yesterday.'

I said, aware of mustard on my face but too hungry to do anything about it, 'Smart choice, this location.'

Mother leaned across the little table to dab my mouth like I was a toddler.

'Absolutely,' Nick said, adding, 'Although there's always a dry spell after the first of the year.'

'Push the chili dogs, dear,' Mother told him. 'And add a creamy broccoli and cheese soup for the duration.'

She had an opinion on anything for anyone. At least they came free of charge.

He nodded. 'Good idea.'

'Nick,' Mother said, 'did you happen to notice Cary Hudson leaving the theater after the children's show?'

His several nods came quick. 'As a matter of fact I did. Things had just let up here, and I glanced out the front window and saw him rush out in a hurry.'

'What time was that?' Mother asked.

'Oh . . . about one. He was carrying a suit bag, and a big bulging red sack. Either it was Cary or the real Santa Claus.'

He grinned and Mother returned it, saying, 'Thank you, dear.'

The owner moved on.

I looked at Mother. 'That jibes with Cary's account. The suit bag was his costume, and the red sack was probably filled with wrapped, empty boxes.'

'But perhaps not *all* of the boxes were empty,' she replied.

Green Acres, a mobile home park in the south end of Serenity, was about as nice as such areas come: paved streets with lights, better-than-average-sized lots, attractive landscaping, and uniform curbside mailboxes.

Darkness was closing in by the time we parked our van behind a late-model gray truck in front of number seven. A sidewalk led to the front door of a double-wide where I ascended cement steps to a small stoop, and rang the bell, while Mother waited below.

Shortly, an outside light flicked on.

The door was opened by Peter Harris, sporting a blue flannel shirt and jeans, his feet bare.

He didn't recognize me for a few moments, then smiled, barely, and said with a nod, 'Brandy. Hello.' Not friendly, not unfriendly, just not committing himself yet.

'We're here to see how Megan is doing,' I said, then gestured behind me. 'You remember my mother? Chief Cassato was talking to her in the hallway outside the recovery room.'

'Yes,' he said, stepping aside. 'Come in.'

The interior was surprisingly spacious, what you call an open concept plan, the living room flowing into the dining area and kitchen. The flooring was walnut, walls white, and the furnishings tasteful. If you didn't know this was a mobile home, it might be any standard housing-addition residence of an upper-middle-class family.

Megan was at a kitchen counter preparing their evening meal, chopping vegetables on a board, a head of iceberg lettuce awaiting its turn.

Peter said to his wife, 'Honey, they're here to see how you're doing.'

There was something guarded in his tone.

She wiped her hands on a towel, then came out to greet us. No longer a pale picture of death – nor an invisible waitress in a white shirt and black slacks – this was the real Megan: pretty, perky, her retro clothing of exaggerated '70s corduroy bell-bottom jeans and '80s off-the-shoulder *Flashdance* top revealing her playful side.

Speaking to me, she said, 'I'm glad you stopped by. Brandy – right?'

'Right.'

'I didn't have a chance to thank you properly for keeping Peter company throughout my ordeal. Sit down, please.'

Mother and I settled on to the gray couch while Megan sat in a gray-and-white striped armchair, separated by a glass-and-chrome coffee table. Peter stood near his wife, arm around the high back of the chair. Protective.

I asked, 'When do you think you'll be returning to work?'

'Actually, I feel well enough to go back tomorrow.' Megan

looked up at her husband. 'But Peter wants me to take a few more days off.'

He apparently considered her well enough to make him dinner.

'Would you mind,' I asked, 'if we ask you a few questions?'

'Not at all. I'm aware of the murders you've helped solve here in Serenity . . .'

Mother stiffened a little at the 'helped.'

'. . . and certainly would like to know who put poison in the candy I ate.' She shifted in the chair. 'It *was* poison, wasn't it? I remember hearing a nurse say arsenic.'

'Yes,' I said. 'Added to the candy in a powder form.'

Megan frowned. 'Am I in further danger, do you think?'

Mother took over. 'Highly unlikely, dear. You were simply an innocent bystander, who happened to find a box of chocolates in the garbage and helped yourself.' That was Mother's revenge for 'helped.' She raised a forefinger. 'That is, *unless* you happened to see who threw it away.'

Megan shook her head. 'I'm afraid I didn't.'

Mother sat forward a bit. 'The police have it now?'

Megan nodded.

'Was there a name attached to the box?'

'No. Not unless you mean the Les Chocolats logo.'

Mother paused, then asked, 'How did you feel about Norma Crumley?'

Our hostess shrugged. 'She was always all right to me.'

'And Ellen Fridley?'

Peter stiffened. 'Why do you want to know about her?'

Mother looked at him. 'Because Ellen received a similarly tainted box of chocolates, which she gave to Norma, who then died.'

Megan's mouth dropped. 'I . . . I thought she had a *heart* attack,' adding, 'although the police *did* ask a lot of questions.'

Mother asked, 'Did Ellen try to get you fired?'

Peter, on the edge of irritation, put a hand on his wife's shoulder. 'You don't have to answer that.'

'It's all right,' Megan said to him. Then to Mother, she said, 'Before I moved here, I got into some serious trouble, and spent some time in the county jail.'

'For?' Mother pressed.

'Assault.'

'Simple, serious, or aggravated?'

Mother became knowledgeable about various criminal charges during her several stays in the county jail.

'Whichever one landed me twelve months,' Megan replied with a resigned shrug. 'I was drunk and in a bad place, and got in a bar fight with another woman, who I cut with a broken beer bottle.'

She didn't seem the type, but enough alcohol can make some people do things they wouldn't do normally; and who's not to say the other woman hadn't started the fight, and Megan had just been defending herself. Moral: if you can't say something good about somebody who gets in a bar fight, don't say anything at all.

Mother was saying, 'I suppose working at the club is one of the more desirable service jobs in town.'

Megan nodded. 'The pay is better than anywhere else, and tips are typically generous. Plus, because of the hours I put in, I get health benefits, which is important because Peter is a freelance contractor.'

'So,' Mother concluded, 'losing your job would have been a real hardship.'

I had been watching Peter out of the corner of an eye, and could tell he was becoming more and more uncomfortable, especially with Mother.

And he made that point, saying, 'I don't like where this is going.'

'Oh?' Mother asked innocently.

'It sounds to me like you're accusing my wife of, well . . . murder or something! Have you forgotten she almost died?'

Mother raised a conciliatory hand. 'We haven't forgotten. But remember – whoever poisoned the chocolates Norma ate is the same person who tampered with the box Megan found.'

His face was flushed with anger. 'Well, that person is not my wife! I think it's time for you to leave.'

'Peter,' Megan said, 'would you finish preparing the salad while I see our guests out? *Please?*'

He huffed. 'OK, babe. OK.'

Reluctantly he retreated to the kitchen.

Megan, accompanying us to the door, whispered, 'Please forgive him. He's upset about what happened to me.'

'Of course,' Mother replied. And for once that seemed sincere.

We were out on the stoop when the young woman said, 'Oh, and Mrs Borne? Thank you for saving my life.'

'My dear . . . how did you know? I was incognito, after all.'

'When you think you're dying, you notice the smallest details . . . like that scratch on the right lens of your glasses.'

Then Megan slipped back inside.

'Sherlock Holmes,' Mother said, with a shake of the head, 'out-deduced by a suspect.'

By the time we'd been talking to the Harrises, night had fully enveloped the city. Inside the van, I was about to start the engine when Mother's cell sounded.

Mother checked the call ID and then asked the phone, 'What is it, Alice?'

'I've just returned from the grocery store, and my house guest – *Ellen* – is gone. So is her car.' The former teacher rushed on, 'And there was a note saying she was going home, to get a few things.'

'Did you try calling her cell?'

'Yes. No answer.'

Anxiously, Mother asked, 'How long have you been away?'

'Less than an hour,' Alice said. 'So it might not be anything to worry about. Ellen could be driving back here now, and that's why she's not answering. Do you want me to keep trying?'

'No, but call me immediately if she shows up,' Mother said. 'In the meantime, Brandy and I will go to her house.'

While I navigated the icy streets as fast as I dared, Mother continued speed-dialing Ellen, each attempt going to voicemail.

From the south end of town, I returned to Pearl City Plaza and began the drive up West Hill to the mansions, architectural masterpieces in styles of baroque, Gothic Revival and Greek Renaissance.

But Ellen's house – built on land purchased by her first husband after an original mansion had burned down – was nothing anyone would look at twice, unless they were enamored of 1970s French Provincial.

Mother was saying, 'That's Ellen's car in the driveway.'

I pulled the van up behind an older model burgundy Cadillac sedan, and we got out.

The house – constructed of tan bricks with black wrought-iron-covered windows – had a few lights on, including the porch and what I assumed was the living room. We followed a short walk illuminated by solar panels to the front door.

Mother tried the knob, which turned.

'Unlocked,' she said, with a wary glance toward me at her side.

Once inside, Mother called out, 'Ellen!'

When no answer came, she tried again, receiving similar silence.

Fearless Vivian Borne moved forward, with cowardly me close behind, into a formal living room which seemed to have been frozen at the time it was first decorated. The carpet showed signs of wear, as did the fabric on the arms and seats of chairs, the couch's cushions sagging from years of use, on which lay Ellen's coat and purse.

'There she is,' Mother said, across the room from me.

Do you know how it is when you drive by a bad wreck and you think you're not going to look, then you do?

I looked.

Ellen lay sprawled on her back by the fireplace, face and head beaten, a bloodied poker discarded beside her.

Brandy's Trash 'n' Treasures Tip

Original vintage movie posters such as *White Christmas* or *Miracle on 34th Street* are a good investment because their value tends to appreciate over time, and are fun to display during the holidays. For some reason, Mother brings out a poster of *The Gorilla* starring the Ritz Brothers, perhaps because there's a Christmas tree in one scene.

EIGHT

Mistletoe-Tag and Folly

Vivian once again at the helm of the Borne Express, chug-chugging down the line. Casey Jones, eat your heart out!

I think a little levity is in order after all this unpleasantness, don't you? Toward that end, I'd like to thank those who contacted me through social media, snail-mail, and our publisher, Severn House, with their positive response (with the exception of Mrs Earl Peabody of Walla Walla, Washington, who clearly doesn't have a sense of humor) to my little joke in *Antiques Ravin'* about an elderly chap whose mates hired a lady of the evening to go to his flat on his eightieth birthday, whereupon answering his door, she said, 'I'm here to give you super sex,' to which he replied, 'I'll take the soup.'

Anyway, boys and girls, I have another knee-slapper for you. As before, in order not to careen into the overly risqué (although our readers are sophisticated and seasoned in the ways of the world), I will once again deliver my jest in a formal British accent, which you won't be able to hear, unless listening to the audio version, so *think* upper crust as you read.

Ready?

There was a wealthy elderly gent who lived in Chelsea or Knightsbridge or one of those posh London neighborhoods, who was about to wed a nubile young lass, and, on the advice of his physician, came in for a check-up.

After the exam, the doctor got around to the upcoming nuptial. 'I'm concerned about the differences in your ages,' he said.

'Oh, why's that, old chap?' the elderly gent asked.

'You're ninety-five and your fiancé is eighteen, and too much fadoodling on your wedding night might well prove fatal.'

The gent sighed, then replied, 'Well, doctor . . . if she dies, she dies.'

Isn't that cute? Isn't that true? Although, it does seem like I'm picking on elderly gentlemen. But let's face it ladies, older gents do make the best foils.

Back to the murder at hand. (You may cease with imagining my British accent – unless you enjoy it, in which case, Tally-Ho!)

Having discovered Ellen Fridley on the floor near her fireplace, bludgeoned with a poker, I pulled off my winter gloves, then knelt to check a limp wrist for a pulse.

Finding none, I got to my feet using a technique I'd learned watching a cable exercise show: from a position on both knees, bring your strongest leg forward with the foot flat on the floor, then put both palms on that knee and use it for support to push yourself up.

Brandy was asking, 'Is she dead?'

'Yes, dear.'

'We need to call Tony.'

I bestowed a patient smile upon her. 'Eventually, dear. But first we'll have a look around. Once the police arrive, we'll be thrown out like yesterday's table scraps. Besides, a few more minutes aren't going to matter to Ellen.'

Brandy sighed, rolled her eyes and said, 'All right . . . but just a few minutes. What are we looking for?'

Never a self-starter at a murder scene, Brandy needed direction.

'See if you can determine how the killer made entry,' I said. 'I doubt he – or she – waltzed in the front door the way we did.'

While Brandy went off to check other rooms, I took a few crime-scene photos with my phone, then had a look around the living room, which appeared tidy, except for an antique walnut secretaire whose hutch had been opened, the contents of drawers and cubby holes scattered on the drop-down writing panel. On the carpet was a small pile of unopened mail that looked as if it had been unceremoniously dropped.

I crossed to the desk, and took some pics of the writing panel, then slipped my gloves back on to carefully sift through the papers – blue stationery, paid receipts, bank statements, current bills, along with such items as paperclips, rubber bands, stamps, and a metal letter opener – but nothing much of interest. Beneath all that, however, I discovered a few red dots, along with several more spots on the carpet leading to the fireplace.

A picture was forming in my mind, and not a pretty one.

Ellen, arriving on the porch pauses to remove the contents of the mailbox, then unlocks the front door (if unlocked *she surely would have been alarmed). Inside, she deposits her coat and purse on the couch, then crosses to the secretaire, still holding the mail. She pulls down the writing panel, and is struck from behind, dropping the mail, then staggers toward the fireplace, falling, the assailant finishing the deadly job.*

Brandy had returned. 'The back door in the kitchen was forced open.'

Which intimated the intruder had already been in the house, either waiting for Ellen – which meant the killer had prior knowledge she was coming – or looking for something and got surprised by her arrival.

Brandy asked, 'Should I check upstairs?'

'No, I will. You call the chief, dear. He'll respond better to you.'

She raised her eyebrows in apparent doubt to that observation. But she was using her cell as I climbed the well-trodden carpeted stairs to the second floor, where two of four doors were closed, perhaps to save on heat. Standing open were doors to the bathroom – to which I gave the dated fixtures a cursory look – and what I presumed to be Ellen's bedroom.

Like the living room, this too was tidy, bed made, bureau drawers closed, nothing on the vanity appearing disturbed.

What I was looking for was Ellen's jewelry box, which turned out to be a piece of furniture, about three feet high and one foot across.

I opened each of its ten drawers, starting from the top. The first contained the good stuff: precious and semi-precious stone rings, pearl necklaces, gold bracelets, and a few nice watches, including a Rolex. The other drawers held costume jewelry;

the farther down I went, the junkier Ellen's stuff (and tastes) became. No Iris Apfel was she.

But that the Rolex and other valuable pieces were still here told me the intruder wasn't after pawn-worthy items. *Unless*, surprised by Ellen, the interrupted killer had fled after dispatching her, abandoning any further search.

I could hear the increasing wail of a police car's siren and went downstairs to join Brandy.

The first responder was Officer Munday, a tall, slender, long-faced man who reminded me of actor Fred Gwynne, who played Officer Francis Muldoon in the old TV series, *Car 54, Where Are You?*, with whom we had a less-than-positive relationship (not Mr Gwynne as he died in 1993).

At this juncture, even though more word count is needed to beef up this book to satisfy the publisher's requirements, I will fast-forward because who needs another post-murder scene where the reader is subjected to information she/he/they/them already know/knows. Besides, a story has its own integrity, and savvy readers (which ours are) realize when a writer is padding. Just as a good actor understands when to get off the stage, prompted by dwindling applause or tossed fruit, and a great director intuits when to end a film (don't you hate movies that conclude but then go on, and on, and on, and on?) (I do!)

On a smaller but no less important scale, think of the ending of each episode of the original *Perry Mason* television show . . . the murderer (usually the name actor who has little to do, smiles too much, and is always accommodating) confesses his or her guilt on the witness stand – cut to Perry, Della, and Paul having coffee in the office or some restaurant where loose ends are tied up in thirty seconds . . . aaaannnnddd *print!*

Anywho, as predicted, Brandy and I were quickly ejected from the crime scene.

So it was around nine in the evening when we returned home after quite the long day, beginning with our trip to St Mary's and ending with the discovery of Ellen's battered corpse in her home. You can get a lot done in a day if you try!

I left Brandy to attend to a neglected Sushi and made for the library/music/incident room to have another go-around at our big board (isn't MSNBC political analyst Steve Kornacki simply adorable when tallying up electoral votes on election night – what enthusiasm!).

From the suspect list – now with a new heading – I erased Megan Harris, convinced she hadn't poisoned herself. Also Ellen because she was deceased, almost always a convincing alibi.

SUSPECTS IN THE MURDER OF NORMA CRUMLEY AND ELLEN FRIDLEY

(in alphabetical order)

NAME	MOTIVE	OPPORTUNITY
JARED EGGLER (created gift list)	?	YES
YVETTE FONTAINE (made chocolates)	?	YES
CARY HUDSON (oversaw gifts table)	?	YES
SHEILA WHITE (drew Ellen's name)	?	YES
MILDRED ZYBARTH (drew Norma's name)	?	?

(Lydia Kincaid would remain on hold until I could establish if the boutique owner had really been out of town during the fateful luncheon.)

I went to locate Brandy but she had already gone upstairs to bed.

Feeling a little tuckered myself, and knowing I wanted to rise bright and early, I followed suit. That canine hot-water bottle, Sushi, must have known my spirits had brightened, as she did not join me. Ellen's death was tragic, of course, but the elements were coming into sharper focus now.

Monday morning, I showered, dressed, and was out the door by eight. With the shop closed on Mondays, Brandy was still asleep. Sushi had come down to see what I was having for breakfast and, when she discovered it was nada, the little doggie trotted right back upstairs.

During winter months my mode of Brandy-less transportation was the trolley, a relic from bygone days that had been reconverted into just another gas-guzzling vehicle. The brainstorm of the Downtown Merchants Association, the trolley provided a free ride from anywhere in the city to their stores, thereby encouraging folks to spend money with them, rather than at the Serenity Mall.

In my woolen coat, knitted hat, leather gloves, and my feet as snug as a bug in Brandy's UGGs, I trod the few blocks to where I could flag down the trolley, bunion surgery be darned.

At this point it's unclear, even to me, whether or not I was still banned from riding the vintage vehicle, due to some prior incidents which definitely were not my fault, or at least not entirely. So my fate this morning was in the hands of whomever might be the driver. If it was Maynard Kirby I would be thumbing a ride with the next car that came by, like Claudette Colbert in *It Happened One Night*, though skirt-lifting in this inclement weather was out.

So it was with some trepidation that I watched as the red trolley pulled up to the curb, only to be relieved to see Mary McBride behind the wheel, as I had managed to convince her it was Brandy who'd been banned.

The doors opened and I climbed aboard, giving Mary a cheerful 'And how are you this frosty morning?'

A bottle-blonde in her forties, Mary was bundled up against the cold – doubly so because of her close proximity to the doors, and the fact that the trolley had no heat.

'Fine,' the woman said.

Mary wasn't much of a talker, which was okey-dokey by me, as when she was in the mood for conversation, she was the type who'd rather tell you her troubles than listen to yours. What were my woes, chopped liver?

A few seats were taken, but even with the high price of gas these days, folks would rather pay extra at the pump than sit in a freezing-cold old trolley car. But the ride downtown was short and sweet, a mere five minutes, with few people waiting in the chill to be picked up. Soon the trolley was pulling up in front of the grand old courthouse, its last stop.

From there I hoofed it over to the Riverside Café on Main, where I knew the ROMEOs (Retired Old Men Eating Out) would be having their usual leisurely breakfast.

I entered the river-themed diner, its walls arrayed with pictures of boats and barges. Business was slow with only a few patrons occupying the booths, so I easily spotted the gents at a round table for six in the back. Coffee had been served and, since they didn't have menus, they had obviously already ordered.

Back in their heyday, the ROMEOs had a robust roster. Like the men themselves, however, time had taken its toll, their ranks having thinned thanks to the grim reaper, and a desire among some survivors to spend their waning days in warmer weather.

But four of the old guard were hanging in: Harold, an ex-army sergeant who resembled the older Bob Hope, right down to the ski-ramp nose, jutting chin, and thinning hair; Randall, former hog farmer, best described as a less sophisticated Sydney Greenstreet (far less); Vern, retired chiropractor reminiscent of the suave Zachary Scott (if I wasn't wearing my glasses); and Wendell, a one-time riverboat captain, a doppelganger for the actor Leo Gorcey who played the malapropism-prone character in the old Bowery Boys movies (not that there were any new ones).

A recent recruit was present, a semi-retired physician everyone called Doctor Bob. To continue with the male movie-star comparisons, he looked like Errol Flynn, but the older version in the 1959 film *Cuban Rebel*, after the actor had gone to seed due to his wicked, wicked ways. And, although I had turned down offers of matrimony from the other four ROMEOs, a trip down the aisle with him might be worth considering, because the doctor had a wonderful bedroom – excuse me! – bedside manner. And think of the free medical advice I'd receive – nothing to sneeze at, considering the rising cost of office visits.

I sauntered up to the table and, in my usual Mae West-ian manner, said, 'Hello, boys.'

Females were routinely discouraged from pulling up a chair and joining in on their male conversation, but I was an exception, much as Shirley MacLaine and Angie Dickinson had been welcomed by the Rat Pack back in the Swingin' Sixties.

'You're looking good, Vivian,' said ex-sergeant Harold, the first of the men I'd turned down in the marital stakes, knowing he'd have me up at the crack of dawn at reveille, consigned to KP.

Still, as I'm from a generation of women who happen to like compliments, I kept up the banter in Mae's voice: 'It's better to be looked over, than overlooked.'

Which garnered some chuckles and snorts.

A waitress materialized with a carafe of coffee and a mug, and I informed her that was all I wanted. Much as the notion of another big tip disappeared, so did she.

Randall gestured to the empty seat next to him, and I removed my coat and draped it over the back of the chair, having tucked hat and gloves in the pockets.

Usually, I would have maneuvered to get a different table position, but the hog farmer finally seemed to have been out of the business long enough to lose his porcine bouquet.

Vern, on my other side, said, 'I hear you're in the thick of mystery-solving once again, Vivian.'

The chiro had a way of self-administering his own neck-cracking, which could get on my nerves, but such was the price of obtaining information.

Wendell chimed in, 'Yes, Viv, give us the inside scoop on Norma Crumley.'

The jury is still out whether the calliope on the riverboat Wendell had been commanding was playing that ragtime favorite 'Bim, Bam, Boom' or 'Here Comes the Showboat' when he fell asleep at the helm and T-boned a barge. Either way, he lost his license.

Doctor Bob, directly across from me, added, 'Is Ellen Fridley part of your latest investigation? I heard the poor woman was murdered last night.' His wife had divorced him some years ago, citing that bedside manner aforementioned.

Normally, I played a cat-and-mouse game with these codgers, the object being to find out more from them than they learned from me. But, since I needed to wrap up two murders in just a few days (grandson Jake the ticking clock, remember!), I decided to share everything I knew. To open the bag, as Archie Goodwin would say.

I wrapped up my account by saying, 'I believe Ellen *was* the intended victim of the poisoned candy at the luncheon – *not* Norma – and Ellen's death last night was the murderer finishing the job.'

Sitting forward, Vern asked, 'What do you want to know from us?'

'Yes,' said Wendell, leaning back with arms folded, 'how can we help?'

Harold and Randall nodded their willingness to assist; Doctor Bob appeared neutral, fairly new to this game.

'What I need are motives, gentlemen,' I said. 'Grievances which Jared Eggler, Yvette Fontaine, Cary Hudson, Sheila White, and Mildred Zybarth might have had against the late Ellen.'

Harold wanted a clarification. 'Firsthand knowledge? Or gossip?'

'Either,' I said. While hearsay can't be used in the court of Perry Mason, it is admissible in the court of Vivian Borne.

We took a pause while the waitress reappeared to serve the men their breakfasts, and refreshed my coffee. In the past I had timed my arrival to occur after a meal so I wouldn't have to watch them eat – not a pretty sight – but such was the price of expedience. Tick tock!

Vern took a big bite of scrambled egg, and spoke while chewing. 'As a member of the country club, I heard that Ellen spread a rumor about Jared having an affair with the new golf pro.'

Which would get both men fired because there was a strict policy against fraternizing between the staff of any gender.

I asked, 'Anyone else have any useful intel?'

Harold speared a small sausage. 'I suppose you heard about that snafu at the Bijou after Cary showed those "classic" French films during the summer.'

I did. A citizens' committee tried to have the art house shut down, but I rallied a contingent of broad-minded people to prevent the closure.

'What about it?' I asked.

'Did you know,' the ex-sergeant asked, 'that Ellen worked behind the scenes to form that committee?'

I didn't. But if Cary was aware of her involvement, that would make a viable motive for him.

Wendell's offering came next. 'I overheard Ellen in the bank telling another woman that Yvette Fontaine didn't really make her chocolates, but bought cheap ones to pass off as her own.'

Most folks can tell the difference between good chocolate and bad . . . but this tip was worth checking out.

Randall said, 'I did hear something juicy from Ellen at the farmers' market this fall.'

'Well?' Like his former pigs, he needed prodding.

'She said some of the art Mildred was selling at her gallery is fake.'

I frowned. 'Fake how?'

He shrugged. 'Not real.'

Such are the limited communication skills one can develop when one spends most of one's life talking to animals.

I tried again. 'Are you saying reproductions or outright forgeries?'

Randall shrugged.

True or not, that kind of gossip can sink a business.

I had yet to hear from our new recruit – the good doctor. Was he truly a ROMEO? I decided to put him to the test.

'Doctor Bob,' I said.

'Just Bob will do fine, Vivian.'

Oh my. His smile was dazzling. And the teeth looked real, a novelty at this table.

'A question,' I said.

'I'll do my best to provide an answer.'

'Is it possible for you to access someone's lab results if they've had a blood test at the hospital?' Which was where the majority of physicians in town sent their patients.

'It's possible. Why?'

'I've neglected to ascertain one key element in my investigation, which you could confirm.'

Would he feel bound by medical privacy rules to decline?

But there was no hesitation. 'Fire away, Vivian. Catching a murderer takes priority over patient confidentiality, in this instance.'

Suddenly he didn't look quite as seedy as Flynn in *Cuban Rebel*, but more like the actor in *Istanbul*. Still no *Captain Blood*, much less *Robin Hood*.

I asked, 'Can you tell me if – and when – Ellen was diagnosed with diabetes?'

Bob grinned. 'Would you like me to do it right now?'

'Well, yes!' This was wonderful, except when I considered how blithely he treated patient/doctor confidentiality. My records were private, I hoped! For one thing, they listed my birth date. Which is no one's business, including yours.

He was digging out his phone. 'I can tap into the hospital's medical files on my cell.'

He did so, shortly saying, 'Ellen's last blood test was about a week ago . . . which showed a blood sugar level of seven point three. So yes, she is – or rather *was* – diabetic.'

I asked, 'And when was her previous test taken?'

Again Doctor Bob consulted his cell. A few moments later, he said, 'A year ago during an annual check-up. Then it was six point four, within acceptable guidelines.'

So Ellen *had* told the truth about her condition, and must have decided there wasn't time – or was too much trouble – to change her gift request.

Bob surprised me further. 'I can also tell you something about Ellen regarding Sheila White, and it has nothing to do with medical records.'

'Please!'

The doctor paused, as if he might have a change of mind, but then went on: 'You recall her husband George ran an investment company in town?'

'White and Associates,' I said.

The doctor continued, 'And that he died from a heart attack shortly after an external audit turned up hundreds of thousands of dollars taken from clients' accounts?'

I nodded eagerly. 'Go on.'

He leaned forward, voice hushed. 'Sheila said Ellen was behind the rumor that George had taken the money.'

I was already leaning forward. 'But it turned out to be one of the associates.'

'Yes,' Bob said. 'However, by then George had died. A passing possibly accelerated by stress.'

'And Sheila blamed Ellen.'

Bob's eyebrows rose. 'Wouldn't you?'

I took a final sip of coffee, then stood. 'Gentlemen, thank you for the information, and should you think of anything else, you have my number.'

Everyone but newbie Doctor Bob said, 'We all have your number, Vivian.' They overlapped a bit.

Vern asked, 'Will you keep us in the loop?'

'Yes,' said Randall, 'we'll want to be kept abreast of your progress.'

Harold chimed in, 'It may help us recall something else.'

Was he withholding something?

'Rest assured everything will be kept strictly confidential,' said Doctor Bob, who had so recently violated the Patients' Privacy Act.

'So what do you say, Viv?' asked Wendell.

I smiled. 'I most certainly will, gentlemen.'

Most certainly not. They'd served their purpose, and I hardly needed any more collaborators on this case. Besides, the men would be texting on their phones like teenage girls as soon as I'd left.

If we'd established anything today it was that these old boys could not be trusted to be discreet.

From the restaurant I trotted several blocks to the police station, where I hoped to find the chief on the job.

Bypassing the front entrance, with its depressing waiting room, sullen receptionist Dawn and needy banana tree, as well as another trip down former-police-chief Memory Lane, I went directly to the back emergency exit and banged on the steel door.

A few more whacks with my gloved fist brought the big man himself.

'Vivian!' the chief growled. 'You know you're not supposed to—'

I pushed passed him. 'I have time for neither formalities nor niceties.'

His office was mere steps away and that's where I headed, plopping down in a visitor's chair.

The chief followed, irritated but interested as he closed the door behind him.

'What's this about?' he asked.

'I want to know what you know about Ellen's murder last night . . . and I'm not leaving until you spill.'

In prior (voluntary) visits, I was the model of diplomacy and tactfulness, but I didn't have time for such luxuries.

The chief went behind the desk and sat, unburdened himself of a sigh, and said, 'All right, Vivian, let's get this over with. What questions do you have?'

Do you know what I loved about the early *Dragnet* radio shows (available from RadioSpirits.com)? The rapid-fire dialogue dispensed by police detective Joe Friday, which made his line, 'Just the facts, ma'am,' so memorable. (Of course there's always a bit of trivial malarkey at the beginning of each episode where Joe's partner has a toothache, or Joe's mother calls to remind him to bring home some milk, just before the 'hot shot' phone rings and all heck breaks loose.)

Therefore, in honor of the late great Jack Webb, actor/writer/director once married to singer Julie London, creator of the unforgettable Joe Friday, here are just the facts of the scene between myself and the chief.

(VB = Vivian Borne; CC = Chief Cassato.)

VB: Do you concur that Ellen was first attacked from behind while standing in front of the secretaire?

CC: Yes. And the fatal blows were administered after she'd fallen by the fireplace.

VB: Were any fingerprints found on the poker?

CC: No. Either it was wiped clean, or the assailant wore gloves.

VB: Could Ellen have recognized this person?

CC: Doubtful, struck from behind as she was. She did make it to the fireplace, meaning she might have seen the intruder before the fatal blow.

VB: Getting back to the secretaire, what do you think the killer was looking for?

CC: Hard to say. But he or she did take the time to go through its contents, which means they were searching for something.

VB: There was a letter opener in the hutch – which I assumed would be easily accessible. Why wouldn't Ellen have reached for *it* for protection?

CC: She may have been too stunned by the initial blow to think of it.

VB: But why stagger over to the fireplace? Yes, I know there were other tools there she could use such as the tongs and shovel . . . but the letter opener was right there.

CC: Don't know the answer to that, Vivian.

VB: What can you tell me about the arsenic Norma consumed?

CC: Not much until lab results come back, other than that the chocolate Megan Harris had tasted contained less than the one Norma ate.

VB: When are you and Brandy going to patch things up?

CC: I don't believe that's any of your business.

VB: Anything that affects my life in a detrimental way *becomes* my business. And her moping around is cramping my investigative style. (pause) Just apologize, even if you don't mean it. Just cross your fingers behind your back. That's what I do.

CC: We're done here.

From HQ, I jaywalked across the street to the courthouse, where I caught the noon trolley, which made a regular stop at the hospital. Sometimes people ask me, 'Where do you get off, Vivian Borne!' Well, right then I got off at the Serenity General. On the lower floor, I entered the autopsy room, which is similar to a regular operating theater except that it contains different procedural apparatus and refrigeration for the bodies.

The last time I was here (*Antiques Liquidation*), Brandy and I had broken in to obtain some information denied us, and when the cleaning lady's cart came to a halt in front of the door, I had to jump inside a cooler while Brandy hopped up on a gurney and made like a covered cadaver. Thankfully, the cleaner didn't stay long – it's cold in them thar lockers! – because quick-thinking Brandy suddenly sat up, scaring the lady, who ran off, allowing us time to escape.

My daughter may not be the best actress in the family, but her performance in the autopsy room would be tough to beat!

Medical examiner Tom Peak, in green scrubs, was standing next to a stainless-steel examination table that had a perforated top for the drainage system, plus a small sink with faucets at one end. On the table lay Ellen Fridley, her torso discreetly covered with a white sheet, a beige-colored ID tag tied to one big toe. Her face, washed of blood, wore a serene expression, despite the lacerations caused by the blows from the poker.

Peak, a tall, middle-aged man with salt-and-pepper hair and a lined face, didn't seem at all surprised to see me.

Confirming as much, he said, 'I figured you might show up.'

Although we'd had a contentious past, I believe he'd come to have respect for my investigative skills.

In *Antiques Fire Sale*, I offered readers an opportunity to attend an actual autopsy with me – those who weren't squeamish, that is, while the faint-hearted could skip to the next scene. Unfortunately, I interrupted Tom's verbal recording of the process with my questions, and got ejected before anything really neat had happened. Well, here is another chance!

Then I noticed the medical examiner wasn't wearing protective goggles and latex gloves. 'Don't tell me the show is over?'

'I only performed a preliminary examination,' he replied.

Which would include such basic information as height, weight, hair and eye color, and cause of death.

Peak was saying, 'The autopsy will be done at the University of Iowa Hospital, since this has been ruled a homicide.'

Dear reader, I must apologize once again for my bungle. But I'm sure there will be another occasion to attend an autopsy in the near future.

'Surely,' I said, 'there's something you can tell me that might help my investigation.'

A perfect time for Peak to answer my question, and follow it with, 'But don't call me Shirley.' As in the classic comedy *Airplane*. He missed this opportunity, however.

Instead he merely said, 'If you mean, which was the fatal blow . . .?'

'Not that. Didn't your laboratory conduct any tests on the arsenic found in the chocolates both Norma Crumley and Megan Harris ate?'

Peak hesitated.

'Come, come, doctor,' I cajoled. 'There's a killer on the loose. Let us not stand on ceremony.'

A crisp nod. 'Yes, I did run a microscopic evaluation to see if the properties were the same in each.'

'And?'

'They were. Except . . . the arsenic in the candy Norma ate contained an anomaly.'

He might have said 'nougat.'

I asked, 'What *kind* of anomaly?'

'A contaminate.'

'Do you know what it was?' I asked, excitedly.

Peak shook his head. 'That will require further testing.'

I pressed: 'Can you give me an example of a contaminate?'

He mulled a moment. 'If I wanted to fill some chocolates with arsenic, I would first pour a small amount of the powder on to a surface from which to work.'

'The contaminate already being on this surface, you mean.'

He nodded. 'A countertop, or workbench, most likely.'

'Thank you, Tom.' I paused. 'May I have a moment alone with my friend Ellen?'

He mulled again, then nodded. 'Certainly. I'll be outside.'

After the door had closed, I turned to the shell that had once housed a human being.

'Dear, I'm beginning to think you were not a very nice person and certainly not up to the high standards of the Red-Hatted League mystery book club. If you were alive, I might well rescind your membership in our organization. But no one had the right to rescind your pending membership in the human race. I *will* find your killer.'

Vivian's Trash 'n' Treasures

Many people such as myself have treasured memories of reclining on the floor by a Christmas tree while a model train goes round and round on a track. Although antique trains are still considered a good investment, even modern ones such as the Lionel Polar Express set are collectible and sell for as much as five hundred dollars. Every year in December, the Canadian Pacific Holiday Train makes a stop in Serenity on a Midwestern route to fill its decorated, illuminated box cars with donations of non-perishable items (or cash) for food banks. If that doesn't get people in the right mood for Christmas, I don't know what does!

NINE
Winter Blunderland

Mother returned home about noon. I had just gotten up, having slept fifteen hours, and was in my pajamas and furry moose slippers, sipping coffee at the Duncan Phyfe table.

She blew into the dining room like a gale wind and the needle on my barometer began to drop, signaling a storm was brewing. No quiet Monday afternoon for me.

'Ah, good,' Mother said. 'You're up and around. You need to get dressed. Time for a road trip!'

'Where are we going?' Why fight it?

'Davenport.'

Davenport, one of four municipalities – two on the Iowa side of the Mississippi, two across the river in Illinois – that had come to be known as the Quad Cities.

'Chop chop,' Mother commanded. 'Time and tide wait for no man! Or woman.'

I downed the last of my coffee, then went upstairs to shower and dress, skipping make-up and the blow-drying of my hair. I got into a sweater and jeans and UGGs and we were out the door in twenty minutes, leaving a disappointed Sushi behind.

The weather had warmed, the bright yellow sun in a cloudless blue sky melting away the snow, inspiring me to take the scenic River Road north and not the boring four-lane through flat barren land.

During the thirty-minute trip, Mother filled me in on her morning adventures. But I was only half-listening, keeping an eye out for deer even as I savored the sparkling river, snow on the boughs of the pines sliding off, going *plop!* on the ground like whipped cream.

Finally I asked, 'Where am I heading exactly?'

We had entered downtown Davenport, continuing to follow the river.

'Les Chocolats factory,' Mother said.

'Oh. Where Yvette has her candy made?'

'Exactly.'

'Why?'

'Weren't you listening?'

'Sort of. I like to concentrate on my driving.'

Mother twisted toward me. 'When are you going to let Tony resume his exalted position in your life?'

'Maybe when he apologizes.'

'You're being very foolish – turn here!'

I made a right on to Riverfront Trail, where a path of asphalt led to a few off-the-grid businesses whose only protection against a rising river was a six-foot cement wall with cracks in it.

'Unusual place,' I said, 'to have a chocolate factory. Willy Wonka would not approve.'

The building had turned out to be a tan cinder-block structure not much larger than a four-car garage.

'Perhaps not,' Mother answered. 'But Yvette's venture is a small one, and if she owns the building, our pretty entrepreneur would probably have got it for next to nothing.'

The neighbor on the right was a sailing boat club, its glorified shack shuttered for the season, a dozen or so covered boats stored next to it like beached baby whales.

To the left was a rundown auto-repair shop, the outside littered with old tires and discarded car parts. I pulled the van up to the front entrance of the factory, where a sign in fancy letters said: *Les Chocolats, by appointment only.*

I frowned. 'There aren't any other vehicles here.'

'Perhaps they're closed on Mondays,' she replied. 'After all, many shops are, ours included.'

We got out and, while I waited by the van, Mother approached the entrance and tried the door, finding it locked.

A man outside the auto-repair shop was adding another bald tire to a pile when Mother headed over to him, gesturing for me to follow. The worker was in his early twenties, wearing a grease-stained gray sweatshirt with hood, dark jeans, heavy boots, and work gloves.

Mother called out to him, 'Excuse me. Would you happen to know if the chocolate factory is closed?'

'I never saw anyone go in or come out,' he said, barely looking at us, and turned to go back into his shop.

To me, Mother said, 'Let's check the rear of the place.'

We walked around to the back of the building to find nothing more than another locked door. The snow had melted enough that there was no sign of footprints indicating anyone had been around. And the windows were composed of frosted glass, giving away nothing of the interior.

Hesitating not at all, Mother produced her packet of lock picks from her coat pocket.

'What do you think you're doing?' I whispered harshly. 'Do you want to get us arrested? There are probably outside security cameras posted!'

She shrugged, blissfully unconcerned. 'I saw no indication of any. Are you doubting my eyesight?'

This coming from a woman whose eye-glass lenses magnified her peepers to near Mr Bug size. Well, Ms Bug.

'In any case,' I insisted, 'that auto-repair guy can identify us!'

'He hardly gave us a glance. If you'd spiffed up a little and thrown on something more fetching, perhaps he would have noticed us.'

I clutched her sleeve. 'Mother! You're the one who mentioned Tony, and he's been good enough to authorize our investigation, more or less. And now you'd alienate him with conduct like this?'

'Very well,' she sighed, brushing off my hand. 'We'll do this the hard way.' Mother withdrew her cell phone from the other pocket.

After a moment, a female voice said, '*State your emergency.*'

'Vivian Borne here, Serenity Sheriff's department.'

Oh, brother. Or I should say, *Oh, Mother*.

She continued: 'Burglary in progress at the Les Chocolats factory on Riverfront Trail in Davenport . . . Yes, that's right . . . Fine.'

She ended the call.

I stood agape.

'When the police get here,' Mother said, 'I'll do the talking.'

'You *bet* you'll do the talking,' I snapped. 'And you'll do the jail time, too! Sheriff's department my—'

'Let's not be vulgar, dear.'

Her lock picks remained in hand.

Dumbfounded, I kept goggling at her. 'You mean, you're *still* going to break in?'

'I'm only making entry easier, dear. We can't have the officers using a battering ram, which might make us liable for damages once they discover there's no robbery.'

That had a certain logic. I guessed.

After picking the lock, Mother said, 'We'll stay out here and await their arrival, like the good citizens we are.'

A black Chevrolet SUV – lights flashing, but sans siren – wheeled into the gravel parking area, coming to an abrupt halt, scattering small stones.

Two male patrolmen in black uniforms and jackets exited their vehicle, a young Black officer and a fiftyish White one.

While I stayed by our car, Mother approached them with her hands held high, one bearing her Honorary Deputy Sheriff ID.

Dear Lord, grant me the serenity to accept the things I cannot change (about her)*, the courage to change the things I can* (sometimes)*, and the wisdom to know the difference* (who am I kidding?).

'Good afternoon, gentlemen,' Mother said cheerfully. 'Your quick response is most commendable.'

'What's this about?' the older cop asked gruffly.

The younger officer was more diplomatic. 'You can put your hands down, ma'am. Could I have a look at that ID?'

She handed it toward him without releasing it. 'Don't be dissuaded by that honorary designation. I am the former sheriff of Serenity County.'

The older officer said, softly, with just a touch of horror, 'Vivian Borne . . .'

'That's correct. I see my reputation has preceded me.'

It sure had.

She was saying, 'I arrived for a scheduled appointment. Uh, this is my daughter, Brandy, a former deputy who continues to serve as my driver.'

They just looked at her, which was something I couldn't do right now. The older cop was coming to the realization that in a lot of years on the department, it turned out he *hadn't* seen everything.

Mother explained, 'We found the front door locked with no reply to my knocking. And yet, we could hear someone moving around inside. I took that as a red flag!'

My thoughts turned to the hope that we wouldn't be sharing the same holding cell.

The officers exchanged glances, the older cop wary, the younger one confused; then they walked to the front entrance, where Officer McGruff banged on the door. 'Police, open up!'

When the command was met with silence, Officer Diplomatic said, 'I'll check the rear.'

A few moments later, his voice came over the senior man's walkie-talkie. '*There's another door here that's unlocked . . . I'm going in.*'

Officer McGruff, anticipating the burglar would flee through the front, withdrew his weapon, taking a combative stance, ready to take a bite out of crime.

He said, 'Stand back, ladies.'

Officer Diplomatic's voice came through his partner's shoulder mic. '*All clear!*'

Officer McGruff relaxed, and holstered his gun.

Seconds later, the front door opened, Officer Diplomatic filling the frame. The two spoke for a moment, but I couldn't hear the exchange.

Officer McGruff turned his gaze on us, his expression less than happy.

'Can you explain,' he asked, 'why you called in a robbery when the building is completely vacant except for cobwebs and dust?'

Mother pressed a gloved hand on her chest. 'Oh, my goodness gracious! Vacant, you say? I'm positive we heard noise inside . . . didn't we, Brandy?'

If she'd been closer, I would have stepped on one of her recovering bunions.

I shrugged and my smile must have been dreadful. 'A river rat maybe?'

Mother stroked her chin, looked in the direction of the Mississippi. 'You know how sound can play tricks, bouncing off the water. That must be it.'

'Riiiight,' McGruff said.

'What were you doing here?' Diplomatic asked.

Mother said, 'We had an appointment at Les Chocolats.'

An appointment at an empty building?

I should have let her dangle, but we were tied to the same rope. So I said, 'It came in as a message on our phone, to stop by Les Chocolats. Maybe it emanated from the *retail* store in Serenity, not here.'

'Of course!' Mother said with a smile that threatened to burst her face. 'I'm sure that's exactly what happened!' She addressed both officers, 'Please accept my apologies for the blunder, and for wasting your valuable time and resources. And thank you for your service and dedication to upholding the law at a salary that does not begin to be commensurate with the frequently dangerous duties you are sworn to carry out. As former sheriff of Serenity County, I salute you.'

And she saluted them. I swear she did.

This malarkey was as transparent as cellophane, but Officer McGruff nonetheless seemed to mellow a bit.

'Well,' he said, 'your vigilance is appreciated. As a former sheriff, no less would be expected of you.'

Before this nonsense could go any further, I asked, 'Is there anything else you need from us, officers?'

'Just your contact information for the record,' the young Black officer said.

While Mother complied with his request, I climbed into the Equinox and started the engine.

On the ride back to Serenity, I was fuming.

'You know those officers,' I said, 'will check up on us and before you know it, Tony will bench us as the nuisance we're becoming.'

'He's tried that before, with little success,' Mother replied. 'What's important is that now we know who the killer is.'

'Yvette Fontaine, you mean.'

She nodded. 'Yvette Fontaine. It all fits – opportunity, and now motive.'

'The police will likely contact Yvette, since she likely owns the building. And they may mention us in the process. That would alert her we're on to her.'

Mother was nodding. 'That's why it's imperative we reach Yvette before they do. Pedal to the metal, dear! And take the four-lane, it's faster. We've seen enough scenery for one day.'

By late afternoon when I had parked in front of the chocolate shop, a winter sun was beginning to set, painting the horizon broad strokes of purple and pink with its big brush, in the sort of sunset onetime resident Samuel Clemens had so extolled.

When we entered the shop, Yvette was waiting on a male customer who I recognized as Mr Fusselman, the kind of perpetually crabby man who would yell at kids for walking across his lawn – an Old Man Shouts at Clouds type of individual.

But when he turned and saw us, we – surprisingly – got a nice smile and cheerful, 'Merry Christmas!' proving even the hardest of hearts could be touched by the holiday season.

Of course, with a murderer to bag, the spirit of Christmas might be temporarily dimmed at least.

When he'd gone, the bell over the door ringing (another angel getting its wings?), Mother turned the sign on the door to **CLOSED** and gestured for me to stand guard should anyone else try to come in.

Yvette was a vision in a red velvet pants suit, her long black hair worn in a high ponytail, lipstick matching the outfit.

Frown lines creased the porcelain skin between the blue-green eyes. We were clearly not a welcome sight. 'Mrs Borne, is there something I can help you with?'

'*Oui oui, mademoiselle* – you can answer some questions.'

With a little edge, Yvette replied, 'I'd be happy to – *after* the store closes.'

'It's closed now, dear. I took the liberty.'

The woman, perhaps sensing danger, gave Mother a conciliatory smile. 'If what you'd like to discuss is *that* important, go right ahead.'

Mother asked, 'Have the Davenport police been in touch with you?'

'No.' The frown lines appeared again. 'Why *would* they?'

'I have it on good authority that your little factory was broken into earlier today.'

Her eyebrows went up and her eyes widened. 'Oh?'

Mother went on, 'I do hope there wasn't much vandalism, as I'm sure the equipment must be expensive.'

'Yes, well, thank you for telling me, but you needn't be concerned. Everything is insured and I only rent the building. Now if that's all . . .'

Mother stood her ground. 'Not quite. You see, Brandy and I were at the factory when this occurred. And what do you suppose the *gendarmes* found inside?'

The woman went on the defensive. 'Mrs Borne, I'll have to ask you to leave, and please turn that sign back around to OPEN as you go. I can't stand here yammering with you about your amateur sleuthing when this is my busiest time of year.'

'Or what, dear? You'll call *our* police? I'm not stopping you.'

Yvette tossed her head, the ponytail swishing like a scythe. 'All right. So *what* if the building is empty? Is that a crime?'

'No, it's not a crime,' Mother said softly. 'But poisoning someone with something as deadly as arsenic certainly is.'

The woman's bravado deflated like a punctured tire. She crossed to the little ice cream table-for-two and sat down.

Mother followed, taking the other chair.

'When was it that you made the decision?' Mother asked softly but firm. 'After Ellen threatened to expose the fact that you didn't make your own chocolates, as you had claimed?'

Yvette sighed; it took her a few beats before she managed to reply: 'It wasn't *only* that I was buying the chocolates elsewhere. She was going to reveal my real background. The fact that my parents weren't French, and we never lived in New York.'

'Where are you really from, dear?'

No faint French accent now – strictly Midwest, flat as the plains. 'Boise, Idaho. I grew up on a potato farm . . . although I did take a year of French in high school.'

Like that somehow made *la différence*!

Yvette went on, 'I knew that woman's wagging tongue was going to ruin me . . . make me a laughingstock after I, well, selected Serenity to, to—'

'Hoodwink people?' I said.

Yvette looked over at me. 'No. I really *had* come through Serenity on a trip with my parents, and simply fell in love with it. That was very much true. And I *did* make my own chocolates when I first started! I was planning to open several Quad Cities shops and looking at other locations around this part of the country. But then Covid came along and business suffered and I had to lay off workers and close the factory, and sell the machinery.' She paused. 'The idea to get back at Ellen started as a fantasy after Lydia Kincaid called the shop and said she wanted a holiday box delivered to the country club with a card for Ellen. But then, the idea took hold and somehow I just . . . just couldn't shake it.'

Mother said, 'You used the rat poison offered through the association.'

'Yes. I had some left over from last spring. I . . . I had no intention of killing Ellen, just to punish her, to make her sick . . .'

How does one determine how much arsenic to use to just make someone 'sick'?

'. . . then when I found out she'd given the box to Norma Crumley—'

Yvette buried her head in her hands, and began to sob.

I was almost feeling sorry for her. Almost.

Mother asked, 'And what about Megan?'

Yvette looked at her with tear-stained cheeks. 'Who?'

'Come, come now, dear,' Mother said. 'Megan Harris. The intended *second* victim of another box of chocolates you had poisoned.' She paused. 'Attempted murder isn't going to add much more to a sentence of first-degree murder.'

'I don't *know* anyone named Megan,' Yvette said firmly. 'Honestly. I don't know anything about a second box of poisoned chocolates.'

Either she was a fine actress, or really was on the level.

Mother said, 'In any event, you'll have to accompany us to the police station.'

Yvette nodded, and rising, said, 'I'll get my coat and purse in the back.'

When I moved to follow her, she said, 'Don't worry, I'm not going to run. And I'm not going to feed myself an arsenic-laced chocolate, either. I got sick of chocolate a long time ago.'

I looked at Mother, who motioned for me to stay put.

After Yvette disappeared behind the curtain separating the front from the rear, Mother produced her cell phone.

'Chief, I'm bringing in someone who knows about the arsenic in the chocolates. But there's something I need you to do . . .'

In the station's conference room, Mother and I sat across from Yvette while Tony stood at the head of the oval table. The chocolate shop owner had already been read her rights.

'Miss Fontaine,' he said, 'I'm going to show you two photographs, and I want you to pick which box of chocolates you made for Ellen Fridley.'

Tony placed the pictures in front of Yvette, depicting both boxes open.

She leaned forward, and tapped one. 'This is the one.'

'You're sure?' asked Tony.

'Yes. In the box Lydia ordered, I had to use a few other chocolates than would normally go into the holiday edition because I'd run out of them.' Yvette paused. 'And there should have been a business card attached with Ellen's name.'

Tony pointed to the other photo. 'Then can you explain why *this* box – the one with *all* the holiday chocolates – ended up in the trash with no card?'

'No. I can't.'

I could. 'There were two poisoners – one intending to hurt Ellen but not kill her, the other intending to murder her – both poisoners not knowing about each other.'

Yvette's eyes grew big. 'Does . . . does that mean I *didn't* kill Norma Crumley?'

'Yes, dear, you did not,' Mother said. 'You merely committed assault. Or perhaps it may be considered attempted assault, since some unknown party interfered.'

'After all,' Tony told the prisoner, 'you did make a waitress named Megan very ill . . . after she found Ellen's box thrown in the trash and took it home.'

Yvette sat forward. 'But . . . but this Megan's all right?'

Mother nodded.

Yvette covered her face with her hands, and again quietly sobbed.

Tony motioned for Mother and me to follow him into the hallway.

With the door closed, he turned to Mother. 'Do you have a suspect in mind?'

'I have several, but need to question them further.'

'What can I do to help?' he responded, which was as co-operative as he'd ever been with her.

'Tom Peak said he detected some kind of contaminate in the more lethal chocolate,' Mother told him. 'So I need to know the analysis of that arsenic ASAP.'

'I can make that happen,' Tony said.

I asked, 'In the meantime, can't samples be taken of rat poison that might be in the possession of suspects, to make a match?'

Tony shook his head. 'That would require a slew of search warrants.' He paused. 'I could probably get *one* – based on your best guess – but more than that looks like a fishing expedition.'

Mother sighed. 'I can't give you just one name at the moment.'

'All right, then,' he said. 'What else?'

'Can you verify if Lydia Kincaid – she owns The Perfect Closet – was in Des Moines Friday night, and didn't return until late Saturday as she claims?'

'The reason being?'

'Lydia took Ellen's name after Sheila White asked her to switch. It was Lydia who called Yvette to deliver the chocolates to the club because she couldn't attend the luncheon.'

He nodded, eyes narrow. 'I'll put someone on that.'

'Tony,' I asked, 'what's going to happen to Yvette?'

'She'll be detained for further questioning, and then charged.'

I wondered what that might be. 'For a misdemeanor, or attempted murder?'

'That will be up to the district attorney.'

Mother said, 'If it *is* attempted murder, Yvette should plead not guilty and go to trial! I'll be happy to testify.'

She relished the notion of taking the stand as a witness (prosecution or defense, it didn't matter), but rarely did any criminal attorney in his or her right mind ever call her.

Tony touched his forehead, his 'tell' that Mother had exceeded his patience. 'All right – that's all for now.' He waggled a finger at her. 'And Vivian? The next time you call in a false robbery, I will *not* cover for you.'

So he knew.

She opened her mouth to speak, but thought better of it – a rare occurrence, but it did happen from time to time.

'Go,' Tony said. 'But I want a word with Brandy.'

I braced myself for a scolding, but his demeanor had softened.

'I was wondering if you would have a dinner with me at my cabin Christmas Day,' he asked, adding, 'That is, if you don't have other plans.'

I pretended to think about it; but no thought was required. 'I don't,' I said. 'Jake won't arrive until the day after Christmas, so that would be fine.'

Maybe there was hope for us yet.

Mother and I returned home to find that a neglected Sushi had been under the tree and ripped open all the gifts. Was it my imagination, or did she have a smug smile?

Mother stood with hands on hips, surveying the damage. 'Well, dear, we might as well have an early Christmas.'

Which made sense since now that we could see what we'd gotten each other.

She was saying, 'But first . . . another update.'

I trailed her into the library where she added motives to the board, gleaned from the ROMEOs. Most of these reflected Ellen's blackmail-worthy threats.

SUSPECTS IN THE MURDERS OF
NORMA CRUMLEY AND ELLEN FRIDLEY

(alphabetical order)

NAME	MOTIVE	OPPORTUNITY
JARED EGGLER	reveal affair with golf pro	YES
YVETTE FONTAINE	expose chocolate business	YES
CARY HUDSON	attempt to close movie theater	YES
SHEILA WHITE	cause of husband's death	YES
MILDRED ZYBARTH	threat to gallery reputation	YES

I asked, 'Shouldn't Yvette come off the list?'

'Not until her story is confirmed.'

'And Lydia?'

'We'll wait for Tony's report. And I have no motive for her as yet.'

'What now?'

'Round two of questioning in the morning,' Mother replied, adding, 'Except for Yvette.'

Relieved we weren't rushing out into a dark night that had turned bitterly cold again, I asked, 'Shall we have some of the plum pudding with our presents?'

'Yes, dear. And put on the kettle.'

Nothing dangerous about that, right?

Brandy's Trash 'n' Treasures Tip

Nutcrackers began as utilitarian tools, but by the fifteenth century elaborate ones were being made of boxwood. The first commercial nutcrackers were sold in Germany in the late eighteen hundreds, and those remain the most sought-after by collectors. Today nutcrackers can be found most anywhere in a huge range of prices, sizes, and characters. (Check out the Alice in Wonderland series created by Hollywood Nutcrackers, and try to resist. I couldn't.)

TEN
Holly Jolly Chrismess

Since the Trash 'n' Treasures shop was open on Tuesday, and Mother and I couldn't afford to lose any more holiday income, I called Joe Lange to see if he could fill in. (I mentioned him earlier in Chapter Three. Friend from community college days? Self-styled oddball? Lives with his widowed mother? Served in Afghanistan and came back with PTSD? Uses military speak?)

Anyway, our phone conversation was brief, as usual.

'*Lange here*.'

'Can you work at the store today?'

'*Affirmative*.'

'Civilian clothes, please.' (He had a tendency to wear camo fatigues and military boots.)

'*Negatory*.'

'All right. But leave the hardware at home.'

'*Affirmative. H-hour?*'

'Ten. Close at five.'

'*Lima Charlie. Oh-ten-hundred to oh-seventeen hundred*.'

'Tango Yankee.' Now he had me doing it!

Joe ended the call abruptly as there's no military jargon for 'goodbye.' Unless maybe 'over and out.'

At oh-nine-hundred – I mean nine in the morning! – Mother came downstairs dressed in her most comfortable outfit, an emerald-green velour top and slacks, which signaled another long round of investigating awaited.

I was also dressed for the duration in a stretchy black tunic top, warm leggings, and black puffer coat. We'd left Sushi alone, either at home or the shop, so many times lately that she was having none of it, blocking the door stubbornly. I caved, helping the little rascal into her cute pink coat with a hood I'd bought her for Christmas that came with matching booties. She was so eager to come along that she put up with such anthropomorphic indignities.

Speaking of booties, I'd given Mother a gift of her very own UGGs – short black ones she could slip into – so she would stop wearing (and stretching out) mine.

Anyway, we had fed and med ourselves and – after Mother donned her outerwear – were ready to go out and brave the cold, white world. This was one of those 'wind-chill advisory' mornings that came with instructions not to stay out too long, yesterday's warmth and sunshine but a distant memory.

Our first stop was the country club, where Owen, the groundskeeper, was riding a small tractor-plow to clear the parking lot of the overnight snow accumulation.

Mother had me drive slowly alongside him until he noticed us, stopped the tractor, and turned off the engine.

I stopped the van, got out and approached the heavily bundled up figure, the hood of his heavy green parka pulled tightly around his head, a long woolen scarf covering his face except for his watering eyes which threatened to freeze over. Or maybe that was just who he'd seen come calling.

I said to him, 'Vivian Borne wants to talk to you.'

It came off as a threat, which in this instance couldn't really be helped.

He pulled down the scarf, revealing chapped lips. 'Should be done in about half an hour.'

I crinkled my nose, nodding to the van. 'Best to get this over with. Like tearing off a Band-Aid. Besides, it's warm in our van and we have a thermos of hot coffee and some fresh baked scones waiting.'

First the threat, now a promise. Stick, carrot.

The groundskeeper – either knowing Mother, or in need of sustenance – abandoned the tractor.

Moments later, Owen was sequestered in the back seat of our warmed-up Equinox while I returned to the wheel.

Mother, handing Sushi over to me, turned to ask our guest, 'Cheery good morning, Owen. How do you take your coffee?'

'Black.'

Which was good because I'd forgotten to bring the packets of sugar and cream. And a spoon.

'Scone?' she offered.

'What kind? I have to curb my carbs.'

'Make an exception. It's caramel apple.'

'Oh!' he exclaimed. 'That's my favorite.'

Somehow she'd known that, of course.

'Butter?' Mother asked.

'No, thanks. I have to watch the cholesterol, too.'

Another good thing. I'd forgotten the butter, as well. And a knife. At least I remembered the scones.

From the floor in front of her seat, Mother (like a magician performing a trick) produced from her tote the thermos of coffee, a tin with the scones, a Styrofoam cup, and small paper plate with napkin.

She, at least, had come prepared. The bribe assembled, she passed it back to Owen.

Taking a sniff of the coffee, the groundskeeper said, 'Thanks, Vivian! This coffee smells delicious . . .'

Mother made an 'OK' sign with her gloved thumb and forefinger, as if a skilled wine taster. 'It contains notes of milk chocolate and toffee with hints of dried fruit.'

Owen took a sip. 'Not bad!'

I gave Mother my best 'get on with it' look, which involved crossing my eyes.

'Now, Owen,' Mother said, turned halfway around in her seat, 'remind me how long you've been groundskeeper here at the club, hmmm?'

His response was muffled due to a mouth full of scone, but I could still make out that he'd said fourteen years.

'And you have no assistants?'

'Just me, myself and I.' He swallowed. 'Can I have this scone recipe to take home for the wife?'

'Certainly, dear.'

Knowing Mother, it wouldn't be *this* recipe, which she had gone to a great deal of trouble to steal from the chef at the Hotel Pennsylvania by bribing a waiter when we were in New York attending a comics convention (*Antiques Con*).

Caramel-Apple Scones

2 cups all-purpose flour
2½ tsp. baking powder
1¼ tsp. ground cinnamon
½ tsp. salt
½ cup unsalted butter, frozen
½ cup heavy cream (plus 2 tbsp. for brushing tops)
1 large egg
½ cup dark brown sugar
1 teaspoon pure vanilla extract
1 heaping cup peeled and chopped apple (Pinata for a tropical twist)
½ cup homemade salted caramel sauce (Mother cut a corner here buying store-bought)

In a large bowl, whisk the flour, baking powder, cinnamon, and salt together. Grate the frozen butter and add to the bowl. Using a pastry cutter, combine the mixture until it forms pea-sized crumbs. In a smaller bowl, whisk the ½ cup of heavy cream, the egg, brown sugar, and vanilla extract together, then pour over the flour mixture, adding the apples last. Gently mix together until moist, then pour out dough on to a floured cutting board, forming a large ball. Press ball into an 8-inch disc, and cut into eight wedges with a sharp knife. Brush scones with the 2 tablespoons of heavy cream. Place disc on a cookie sheet lined with parchment-paper, and refrigerate for 15 minutes while the oven is preheating to 400 degrees Fahrenheit. Take out the cookie sheet from the refrigerator, remove the disc, and arrange the eight scones 2 inches apart. Bake for 22–25 minutes or until edges are golden brown. Cool scones for a few minutes before drizzling with the caramel sauce.

Mother was asking, 'Owen, how do you deal with vermin when you see those rascals making an appearance on the course?'

He shrugged, chewed, swallowed. 'Usually I shout at them first,' he said, 'then if they don't leave, I call the police.'

I clarified: 'She means gophers not kids.'

'Oh.' He paused. 'I have rat poison in the maintenance building to deal with those.'

Mother asked, 'The kind the downtown merchants use for river rats? Purchased by and provided for the city?'

'Why, yes. Why do you want to know?'

Mother continued, 'Who has access to the maintenance building?'

He shifted, concentrating on Mother's new, no-nonsense tone, not a scone. 'Well, I have a key, of course. And Jared Eggler has one.'

I had been watching him in the rearview mirror, but now I twisted my head to look directly back at him. 'Why would Jared need access to maintenance?'

'Christmas decorations are stored there,' Owen replied. 'The trees and wreaths, along with boxes and boxes of ornaments. Mr Eggler is fussier about how the club is decorated for holidays and such than Mrs Crumley was. He's very particular that way.'

Which gave the social director access to arsenic trioxide.

Mother, having gleaned all the usefulness out of Owen, said, 'Thank you, dear. Sorry to have kept you from your work.'

'Well, thank you for the coffee and scone.' He reached for the door handle. 'And you'll remember to drop by with that recipe?'

'Indubitably.'

'What say?'

'Beyond a doubt.'

No doubt a reasonable doubt.

Owen opened his door, a gust of frigid air immediately displacing any warmth, and I waited until he'd started up the tractor plow and chugged back to work before I pulled away.

'Jared now?' I asked. 'I spotted his car in the front parking lot.'

'Yes, dear. You're learning.'

If I could have parked any closer to the club's front entrance, our van would have been blocking it. We exited and made for the door, me clutching Sushi, grateful for her shared warmth.

Inside, I waited for my teeth to stop chattering before saying, 'It doesn't look like he's in his office.'

The window blinds were open and lights on, giving us a decent view inside.

'Let's find him,' Mother said, moving into the corridor that led to the ballroom.

We passed by the bar, finding it empty, as well as the ballroom, and kitchen. No sign of the social director.

'But his car is here!' I said, frustrated.

'We'll check downstairs.'

Backtracking, we took stairs down to the smaller dining area and bar, also finding no one. Finally, I checked the women's locker room while Mother took the men's.

Meeting up, she said with a frown, 'He *has* to be around . . . that car didn't drive itself here.'

I shrugged. 'Let's go back to his office and wait.'

Which we did, sitting in chairs in front of the desk. I looked over at a coffee cart holding a one-cup drip machine that used pods, an assortment of flavors in a holder beside it, and considered making myself some . . . then decided I'd had enough coffee before we left.

Since Sushi's warmth was no longer needed, I put her down, noticing that one of her booties had already gone missing, and she immediately disappeared behind the desk. I don't know if it was the saucer on the desk that had no cup, or Sushi's sharp bark, that told me Jared had been in the office all along . . .

Mother sensed it, too, and stood, and went to investigate.

But I stayed put. There was no need for me to see the man's contorted face, foamy mouth, and twisted body, or the spilled coffee cup that apparently had been fouled with arsenic. I was glad I hadn't helped myself to one of those coffee pods!

Mother bent and disappeared behind the desk. For a moment I thought she was checking for signs of life, but when she straightened, her hand held a ring of keys.

'What are you doing?' I asked.

'Something we must do before the police are called.'

I retrieved Sushi and followed Mother out of the office, then down the stairs to the lower level, where we went out an exit, then along a walkway leading to the maintenance building.

A side door was locked, and it took her a few tries to find the correct key; but then we were inside.

The cement-floored area was well-organized: equipment such as rider-mowers stationed near a garage door (a space left for the in-use tractor plow); smaller electrical tools like hedge trimmers, weed cutters, and leaf blowers arranged on metal shelving. Other shelves held a variety of gardening necessities, from outdoor hoses to sacks of garden soil and fertilizer, which is where we found the bag of rat poison, identified as such with a cartoon on the front of a dead rodent on its back, clawed feet in the air. All it was missing was an X over each eye.

Like other seasonally dormant items on the shelving, the bag was covered with cobwebs.

'Doesn't look like it's been disturbed for some time,' Mother said, her breath visible in the unheated building.

I nodded. 'Jared certainly didn't use this bag to poison any chocolates.'

'Or *himself* either,' Mother added, 'committing suicide aware that justice was closing in.' On the word 'justice' she thumped herself in the chest. 'Which in a way clears him of Norma's extermination.'

I frowned. 'If Jared didn't take his own life, he must have seen or heard something at the luncheon that made the killer believe he was a threat.'

Mother turned toward me, one eyebrow rising above a glasses lens. 'And after all, what was one more murder? They can only fry you once!'

Actually, there was no capital punishment in Iowa, but Mother was always saying things like that.

We left the building, Mother relocking the door, and returned to the social director's office. I stood near the door, not sharing her comfort around corpses.

She was about to use the desk phone to call Tony when a crimson-cheeked, watery-eyed, red-nosed Owen entered, his hat, scarf, and coat covered with blowing snow.

Before the groundskeeper could speak, Mother asked quickly, 'Has anyone else been here this morning besides you and Jared, and us?'

Compelled by her urgency, Owen said, 'No. I got here about seven, and Mr Eggler arrived at eight. The rest of the staff won't be in till ten.'

Which meant the coffee pods – or pod, as in Russian roulette, if we were right to assume a poisoned pod had been the murder weapon – had been tampered with earlier, when the killer would have an alibi at the time Jared died.

Owen asked, 'I need to tell Mr Eggler the lot is plowed. Do you know where I can find him?'

'Yes,' Mother replied, casually. 'He's right there behind the desk, quite dead. Do be a dear and call the police, as the man's obviously been murdered. And don't – I repeat, *don't* – use any of the coffee pods, no matter how cold you might be. Or you might wind up colder.'

We left Owen, his chapped-lipped mouth frozen open.

Sheila White lived in one of the grand old homes that surrounded Weed Park, so named not because the park was weedy but because a family with the last name of Weed had generously donated the land back in the early nineteen hundreds, when apparently weeds were not as unpopular as they are today. Either that or the Weed family were incredibly lacking in self-awareness.

The large wooded park set on gently rolling hills sported an aquatic center with all the thrills of a state-of-the-art outdoor swimming facility, several elaborate playgrounds to tucker kids out, and even a good-size duck pond perfect for ice-skating in the winter. During the 1950s a zoo was established that grew to expand from a monkey house and an aviary to cages and enclosures including lions and tigers (and no bears) (oh my), antelopes, peacocks, goats, and even an elephant, as well as the same assortment of ill-mannered monkeys who apparently resented their new lesser place in the pecking order, and a collection of creepy snakes housed in an old log cabin that included rattlers.

But the menagerie came to an abrupt end in the 1980s when, one dark night, animal activists released all the captives, which promptly overran the town, snakes included. Fortunately, the animals had been previously well-fed and no citizens were harmed or eaten, and all were captured and returned to their cages, except for one MIA rattlesnake. For years afterwards, pranksters would go out at night and shake a baby rattle outside open bedroom windows, creating shrieks from within, and the switchboard at the police station would light up. (As a kid, I may or may not have taken part in one or more of these escapades. Anyway, surely the statute of limitations has kicked in by now.)

Sheila lived at an edge of the park opposite the old brick bandshell, in a grand white Victorian home with conical turrets and a wraparound front porch that had been built by the aforementioned Weed family and was in the state's registry of historical homes.

An old turn-crank bell in the center of the front door summoned the manor's mistress, who was still in her bathrobe with curlers in her hair (an ungodly form of torture if slept on, especially the ones with bristles).

The nice thing about our surprise visits in sub-zero weather was that even an unsuspecting resident wouldn't keep us waiting outside for long in the cold we were letting in, assuring us a foot in the door.

From there, if further access was denied, Mother would feign feeling faint and ask for a glass of water, and when the helpful subject returned with the revitalizing drink, we'd be found securely ensconced on their couch.

Another tactic of Mother's was to bring something by way of an offering – the person's favorite food perhaps, or an antique that hadn't sold at the shop, or free tickets to some event neither of us wanted to attend.

But we didn't need to employ any of those gambits, because as soon as Sheila had closed the front door, the woman said, 'Ah – I was expecting you.'

'Oh?' Mother asked coyly.

'You can knock off the theatrics, Vivian,' Sheila said. 'I

know you all too well. Let's talk in the kitchen.' To me, she said, 'Better hang on to your dog . . . I generally don't allow pets inside, but in this weather I'll make an exception.'

The reason for that policy was made clear as we followed her past a parlor on the right and a formal dining room to the left, each home to museum-quality examples of Victorian-era fixtures and furniture.

But the kitchen was another matter. While the decor was meant to invoke the past, it had all the modern conveniences of the present.

Mother and I sat at a glass-topped table.

'Coffee?' Sheila asked.

We both declined, somehow suppressing shudders.

Our surprisingly anticipatory hostess sat down, then said, 'I assume I'm on your suspect list for Ellen's death – which I just heard about – because I'm the one who originally drew her name in the gift exchange.'

'Bingo,' Mother said.

'This time of year it's always a good thing,' Sheila said with a sly smile, 'to get off the "naughty" list. How might I accomplish that?'

'Easily done,' Mother replied. 'Simply answer my questions truthfully.'

'Go right ahead and ask.'

Mother's chin came up. 'I understand that you sometimes assist Lydia at The Perfect Closet.'

'That's right,' Sheila replied. 'Gets me out of the house, and who doesn't like a discount? I don't run the register, but will wait on customers . . . *and* unbox new clothing, which gives me first dibs.'

Mother nodded. 'When was the last time you helped out there?'

'Last Friday, when Lydia received a call about her mother falling. A new shipment of dresses had come in and Lydia wanted them hung and steamed before she left for Des Moines.'

That would have allowed Sheila access not just to a new batch of apparel, but to Lydia's bag of arsenic the day before the luncheon.

Mother moved on. 'What was the reason you switched Secret Santa names?'

There was no hesitancy in the answer. 'Because I blamed Ellen for my husband's death.'

'You disliked her,' Mother said.

'Intensely. But I didn't poison any chocolates or break into Ellen's home and kill her.' She paused, adding, coldly, 'I thought someone else might eventually do me that favor.'

At least the woman was honest on that score.

'But,' Sheila replied, 'I do not make a habit of homicide.'

'Yes, dear,' Mother said. 'Always a good policy. Still, someone did make your Christmas wish come true. Unfortunately, there have been other casualties.'

'You're referring to Norma,' Sheila said, frowning now. 'And I heard a waitress at the club was also poisoned, which is most unfortunate. But at least she survived.'

Mother said, 'That is more than can be said of Jared Eggler.'

Sheila frowned. 'The club's social director? What about him?'

'We found Jared dead in his office an hour ago,' Mother said bluntly. 'His morning cup of coffee did not agree with him. Or at least the condiment he stirred in didn't.'

I knew she was watching Sheila closely for the woman's reaction, which in my opinion couldn't have been faked: a combination of shock and alarm.

'Good Lord!' the previously well-composed woman blurted. 'Am . . . am *I* in danger?'

'I don't know any reason you should be,' Mother replied. 'But I don't really know. Is there anything you haven't told the police? Or something you'd care to share with us now?'

Her coolly confident manner was gone now. Softly, she uttered, 'No. Nothing.'

'Nothing to worry about then,' Mother said cheerfully, and stood. 'Come Brandy.'

She might have been giving Sushi a command.

Behind the wheel again, I passed the doggie over to her, noticing another missing bootie. A canine will shed human clothing, given half a chance.

'You were a little rough on Sheila,' I said. 'And insensitive about Jared.'

'Was I? Should I take it easy on a woman who wished Ellen dead? Or a man who likely knew the killer's identity, and by not coming forward, caused further deaths, including his own? This is no time for sentiment.'

Even if it was close to Christmas.

Because Mother needed to tie off a loose end, we headed downtown, this being the first opportunity to question Mayor Robert Goodall since City Hall had been closed on Sunday, and he was never in his office on a Monday.

City Hall was a three-story limestone structure built around the same time as the nearby courthouse, though minus any of the latter's Grecian grandeur. Small, austere, with chugging air conditioners in the summer and hissing steam radiators in the winter, City Hall seemed to brag, 'No taxpayer's money wasted here!'

Set back from the street, the building had an odd shape, as if having been square until a toothless giant took a bite out of a front corner, the architect allowing for an area on the grounds where citizens, whether cheering or protesting, could gather.

A well-shoveled and salted walkway – preventing the city from lawsuits should some visitor take a tumble – led us along snow-covered grounds dotted here and there with small trees and park benches.

At a human-size replica of the Statue of Liberty painted a garish gold, the walkway split to the left and right, circumventing Lady Liberty before meeting up again. Mother and I always took opposite paths, so she could say 'bread and butter,' an old superstition to prevent something from coming between two people.

We ascended the outside steps of City Hall to a small two-columned portico alongside which American and Iowa flags fluttered valiantly in the icy wind, then went in.

The mayor, whose office was on the second floor, liked to brag that his door was always open to anyone; but first they had to get by his lovely if officious secretary, Gwen, who sat at a desk guarding Goodall's quarters.

Rumor had it there once had been not just mayoral business but funny business between His Honor and the curvy brunette, which apparently came to a screeching halt when His Honor's wife, Martha, found out. To Serenity's First Lady's credit, she didn't insist on Gwen's dismissal. Some say this was because a rumor is just a rumor, others that Gwen was too skilled a secretary to dismiss over a minor flirtation. Mother said no minor flirtation ever got a wife a European vacation – which Martha had taken solo.

Upon catching sight of Mother, Gwen announced, 'I'm sorry, Mrs Borne, His Honor is very busy this morning.'

So much for the 'open door' policy, which had just slammed shut on us.

'That's quite understandable with him taking Mondays off,' Mother quipped. 'But I'm sure he won't mind the interruption on Tuesday.'

Thus had Mother made it clear to the secretary that we weren't leaving.

Gwen pressed a button on her intercom. Her tone was professional with just the tiniest tinge of contempt. 'Mr Goodall, Vivian Borne is here.'

His voice came back, '*Please inform her that I can't possibly see her this morning . . . perhaps this afternoon.*'

Mother said, loud enough for him to hear, 'Gwen, please refresh the mayor's memory as to who put him over the top in the last election.'

'*Send her in.*'

Over the last few regimes there had been some improvements to the mayor's personal area – new carpeting, modern furniture, and custom-made bookcases – but it still retained the transitory feeling of a temp worker's space, making it prudent that all personal items could eventually fit in a single cardboard box. The most recent addition, however, was a framed photo of his wife Martha prominently displayed on the desk.

The mayor, a ruddy-faced man with white hair and neatly trimmed beard, stood as we entered. He wore a navy suit jacket over a white shirt with red tie, faded jeans, and I would guess, running shoes, as if the upper half of him was appealing to the conservative business community, and the lower half to the blue-collar workers who he would smilingly walk to the door after a meeting. Either that, or of someone wanting to give a good impression on a Zoom call, while staying comfortable.

'Vivian . . . Brandy,' Goodall said, working up some warmth. 'What can I do for you?'

Just by acknowledging me, he'd got my next vote.

Mother said, 'We won't take up much of your time . . .'

Still, she plopped down in a chair and got comfy, taking off her gloves a finger at a time.

'. . . but I'd like a list of all merchants who received the rat poison offered through your office and the Maintenance Department.'

The mayor's smile was patronizing. 'We, uh, prefer to use the term rodenticide, Vivian. And I'm afraid Maintenance has those records – you are welcome to contact them.'

'Come, come now Robert,' Mother chided, 'I know you have an interdepartmental computer system to access any file. I *am* the former sheriff, after all.'

As if he could forget.

'That's true,' the mayor admitted. 'But I'd like know why you want this information.'

'To prevent another murder,' Mother said casually.

Goodall sat back. 'Thanks to Chief Cassato, I'm aware that Norma Crumley's death has been linked to the type of rat poison distributed through the city . . . but, as the chief has also informed me, that's not how Ellen Fridley died. Hers was a death by violence.'

'True. But Jared Eggler met the same fate as Norma about an hour ago, apparently after an unfortunate reaction to coffee he drank. You should be hearing about this latest murder from the chief as soon as he . . . catches up.' Mother paused. 'Perhaps you're next on someone's holiday list. One of the merchants you provided the ratty 'cide might be tying up loose ends.'

The mayor swiveled toward his computer. 'I'll get you that information.'

A minute or so later a nearby printer whirred.

'Just so you know,' Goodall said, handing Mother the

one-page sheet, 'I'd already decided to discontinue this service since receiving a recent report from the city Water Department of their concern that this material could start contaminating the river, after the flood recedes.'

Which of course might also contaminate the city's water supply.

'A wise decision,' Mother said.

We left the mayor's office for a powwow in the hallway.

Mother, looking at the sheet, said, 'This is most interesting . . .'

'What is?'

'Everyone on our current suspect list is here, with the exception of Cary Hudson, and Sheila White.' She paused. 'We know Sheila had access to the poison having occasionally worked for Lydia. But Cary said he already had a bag.'

Yet the owner of the Bijou had said he used the same city-provided pesticide.

'Why would that be?' I asked, adjusting Sushi in my arms, a third bootie having gone AWOL.

'I don't know, dear. Why don't we ask him?'

Brandy's Trash 'n' Treasures Tip

The history of Santa Claus dates back to the fourth century and the patron saint of children, Saint Nicholas. But it wasn't until Clement Clarke Moore penned 'A Visit from St Nicholas' that the modern version became popular. But no matter what he is called – Father Christmas, St Nicholas, Kris Kringle, or Sinterklass – Santa collectibles are easy to find, fun to collect, and fit every price range. The one that Mother and I have next to the fireplace is a vintage plaster statue of the jolly old elf once used to advertise Old Harper Whiskey, and to which we toast every Christmas by tossing back a healthy shot of . . . what else? Coca-Cola.

ELEVEN
Silent Fright

On our way to the Bijou to see Cary Hudson, Mother's cell sounded its restored 'I Fought the Law (And the Law Won)' ringtone. Perhaps that was a harbinger of the murderer's future, whoever that murderer might be.

'What's up?' Mother asked the phone, as my mind filled in the rest of the Bugs Bunny catchphrase: 'Doc.'

'*Why did you and Brandy leave the country club before we arrived*?' Tony irritably asked, his voice coming through loud and clear without Mother invoking the speakerphone function.

Mother said, 'We were following up an important lead, time being of the essence.'

'What *lead*?'

She back-peddled. 'I'll let you know if it pans out.'

'*Vivian, you said it was "important." You need to keep me informed as to what* you've *learned.*'

I don't know if it was Mother's sixth sense, or the way he emphasized 'you've' that made her reply, 'My Spidey sense tells me you must have some news.'

His deep sigh came across the line like steam rising. Then: '*Lydia Kincaid was in Des Moines from late Friday afternoon until Saturday night, according to her mother's live-in housekeeper.*'

Which cleared Lydia.

Tony went on, '*Also, results came back on the contaminant Tom Peak detected in the chocolates Norma ate.*'

'And that contaminant is?' Mother asked.

'*Trichloroethane.*' He paused. '*A cleaning solvent used by a variety of businesses in a variety of ways, but which can also be found in certain household products.*'

(Regarding household cleaners that boast they kill

99.9 percent of all bacteria . . . what .1 percent is it that gets away?)

I leaned toward the cell. 'I don't know if that helps us narrow our list of suspects, Tony.'

'*What suspects are the* remaining *ones?*' His patience was thinning.

'Down to three,' Mother said. 'Sheila White, Cary Hudson, and Mildred Zybarth.'

Tony's voice softened, grew thoughtful. '*An historic home, a movie theater, and an art gallery. Places any one of which could easily use a product containing trichloroethane. Where are you headed now?*'

'The theater,' Mother said.

'*Stay in touch and take care. This killer is becoming bolder.*'

Mother ended the call without promising to do so.

She said, 'I'm going to look up trichloroethane.' Soon, using her Google app, Mother said, '. . . TCE. A colorless liquid organic chemical solvent.'

'Examples?' I asked.

She scrolled down the screen, then sighed. 'The list is long. It's better to ask what it *isn't* used for. TCE is even found in adhesives, and used as a facial peel, and wart remover. Have you noted any warty suspects on our list?'

'Can't say as I have.'

We arrived at the Bijou, where the figures of Santa and Rudolph in the outside ticket booth had been replaced with Suzy Snowflake, which – according to the accompanying card – was another puppet created by Centaur Productions for the 1953 stop-motion feature of the same name. Suzy was not as detailed as the Santa or Rudolph, and looked like one of those wooden models used in drawing by artists, but painted white, wearing a full-skirted lacy dress and snowflake hat.

Inside I made straight for the concessions counter with Sushi in my arms. Alexis was there restocking for the matinee. Today the teenager's outfit was a short black lace dress that went well with her black eyeliner and lips.

'One ticket, and two Abba-Zaba bars,' I said, pointing to the candy with its distinctive yellow-and-black checkered wrapper. Sushi seemed to be peeking into the confectionary display case herself, tiny nose twitching.

Alexis gave me a knowing smirk. 'Are you actually going to *see* the show? You're a little early.'

'No.'

'I'll just charge you for the candy, then.'

'Really?'

'Yeah. Don't tell the boss.' She rang me up and another angel won its wings. 'That'll be six dollars.'

'Thanks.' I dug in my purse and gave her the cash.

Mother spoke behind me, addressing Alexis. 'Is Cary here, dear?'

The Goth girl pointed with a black-nailed finger toward the auditorium. 'He's in there.'

On our way to the double doors, Mother gestured to the candy bars in my hand. 'I hope one of those is for me. It may have to do for a meal.'

Somebody growled and it wasn't Sushi. 'Get your own,' I said, quickly getting the candy into my purse, a bit of a juggling act with Sushi still in my grasp.

Inside the auditorium, the house lights were up, and every scratch on the wood floor, every threadbare seat, every tear in the velvet curtain, every chip in the plaster of the proscenium was on unforgiving display. Even the high ceiling, which gave the illusion of a starry night sky when the theater was dark, appeared haphazardly painted, with peeling fluorescent stickers. The only thing sadder was closing time in a hard drinkin' bar when the lights came on and last-call dating choices revealed their limitations.

I followed Mother along the slightly declining aisle at right, along which Cary was putting a red cover over another busted seat in the middle section.

'Dear boy,' she called out, 'I do think it's time we have another fundraiser for needed repairs.'

Cary, pausing in his work, looked our way. 'I can't argue with that, Vivian! Hi, Brandy, and . . . I've forgotten the little dog's name.'

'Sushi,' I said. Then asked, 'Is it OK if I let her roam? She's house-broken.'

Unless she was in a vengeful mood, and she wasn't.

'Sure.' He chuckled with an edge of sadness. 'I don't think she can do any more damage to the place. And there's no rat poison put out anywhere.'

As if she understood what he'd said, Sushi jumped down and scampered off to take in new smells.

Suspecting the purpose of the visit, Cary asked, 'You have more questions for me, I take it?'

Mother said, 'If you don't mind.'

He slung a few more red seat-covers over one arm. 'I don't, if *you* don't mind following me around.'

'Not at all.'

I moved to a side seat well within range of their exchange.

Mother began: 'Were you aware that Ellen Fridley was behind the petition to close the Bijou?'

'Yes, I knew that,' Cary replied. 'Meaning no disrespect, she was a rather awful woman.'

I hated to think how he expressed actual respect.

The two voices echoed a little in the cavernous theater as Mother pressed on: 'And how did that make you feel toward her?'

He offered up another sad smile as he continued with his work, Mother trailing after. 'If you mean was I angry enough to *kill* her . . . no, certainly not. And anyway, her petition failed – thanks in part to broadminded people like you and Brandy.'

I was all for the theater, including racy French fare. I wasn't about to let my source for Abba-Zaba bars dry up!

'Anyway, I got together with Ellen whose objection was some of the art films I'd shown. I promised to make it clear in the advertisements if any film contained racy material and limit admission to adults. In return she agreed to let me display her Santa and Rudolph puppets this Christmas.'

'I noticed you have Suzy Snowflake in their place,' Mother said. 'Is she yours?'

Cary nodded. 'I'd gotten her a few years ago at an online auction.' He paused, then brightened. 'But Santa and Rudolph will be back next year.'

'Oh? Mustn't they be returned to Ellen's estate?'

'No. I bought them from Ellen for five hundred dollars not long before her tragic passing.'

'The amount seems reasonable. Perhaps a little undervalued.'

'I have a letter signed from her, accepting my offer, if you'd like to see it.' He sounded a bit defensive.

'Of course not,' Mother replied, placatingly. 'I'm so happy they've found a good home here in this theater. Where better?'

Cary nodded. 'I'll take good care of them. I'd love to have the Hardrock, Coco, and Joe figures, but they were either lost or destroyed.'

These, too, were puppets featured in another stop-motion cartoon from the 1950s, three demented elves that had given little Brandy nightmares. Actually, they still did.

Mother switched gears; I could almost hear them grind. 'You mentioned a rat poison offered through the mayor's office,' she said, 'and yet your name does not appear with other merchants on the purchase order. Is that because you had some ratty 'cide left from the previous year?'

Pausing again, he shook his head. 'No. I split a bag with Mildred Zybarth. Because of her location, she doesn't often get river rats in her art gallery during flood season, but wanted some pesticide on hand, just in case.'

'I see. Then she's who put in the order with the Maintenance people.'

'Yes. And of course we shared the expense.'

Mother cocked her head. 'Was this Mildred's idea, sharing a bag?'

Cary frowned. 'I can't recall, but I believe it *was* Mildred's.'

Mother switched gears again. Her gaze went to the silver screen, absent of any images at the moment. 'What you do here fascinates me, Cary. I particularly relish your silent film offerings, however hazardous the nitrate materials might be.'

He wagged his head. 'We take care on that score.'

Her keen interest obvious, Mother asked, 'How do you clean the old movie projector used to show your silent films?'

He shrugged. 'Not much to it. First I blow out any dust from the machine with a canister of compressed air. Then I wipe the lenses with a lens-cleaner – like the kind you buy for your own glasses at any drug store. And, every so often, I lubricate the parts with sewing machine oil. If there's any film emulsion build-up, I remove that with a cuticle stick. That's all there is to it.'

'Fascinating, dear,' Mother said, smiling. 'Isn't it simply marvelous to find out about things one doesn't know?'

I was between Abba-Zaba bar bites and called out, 'Never too old to learn!'

Mother tossed me a glare, then returned her attention to the movie-house manager. 'Sharper than a serpent's tooth,' she muttered – a mutter that could have been heard in the back row.

Cary was looking at her warily. 'Vivian?'

'Yes, dear?'

'Has . . . something *else* happened? Something bad?'

'How astute you are.'

Mother told him about Jared Eggler.

He sank down in one of the seats he'd just covered in red. 'My God.' He looked up at Mother. 'Why Jared?'

From the aisle, she said, 'If I knew the answer to that, I'd be close to solving these murders.' She paused for a sigh. 'Thank you, dear – we'll see ourselves out.'

I was about to call for Sushi when she jumped into my lap, apparently disappointed by the Bijou not having the magic of the prop room at the Playhouse where she could battle nemeses like the carnivorous plant Audrey in *The Little Shop of Horrors*, or the rabid dog from *The Hound of the Baskervilles*. Sushi had also lost another bootie.

The animal looked at me suspiciously, sniffing my mouth. I had opened the candy bar so quietly, the rustle and tear had gotten past her, on her excursion.

Outside, we were approaching the van parked at the curb when Alexis came dashing out the front doors in her flimsy black lace dress.

'Brandy!' she called out loudly. 'I forgot to give you your change for the candy.'

Which would have been thoughtful, except I had no change coming.

As she held out a hand with nothing in it, Alexis whispered,

'Cary sent *me* to buy that holiday box of chocolates.'

The girl turned and ran back into the theater.

Mildred Zybarth was busy with customers when we arrived at her art gallery, where she was attending last-minute shoppers looking for something unique to tuck under their Christmas trees.

The proprietress's cheerful expression soured upon seeing us.

'Vivian, you couldn't have come at a *worse* time,' Mildred said, striding over, her peevish disposition at odds with the festive red dress.

Sushi and I were ignored.

Mildred continued, 'So unless you intend to *buy* something . . .'

'I do,' Mother replied, like a bride at the altar.

Mildred's demeanor lightened. 'Oh, in that case, I'll be glad to help you, while my other patrons are making up their minds.'

'Very gracious of you.'

What was Mother up to? We certainly couldn't afford anything in this high-end place.

Mildred folded her hands at her waist. 'What in particular were you interested in?'

Mother walked over to a column displaying a bronze statue of a dancing maiden in the art nouveau style. It really would go nicely in her bedroom, if predictably pricey. 'Tell me about this lovely item.'

'Ah,' Mildred replied. 'You have exquisite taste.' A quality rarely attributed to Mother.

The gallery owner went on to explain, 'It's not a reproduction, but an original found at the site of an old mansion in Davenport that had been demolished.'

'Goodness gracious,' Mother said, 'it's a wonder the statue survived. Must have taken a bit of cleaning to get it to look brand-new like this. Just *look* at that shine.'

Mildred nodded. 'It *was* in rather sad shape when I bought it. But I assure you the cleaning solvent did not lessen its value in the least.'

'What did you use?' Mother asked.

'Excuse me?'

'What solvent did you use? I'm concerned about the original patina.'

'The patina is intact,' the gallery owner said with a hint of irritation. 'All it will need in the future is a soft damp cloth.'

'I understand, dear,' Mother responded sweetly, 'but I'd like to know *exactly*—'

'Are you going to buy the statue or not?'

'I'm giving it serious thought. In the meantime, why don't you see to your other customers.'

Mildred made a clicking sound with her tongue, and turned away.

As soon as the woman was occupied, Mother grabbed my arm, nearly causing me to drop Sushi, and pulled us through a velvet curtain that separated the gallery from a backroom work area.

'What are we doing?' I whispered.

'You search for any cleaning products containing TCE,' she said, 'since your eyes are better at reading small print. And keep your gloves on. I'll look for the rat poison.'

Since I needed to free Sushi from my arms, I unzipped my coat and tucked her inside so that just her head stuck out, like I had a furry alien growing out of my chest.

The backroom was surprisingly messy considering the elegance of the gallery and the prim and proper front Mildred presented. Wooden crates and shipping materials were strewn about, a workbench scattered with tools. I located the cleaning supplies on shelves in a closet.

Several products listed trichloroethane among their ingredients, both liquid and aerosols; but one in particular – a solution in a glass bottle – boasted of giving any metal a lustrous shine.

I took the bottle over to Mother.

'More than satisfactory,' she said, one-upping Nero Wolfe. 'Find something to pour a sample in.'

I spotted a small Mason jar that looked clean, and used it to drain off just enough that it wouldn't be noticeable.

Rejoining Mother I asked, 'What about the rat poison?'

Mother nodded. 'I found a plastic container that Mildred

had labeled as such – which confirms Cary's story – so he must have kept the bag.'

'Do we need a sample?'

She shook her head. 'We know it's here.'

Caught up in Mother's whirlwind, I asked, 'Should I see if the coast is clear?' Two heads – mine and Sushi's – looked curiously at her.

'We'll leave by the back door.'

Aghast, I said, 'You mean the one with the sign that says an alarm will sound if it's opened?'

Mother shrugged. 'I'm guessing it's tied into the security system, which should be switched off right now.'

Thankfully, she was correct.

So is a stopped clock, twice a day.

In the foyer at home, I freed Sushi from her little jacket – no need to remove any booties as there weren't any survivors – and she trotted off, probably as glad to be back as I was.

Tired, cold, and hungry, I went into the kitchen to find something that might pass for dinner, and that's when it came to me – *this was Christmas Eve!* Caught up in crime-solving, we almost missed it, even though we'd encountered Yuletide trappings everywhere we went.

Since we hadn't been to the grocery store for a while, I opened the freezer and found two Stouffer's turkey dinners (white breast medallions, stuffing, mashed potatoes and gravy). I checked the expiration date – not that it mattered, because I'd have eaten it regardless – then, because no vegetable was included, opened a can of peas.

In the dining room, I set the table with our holiday dishes (Christmastime by Nikko) and gold flatware that was used only for special occasions because the utensils had to be handwashed. (Once I cheated and put them in the dishwasher and some of the gold came off.)

I located a large silver candelabra that Liberace might have used on his piano, placed it in the center of the table, and lit some mismatched candles.

Returning to the kitchen, I found Mother at the stove tending to the pan of peas.

'If only we had a few more days before Jake arrives,' she lamented, 'we'd have this case solved.'

'Well, if it isn't,' I countered, 'you'd better erase your precious blackboard, because that's the first place Roger will check, to see if we've broken our promise.'

The bell on the microwave dinged.

While Mother poured tap water into our crystal goblets, I arranged the turkey dinner on two plates, adding a generous scoop of peas, then we retired to the festive Duncan Phyfe table. Our largely frozen meal looked downright scrumptious.

Grace was rarely given in the Borne household, but this being Christmas Eve, Mother bowed her head and resurrected (whoops, wrong holiday!) a prayer her Danish mother had said to her: *Lord bless this food which now we take and make us thine for Jesus' sake. Amen.*

Little Brandy for years said 'foodwich,' a kind of sandwich, and we were supposed to 'make a sign' . . . for Jesus' sake!

Our formerly frozen dinner having been blessed, we dug in. And was it ever good, calling into question why anyone would spend holiday hours toiling in the kitchen, followed by more hours cleaning up, and every year wondering what to do with the turkey carcass? Oh, and here's something else an already frazzled hostess wouldn't miss: pass the butter, pass the gravy, could I have some more turkey, and are there any more peas? In this instance, what was in front of you was a frozen dinner and that was it!

Mother, breaking her Nero Wolfe no-talking-business-at-dinner rule, said, 'I believe the killer is either Cary Hudson or Mildred Zybarth.'

I swallowed a mouthful of food. 'I don't disagree. They each had the most to lose by their businesses being threatened by Ellen.'

Mother nodded. 'Regarding the motives of Sheila White, Jared Eggler, and Megan Harris . . . husbands can be replaced, reputations can be restored, and a waitress can always find another job. But an art gallery, and movie house struggling to stay alive? Not so easy.'

'But which is it?' I asked, chasing the last bite of food around my plate, several peas rolling away. 'Mildred or Cary?'

'Women have more of an affinity to use poison,' Mother mused, 'yet bludgeoning a victim is more like the work of a man.' She frowned. 'What are you thinking, dear? You seem lost in calculation.'

I nodded to her plate. 'Are you going to eat the rest of your mashed potatoes?'

Mother pushed the remains of the day toward me, then stood. 'I'm going get the coffee and what's left of the plum pudding.'

'Don't forget the whipped cream,' I said to her back. 'It's kind of icky without.'

I think if a case lasted long enough, I would revert not just to childhood but a crib. And not the MTV kind.

A few minutes later, Mother returned with a tray holding two steaming cups and two slices of the pudding, each with just a dollop of the white stuff, and I somehow resisted getting up and adding more whipped cream to mine.

During the meal I had been feeding Sushi bites of turkey under the table, and now she began pestering me for the cake. I broke off a small piece and held it down to her.

She sniffed the bite, then backed away.

A gold fork speared with the pudding was on its way to Mother's mouth when I lunged across the table and knocked the fork from her hand, the utensil taking flight, then dropping to the floor, where it skittered beneath the buffet table and spun like a top.

'Brandy!' she admonished. 'I *gave* you the larger piece!' Reading my horrified, terrified expression, she uttered, 'Oh, my.' Then, 'You don't think . . .?'

'I *do* think,' I said. 'Arsenic may be nearly odorless to humans, but its garlic scent doesn't pass the Sushi sniff test.'

Using my spoon and fork, I carefully turned my piece of pudding over.

A hole had been cut in the bottom . . .

. . . and filled with white granules.

I said, 'I don't believe that's powdered sugar.'

'I suspect it isn't,' Mother replied.

Still seated, I pushed my chair away from the table with a wake-the-dead screech. 'We need to call Tony.'

'No, dear,' she replied emphatically.

'Mother!' I exclaimed. 'Someone clearly broke into our house, and attempted to murder us! This is no time for grandstanding.'

'I am not grandstanding,' Mother said calmly. 'The killer may be watching, and the moment a police car arrives, along with a forensics team yanked rudely away from their Christmas Eve dinners, the miscreant will *know* this effort to silence us had been thwarted.'

I saw her point. 'And start destroying evidence.'

'Yes. Our perp *must* think we haven't yet eaten the pudding. In which lies the proof of how close we are.' She stood. 'Come. Let's appear festive.'

I put a frozen smile on my face and followed Mother into the living room. The curtains of the picture window had been closed, and she drew back both the drapes and sheer panels.

'Put on some music,' Mother said, seasoned director that she was. 'Play with Sushi. I'm going to find out how he – or she – got in.'

On my cell, I downloaded *The Beach Boys Christmas Album*, setting the volume high. Picking up Sushi for a dance partner, I cavorted around with her in my arms to the first tune, 'Little Saint Nick.' Yes, we looked ridiculous.

The next tune, 'The Man with All the Toys,' was playing when Mother gestured from the dining room.

I danced with my partner out of view for a confab.

'It appears lock picks were used on the back door,' Mother grumbled, disgruntled by the audacity – she hates being topped. 'The door to the basement is locked from the kitchen, so our killer – in our case, would-be killer – couldn't have come in that way. And all the windows on this floor are locked.'

'What now?' I asked. I'd exhausted my dance moves.

'Do you remember the time we used two dummies to make it appear we were home?'

Two dummies were frequently home in this house, but never mind.

After a string of daytime burglaries in the neighborhood, Mother had 'borrowed' the prop manikins from the Playhouse, dressed them in wigs and our clothes, and set them in chairs near the front window.

Mother said, 'They're under some plastic in the attic.'

Meaning I should go get them. Sometimes it isn't easy being Watson.

'And,' she added, 'don't forget the gizmo.'

Meaning a gearmotor.

When I returned from the attic with the dummies and motor, Mother had closed the drapes again, and set the stage in front of the window: an antique rocking chair and Queen Anne armchair placed at an angle toward each other separated by a Victorian table holding a silver tea set.

'Brandy' was placed in the Queen Anne, while 'Mother' was arranged in the rocker. The gearmotor – which made the rocker rock on its own – was attached, and a standing lamp positioned so that the dummies would be seen in silhouette through the layer of sheer curtains.

Mother and I had to be careful not to be viewed in duplicate from the outside, but once we were out of the lamp's light, we could move around undetected.

She and I reconvened in the kitchen, where I took a swig of rum straight from the bottle. Yo ho ho.

Mother, cell in one hand, said, 'While you were in the attic, I revisited the uses of trichloroethane, and far down on the list was its effectiveness for cleaning film.'

'As in old silent movie prints?'

'As in old silent movie prints. I had been concentrating on that old projector, but the clue was the cellulose film. I want to show you something . . .'

As I looked over her shoulder, Mother scrolled through the photos she'd taken the night Ellen was killed, stopping on one of the woman's body, enlarging the area of one hand.

'Doesn't it look like she's pointing to the fireplace?'

'So?'

'Fireplace? Santa? It's a clue, dear. That's why she staggered over there.'

'I think you're reaching,' I said skeptically.

'Well, Ellen certainly is. Here's something else . . .'

She scrolled through more pictures.

'You recall that Cary mentioned he had *mailed* Ellen a check for five hundred dollars for the Santa and Rudolph puppets?'

'Yes.'

'Here's one showing the letters Ellen had brought in from the mailbox and dropped.'

Again, a portion was enlarged, revealing the return address was from the Bijou Theater.

'Notice anything?' Mother asked.

I caught it right away – perhaps the rum had helped. 'The stamp hasn't been cancelled by the post office.'

'Very astute, dear. But Ellen was cancelled all right, and that's the kind of ruthless villain we're up against.'

'Still,' I said, 'Cary could have put the letter with his check directly in her mailbox.'

'Then why put on a stamp?' Mother asked.

I stared at her, agape. 'You're not saying Cary killed Ellen . . . to get those *puppets*?'

Mother opened a hand. 'I'm not implying that was his main, or only, motive . . . but it could have been the catalyst. After all, collecting puppets from old stop-motion features was his obsession, and you know how obsessive collectors can be.'

I did. She was still hunting for a second art nouveau fleur-de-lis red enamel cuff bracelet to complete a pair.

I knew what was coming next. 'Don't tell me. We're going to break into the theater.'

'I don't have to tell you. You seem to already know.'

My moan couldn't have been worse if I *had* swallowed the poison. 'When?'

'The witching hour,' Mother replied. 'Midnight.'

'I know what the witching hour is, and anyway that's the wrong holiday you're invoking.'

She ignored that observation. 'We'll have to leave the van in the driveway and take the Vespa. You'll want to dress warmly.'

Brandy's Trash 'n' Treasures Tip

The snow globe was invented in Austria at the end of the nineteenth century by Erwin Perzy, a producer of medical instruments who was trying to invent a brighter surgical lamp. His first globe was a model of the basilica of Mariazell and sold so well that he began a family business in Vienna that remains in operation. But the most collectible snow globes today are produced by Disney, the value depending upon rarity and popularity. Snow globes do not fare well in the Borne household, tending to break, unless they are completely made of plastic.

TWELVE

Little St Nicked

As planned, at the witching hour, bundled in black, Mother and I snuck quietly out the back of our house where the Vespa was parked.

The night was cold, but the wind still as the moon washed the world ivory. This made the crisp open-air trip to the Bijou not as unpleasant as I'd expected and instead one that encouraged alertness. Mother guided the scooter with a sure hand, neither slowpoke nor speeder, but a woman on a mission.

A block from our destination, we tucked the scooter behind a Dumpster in the alley, then continued on foot, our shoes crunching on thin ice that had refrozen from the day. Well, we'd been on thin ice before . . .

Gaining entrance to the theater through either the front or rear doors would have triggered the alarm, and since the lower windows were wired – indicating the system was not motion-activated – it meant our best . . . perhaps only option . . . was getting in through an old coal chute, located at the back of the building.

The chute's iron door had been sealed shut with caulk, but over the years became brittle, and was easily pulled open, producing an alley echo that made me jump a little. Not Mother.

This was not our first experience going down a chute into a suspect's basement. The last time we'd taken such a trip, Mother got stuck in the opening, and had to be pulled through – but that was a residential home, and this was a business sporting a larger aperture. We didn't even need to remove our coats.

'After you, dear,' Mother whispered.

I went in feet first, sliding briefly and then dropping down about four feet into darkness. Getting my balance under me, I brushed myself off and stood there listening for a few moments, to see if my landing had attracted any attention. It didn't seem to have. I helped Mother make a softer landing and she tottered for a while until she got her bearings. My cell light activated, we stood quietly while I slowly scanned our surroundings.

Usually basements of old Victorian commercial buildings consisted of dirt floors, decaying brick walls, stale air, and scurrying rodents. But the Bijou's lower level had been renovated. There was a cement floor, patched brick walls, ventilation (I could feel air flowing), and no vermin captured by my beam.

The light disclosed a workbench with stool, tools on a pegboard, bookended by metal storage cabinets. Nearby a reinforced-steel vault door with a circular red handle was set into a brick wall of the building, the iron door itself closed of course.

Mother whispered, 'That must be where Cary keeps his silent movies.'

Should any nitrate film ignite, the fire wouldn't spread to other parts of the theater.

'Let's check the work area first,' I whispered back. That was where Cary most likely doctored the chocolates, picking up traces of the trichloroethane he used to clean the nitrate film.

Mother shook her head. 'We'll start with the office. And remember to keep your gloves on.'

My light located a modern metal staircase and we headed toward it. And, with me in the lead, we ascended the steps to a landing. New or not, they creaked, unless that was Mother's knees.

Suddenly I let out a little *eek!* as a hockey-masked, machete-wielding Jason from *Friday the 13th,* ready to strike, filled my beam.

'It's only a standee,' Mother chided.

Still, I needed a moment to regain my composure, not that I had much to begin with.

The door at the top of the second flight was closed but unlocked, and we emerged beside the concessions stand, where

I turned off my cell because its brightness might be spotted through the theater's glass front.

A streetlight bleeding in enabled us to see well enough to make our way to Cary's office, the door of which was locked, necessitating that Mother produce her trusty picks to allow us to gain entry.

With the door closed again, and no windows to worry about in the small office, Mother switched on the desk lamp.

She said, 'While I look here, you check the file cabinet.'

'Checking for what?'

'Anything that might implicate Cary. Think outside the box, dear.'

Since that seemed like a rather broad mandate, I gave the cabinet's four drawers a quick but relatively thorough once-over.

I dutifully reported: 'Nothing but files on invoices, vendors, and contracts.'

'Search elsewhere,' Mother said, now seated in Cary's chair, a pile of papers on the desktop before her.

The only option of 'elsewhere' was the waste basket, which I knelt before and poked around in with gloved fingers. Getting nowhere, I emptied it on to the floor.

Judging by the discarded yellow-and-black checkered wrappers, Cary – like me – was clearly a connoisseur of Abba-Zaba bars. But he also had an affinity for Jujubes – a movie treat I once enjoyed, but es-'chewed,' after losing several fillings to the hard gummy candy. (Did the manufacturer make it that way? Or did it get stale in the box? One of life's little mysteries, yet to be solved.)

Apart from a few crumpled tissues the remainder of the basket contained wadded-up white paper.

I was smoothing one open when Mother said, 'Eureka!'

She held up a sheet of blank blue stationery that I recognized from a photo Mother had taken of Ellen's secretaire on the night the woman was killed.

And I had some evidence of my own. The crumpled paper contained samples of Ellen's signature that Cary (apparently) had tried to mimic.

I passed it to Mother.

'Splendid,' she replied. 'Now, if only the letter he claimed Ellen sent accepting his offer to buy the puppets could be found. I'm *sure* it would prove to be a forgery.'

'It may not exist,' I said, adding, 'Or, he hadn't gotten around to writing it yet.'

Mother made a face. 'I should have called his bluff when he offered to produce it.'

I was beginning to feel uneasy.

'We've got enough to go to Tony for a search warrant,' I said. 'Let's get out of here while the getting's good.'

Mother replied coolly, 'There's still the trichloroethane to find.'

'OK . . . but could we hurry? This place is giving me the creeps.'

'Try not to talk in clichés, dear.'

'All right, it gives me the willies then.'

'Very well.' She folded the blue stationery and white sheet of forged signatures, then tucked them into a coat pocket.

While I refilled the waste basket, she straightened the desk drawers, and turned off the lamp.

We left, Mother relocking the office door.

Retracing our steps toward the concessions counter, I said, 'While we're here, I want another Abba-Zaba bar.' It could very well be my last one at the Bijou with the theater closed after Cary's inevitable arrest.

'Dear,' Mother said disapprovingly, 'that would be theft.'

'What's breaking and entering? Chopped liver?'

But we curtailed our repartee, after I'd selected two more Abba-Zaba bars. (I left a five and a one under the popcorn-salt shaker.) Once the basement door was closed behind us, I resumed my cell light as we descended the stairs. At the bottom, with the beam leading the way, Mother and I approached the workbench area, with a metal four-drawer file cabinet on either side.

'You take one,' she said, 'I'll check the other. Remember, we're looking for trichloroethane.'

As if I had to be reminded.

The drawers I searched held a variety of small equipment

– a film splicer (according to the box), an assortment of cables, and other tech stuff I didn't understand, as well as office supplies and filed away publicity material on various feature films.

But in her cabinet, Mother hit a trifecta in the evidence category.

'I believe this is what we're looking for,' she said, holding up a small dark brown bottle with brown cap that might have been something found in a lab setting, or a cabinet in a doctor's office.

A white label read: 'Spectrum,' and below, among several other listed ingredients was 'Trichloroethane'.

I smiled tightly. 'With Ellen's stationery, the forged signatures, and now this . . .'

Mother, slipping the bottle into her other coat pocket, finished my sentence, '. . . we have enough to convict our jolly old elf.'

All we needed now was to find something to stand on to reach the opening of the coal chute.

Which was when I noticed the vault door was partially open.

'Wasn't that closed before?' I asked, pointing.

Mother frowned as she took in the yawning door.

'I believe you're correct, Brandy. It *was* closed.'

But the response had come not from Mother, rather the dark recesses of a corner.

Basement lights blazed on, temporarily blinding me, but not enough that I couldn't see Cary walking toward us.

He was festively attired in a green Alpine sweater with dancing red reindeer. One hand held a film canister, the other a cigarette lighter.

'It's open now,' he said, 'because that's where you're going.'

'Now, dear,' Mother said soothingly, 'let's not do anything rash . . .'

'Yes,' I added. 'The police know where we are.'

Cary looked around. 'That seems unlikely. There's no sign of them being party to this midnight raid. In fact, I'll take my chances that they're not coming.'

He was correct, of course. I had not texted Tony as I usually did, as a fail-safe should things go awry. After all,

Tony would have almost certainly short-circuited our extra-legal endeavor.

The lid of the canister clattered to the cement.

'You'll recall we spoke earlier of the flammability of cellulose nitrate,' Cary went on. 'Hence the precaution of the vault.'

He unrolled the film just a little, like a fuse leading to a stick of dynamite.

In the past Mother and I had been faced with a variety of weapons: guns, knives, golf clubs . . . even a working antique pistol. But this was a new one on us. All Cary had to do was light the fuse, toss the canister our way, and we'd be as silent as Charlie Chaplin . . . after our screams died down, anyway.

'Empty threats don't bother us,' Mother said. 'How would you explain our demise to the authorities?'

The twinkle in his eyes was Santa worthy. If Santa were a sociopath. 'Easy peasy, Viv. That I arrived at the theater tomorrow morning and was shocked to find you both burned alive in the vault after some cellulose nitrate spontaneously combusted. Which shouldn't be too unbelievable a passing for you two, considering your past history of breaking the law.' He paused. 'Interesting choice, the coal chute. I *had* left the alarm off assuming you'd drop by. But instead you dropped in.'

With Cary waiting for us, ready for a midnight screening. Or was that screaming?

Playing cool, Mother nodded to the film can in his grasp. 'What are you sacrificing, besides a mother and daughter?'

'*Black Oxen.*'

'You can't!' she exclaimed, truly appalled. 'That's Clara Bow's first appearance after she won a beauty contest to get the part.'

He shrugged. 'The film's already starting to degrade.'

Mother frowned sadly. 'I do hope there won't be any other casualties.'

His smile was grotesque. 'Only you two. I've removed most of the other canisters in the vault, leaving only deteriorating ones behind.'

'Will you answer a few questions?' I asked, stalling, hoping some previously unused portion of my brain was coming up with an escape plan.

Cary smirked. 'Like the end of one of those corny old movies where the killer confesses all? Only to be recorded on a tell-all cell phone?'

I turned to Mother, trying to play as cool as she was. '*I'm* not recording, are you?'

Mother's shrug was the epitome of casual. 'No, dear. There's no point. Our phones will be destroyed in the fire with us.'

I nodded. 'And it would look suspicious if we didn't have them on us.'

'I'm sure he's thought of that,' she said. 'He seems to have thought of everything.'

I looked at Cary. 'Well, what about it?'

'About what?'

'Why not share some answers,' I said. 'Show your ingenuity off a little. It'll be your only chance, assuming you get away with this.'

He shrugged his consent, holding the wheel of film in one hand before him like an insufficient if deadly shield.

I nodded to Mother, who said, 'The night you killed Ellen before the evening showing of *It's a Wonderful Life*, had you followed her home? Or was her arrival there a surprise?'

He might have been reporting a trip to the grocery store, enumerating his purchases. 'I'd heard Alice at the club ask Ellen to stay with her, so when Ellen showed up, I had to . . . improvise.' He frowned, just a tinge of worry coming in. 'You're not suggesting that I may have made a mistake in the process?'

The man seemed to want to know.

So Mother told him.

'Yes, dear,' she said. 'What you might call an unforced error. The stamp on the letter you added to her mail . . .'

'. . . hadn't been cancelled,' Cary interjected, nodding, smirking again, wrinkling his chin this time. 'Well, no matter. That mistake will die with you.'

'And the arsenic in our plum pudding?' she continued.

He chuckled. 'Now *that* was a chance I took . . . that you weren't home.'

I said, 'Seems like you took a lot of chances.'

That riled him, his smugness going up in smoke. Bad choice of words.

'I had no *choice*!' Cary exclaimed, a defiant child. More Spanky from *The Little Rascals* than jolly St Nick. 'It was that *woman's* fault! None of this would have happened if she'd sold me those puppets in the first place . . . my offer was *more* than fair! But Ellen wouldn't sell to me at any price. Not because she valued them or loved them. Just to keep *me* from having them! That's why I had to plant the letter, and try to forge one with her accepting my offer.' He paused. 'I sent Alexis to buy a box of the holiday chocolates which I filled with rat poison on my workbench in the basement, then took to the club in my Santa's bag where I switched my chocolates with Ellen's gift, adding her tag to it, later throwing hers in the trash. How was I to know Ellen would trade presents with Norma? Again, not my fault! Jared had to die because I'd asked him what gift Ellen had wanted, then, figured he'd put two and two together and either tell the police or try to blackmail me.' Cary made a face as if tasting something foul. 'What a disgusting horrible experience that Ellen woman made me go through! *Some* people.'

The cigarette lighter flicked on, its flame drawing closer to the exposed tail of the film.

'All right, ladies,' Cary ordered. 'Inside the vault!'

And still I had no plan. If there *was* a previously unused portion of my brain up there, it wasn't showing itself.

But Mother's did. She splashed the opened bottle of trichloroethane in his face, the acid making him cry out, both hands flying to his burning skin, canister dropping to his feet, the lighter landing on top.

There was a *WOOSH!* as the film caught on fire. It didn't help matters that trichloroethane was, in addition to poisonous, also highly flammable.

I can't go into further details of Cary's final moments because as of the writing of this book, I'm still in therapy learning to cope with the memory of the sounds and frankly smells of what I witnessed. Let's just say his screams were as terrible as they were thankfully brief, though Mother said what she witnessed reminded her of *House of Wax*.

I will say, however, that Mother and I did our best to smother the flames with our coats, futile as it proved.

Vivian once again. We'll dispense with the train metaphor and get right to the aftermath of the murderer's demise.

After calling 911, I sent Brandy upstairs to the front of the theater to wait for the paramedics . . . though we were already well past holding out any hope for misguided puppet collector Cary.

When two male medics arrived at the scene – the same pair that had pronounced Norma dead at the country club four days ago – it didn't take them long to come to the same conclusion.

One was dispatched to bring back a body bag.

At this juncture I noticed Brandy, who had accompanied the EMTs down, appeared to be in a state of shock, unresponsive to my inquiry if she was all right, her eyes staring at but not seeing me.

When officers Monroe and Munson descended the steps, I approached Shawntea.

'Would one of you please take my daughter home? She doesn't seem well. We witnessed something quite traumatic. Imagine the burning of Atlanta in *Gone with the Wind* combined with the opening of the box at the end of *Kiss Me Deadly*.'

Two pictures I had seen in revival at this very theater!

I concluded: 'In the meantime, I'll answer any questions you might have.'

'I'll take her,' Munson said.

Shawntea nodded her approval.

Moments later the tall, lanky officer escorted a trance-like Brandy up the stairs. Actually, he had glimpsed the charred remains of Serenity's favorite Santa Claus and seemed a little traumatized himself.

Shawntea came closer to me, her eyes hardened. 'You're killing that girl with your nonsense.'

'It's your opinion that's nonsense,' I said, in no mood for judgmental baloney.

The medics had returned with the black bag, and the pair went down to consign the charred body inside.

Shawntea was saying, 'She can't take these deaths as blithely you can.'

'No one takes murder more seriously than Vivian Borne.'

The officer's communicator crackled.

'*I want Mrs Borne in my office immediately*,' Tony said.

'Chief, I was just about to question her.'

'*I'll do that here*.'

'Yes, sir.'

To me Shawntea said, 'You heard. Get going.'

'My coat is burned, dear, so I'll need to borrow yours.'

She sighed, and removed her outer jacket.

Dear reader, would you think unkindly of me if I admitted it crossed my mind not to give it back? Having an official coat with real insignias and POLICE spread across the back could come in handy.

No answer necessary to that. Call it a rhetorical question, if that helps.

Outside, the cold air felt refreshing as I walked to retrieve my Vespa behind the Dumpster in the alley a block away.

Usually I fought tooth and nail to hang around a crime scene, but not this time. Brandy and I had been in tight spots before, but never a situation coming as close to what might have been visited upon us by Cary, who wound up suffering the very fate he'd intended for us.

It was my fault – something I rarely admit because it is seldom true – but I'd had an expectation Brandy would have texted Tony as to our whereabouts once we arrived at the theater, as she'd done in past cases when we were about to expose a murderer. That would have set him up to intervene in the (Saint?) nick of time.

But due to their ruptured relationship, I should have taken the precaution of sending the chief a text myself.

Consequently, the bottle of trichloroethane in my pocket – whose cap I'd been unscrewing with my fingers – became our only option for escape.

In hindsight, I didn't expect the lighter to fall on to the film . . . only for Cary to be distracted or possibly disabled long enough that he might be subdued.

Considering how circumstances played out – and Cary's love of watching movies – well, it would have been a long and esthetically unhappy life for him in prison had he lost his eyesight when I splashed him with the poison he'd used so readily on others.

I found the Vespa where we'd left it, wheeled the scooter out, and climbed aboard for the short journey to the station.

At the back entrance, I rapped several times before Tony opened the door, his expression as frosty as the night air. I followed him into his office, where he took his place behind the desk, and I the chair opposite him.

The chief looked tired – and why not? – having been dragged from his wee little bed (couldn't resist the Christmas reference!), and forced by expediency to don clothes worn earlier.

He also looked angrier than I'd ever seen him. And I'd seen him considerably put out with me over what he saw as interference in official investigations. But hadn't he given us carte blanche this time? Or at least blanche?

I waited for the tongue-lashing.

'Brandy went home?' he asked.

'Yes,' I replied. 'Office Munson was kind enough to take her,' adding, 'She's fine.'

'*Is* she?'

Was that steam coming out of his ears? Or had I seen too many old Warner Bros cartoons?

I shifted in the chair. 'Well, naturally, it was an unpleasant experience for Brandy . . . but there's no such thing as a fate worse than death, and we circumvented the ol' Grim Reaper. Anyway, I'm sure after a good night's sleep—'

'You think a good night's sleep,' the chief asked coldly, 'is going to reverse the damage you've done her?'

I went on the offensive. 'Brandy wanted to solve this case as much as I – perhaps even more.' I paused. 'Anyway, if you two weren't on the outs, she would have texted you where we were and why.'

His eyes golf-balled at me. 'Now you're blaming *me*?'

'What *else* is different this time around? If you'd patched things up, you and Brandy would be married by now and away from me!'

Had I just admitted I was a bad influence on the girl?

The chief was saying, almost to himself, 'If I told her I was wrong, she'd know I was lying.'

The girl did have a remarkable b.s. detector.

He sat forward. 'Anyway, you're not here to discuss Brandy and me. I want to know what happened tonight.'

'Could I have some coffee? Preferably with cream.'

'No.'

'Very well, if you want to be inhospitable.'

Apparently he did.

I began with the timely discovery of the poisoned plum pudding at dinner – which appeared to erase any hostility from the chief's expression – then proceeded to elaborate on how Brandy and I had deduced the killer was Cary Hudson, and the need to obtain proof before the theater owner realized we were still alive, and destroyed the key evidence.

From one coat pocket I withdrew the blue stationery Cary had taken from Ellen's home, along with the white sheets with samples Cary had made of her signature. From the other pocket I produced the bottle of trichloroethane.

'This is what we found,' I said, placing the items on his desk.

I explained the significance of each, and waited for praise.

It didn't come.

'I should throw you in jail,' he said. (Actually, also included was a reference to my posterior.)

Honestly, I was appalled by this reaction. And annoyed by the man's ingratitude.

'On what charges?' I asked.

'Breaking and entering, confiscation of evidence, interfering with an ongoing investigation.'

'Which was undertaken with your blessing.'

'The investigation, yes. The rest of it, don't be ridiculous.'

I shrugged. 'Well, why don't you make your arrest then?'

'Because you'd like that.'

True. I had fond memories of my stays in the county B & B – except for the time an inmate tried to shiv me during a meal (referred to in jail parlance as 'dinner and a show'). Also, I'd recently heard that a former inmate was back in stir, a charismatic gal who would make an excellent lead in a prison production of *Heathers: The Musical.*

The chief was saying, 'But I won't arrest you, because I'd also have to charge Brandy.'

Who did *not* have fond memories of her time behind bars.

The chief rolled back his chair, indicating the close of the interrogation. 'I want you here first thing in the morning, for a complete statement.'

I stood. 'Which you'll be taking?'

'No. Officer Monroe. I have the day off.'

'And a well-deserved day that will be,' I said cheerfully.

'Leave.'

'Yes, sir.'

You know those old war movies where a pilot sent out on a dangerous mission hears voices in his head like, 'Wait until you're over the bombsite!' and 'Remember, you only have enough fuel for one pass,' and 'The whole country is counting on you . . . *counting on you . . . counting on you!*' (That last part is an echo.)

I didn't hear any of that during my trip home on the Vespa, although years ago I did briefly take flying lessons in a Piper Cub until I clipped a wing on the sock pole.

Bouncing around in my head was what Shawntea had said: 'You're killing that girl . . .' And Tony's retort to my statement that Brandy was fine: '*Is* she?' (*Is she? Is she?*)

The house was dark when I pulled the Vespa into the driveway, except for the Christmas tree's glow behind sheer curtains.

In the foyer, I removed my coat and boots, then picked up Brandy's jacket, which she'd dropped on the floor, and corralled her flung-off UGGs.

Then I padded into the kitchen and turned on the light to make myself a cup of herbal tea. As I did, an open bottle of Ambien on the counter caught my attention.

I'd been prescribed the sleeping drug for tinnitus, but only took one pill after waking the following morning to find the SUV parked on the front lawn, my purse inside.

Quickly I poured the tablets on to the counter and began counting. The bottle had originally contained thirty. Deducting my one-time dose, and another for Brandy tonight, there should be twenty-eight.

And there were.

I breathed a sigh of relief.

Still, the fact that I had immediately jumped to the conclusion that the girl might have tried to harm herself reinforced the opinions of both Shawntea and the chief that what I had been putting her through was hurtful.

I went upstairs to Brandy's room.

She was deep asleep, Sushi cuddled beside her. The little dog raised its head, made the decision not to abandon her mistress (and the warmth of the bed), and lowered it again.

I needed to get Brandy and Tony back together, toot sweet; and married, toot sweetier.

I just hoped he knew she snored.

Bet he did.

Vivian's Trash 'n' Treasures Tip

What is the holiday season without cookies? And what are cookies without a festive cookie jar? Whether you find them at yard sales, flea markets, or online, always inspect carefully for damage before buying. Valuable and rare cookie jars should be used for display only, preferable out of the reach of little hands, although even adults can have fumble fingers. I blame arthritis for the chip in the cap of my vintage McCoy Santa.

THIRTEEN

Home For the Holly Daze

I awoke in a groggy haze, in pajamas I had no memory of getting into, their top damp from night sweats, sheet tangled around my legs, cover thrown off on to the floor in a mess like a skydiver whose chute didn't open.

I reached for my cell on the nightstand, moving with all the speed and grace of a sleepwalker.

The phone reported that it was a little after three in the afternoon on Christmas Day. Merry Christmas, Brandy. I'd slept nearly twelve hours.

A text from Tony asked how I was . . . and if he could expect me for dinner at his cabin tonight.

My response was OK and yes.

On unsteady feet, I staggered downstairs, drawn to a clatter in the kitchen. It wasn't St Nick.

Mother, in her favorite green velour slacks and pullover, stood at the counter, rolling out dark-colored dough, old-fashioned cookie cutters (aluminum with little wooden knobs) waiting nearby to perform their Christmas duty.

Also nearby was Sushi, eyes laser-focused on Mother, any concern for her mistress long gone with only one thought in her canine mind – getting some of that dough!

Without looking at me, Mother said, 'Jake would be disappointed if I didn't make *brunkager*.'

Which was (and is) a thin, crispy spiced cookie that her grandmother used to bake.

Brunkager
(Danish gingerbread cookies)

½ cup unsalted butter
½ cup brown sugar

⅓ cup molasses
1 cup all-purpose flour
½ tbsp. cinnamon
1 tsp. ginger
½ tsp. cloves
½ tsp. baking soda
pinch of salt

In a saucepan, melt the butter, sugar, and molasses over low heat until the sugar dissolves. While the mixture cools, in a large bowl combine the flour, cinnamon, ginger, cloves, baking soda, and salt. Add the wet mixture into the dry ingredients, combining completely. Wrap the dough in cellophane and refrigerate overnight. On a floured board, roll out the dough very thinly, and use cookie cutters for the shapes desired. Transfer the cutouts to parchment paper on cookie sheets. Bake at 350 degrees Fahrenheit for between 5 to 8 minutes, depending upon thickness, watching closely so they don't burn. Cool completely before storing in an airtight container.

What is it about grandmothers and cookies that made Christmas so special? Would I be a grandmother one day whose Christmas cookie recipe would be: 'Find a convenience store that's open and buy something packaged. Check the sell-by date. Enjoy!'

'There's a fresh pot,' Mother advised.

I poured myself coffee in a Christmastime cup, then sat on a vintage red step-stool chair at the counter, like little Brandy used to, watching Mother mix some dessert, waiting patiently for the spatula and what was left in the bowl.

I wanted to cry. Hard to imagine a more traumatic build-up to the big birthday.

'Did you get a restful sleep?' Mother asked, pressing a cutter shaped like a bell into the dough.

'I got plenty of sleep, but I don't know how restful it was.'

'I've thrown the Ambien pills away, so neither of us will be tempted to take them again.'

'. . . OK.' That seemed strange, but since I didn't like the aftereffects of the drug, that was fine with me; and Mother had a bad experience the one time she took it.

Ignoring the recommended parchment paper, Mother placed the bell on a sprayed cookie sheet. 'I've been thinking . . .'

Uh-oh.

'. . . now that Jake is coming to stay for a while, and I'm hanging up my deerstalker cap and magnifying glass, I'll need to occupy my time with other endeavors.'

I waited for her list of other endeavors, not wanting to bother guessing what she had in mind. One of her ventures between cases had been running for sheriff, and we know how that turned out.

She was saying, 'There are lots of opportunities for volunteering in our community.'

Now, the only time Mother 'volunteered' for anything was by court order to complete a sentence via community service. Oh, she gave money to many local charities, and campaigned for civic causes, but wouldn't – couldn't – be involved in anything where she wasn't in charge.

She went on, 'And you, dear, need to get on with your life.'

Meaning marrying Tony.

Something had changed between us. I could feel it. From a very early age I'd become attuned to her moods and methods. I knew when she was off her medication; when to go along with her antics; when to call her psychiatrist; and when to have mental health advocates intervene when there was no other option.

But this was different. She was pushing me away.

I didn't know whether to be hurt, or relieved.

Maybe both.

Mother was saying, 'Santa arrived during the night and filled your stocking – it's under the tree.'

I hadn't had stocking gifts since putting a stop to it after I turned thirteen. Here she was, treating me like a child again, but in an uncharacteristically loving way.

I stumbled into the living room, still suffering an Ambien hangover.

And there it was, with red and green stripes and a big Santa face and my name at the top. Despite the dropped stitches, inconsistent stripes, and a Santa that looked demented, I had a great fondness for that sock and was glad she'd hung on to it – Mother's first – and, as far as I knew, last – attempt at knitting anything.

I reached inside.

And pulled out some vacation brochures.

A note was included. Your destination wedding will be at my expense! Signed, Mrs Claus.

Not too subtle, was she?

Upstairs, I had a long, leisurely bubble bath, thinking about my rift with Tony. Did feeling a certain way automatically justify it? If so, we both were right.

Ultimately, I came to no tub conclusion.

I took extra care with my hair and make-up, and put on a white silk shirt, black slacks, and Kate Spade shoes that my BFF Tina had given me last year for Christmas: black flats with embellished martini glasses.

Curses! I'd only worn the shoes a few times, and already had lost some of the crystals!

Dear Kate Spade Company,

Please include spare beads and/or crystals along with your shoes and bags. Thank you.

Brandy Borne.

My preparatory intention was not to be alluring, but to look presentable in the snapshot within Tony's mind, if this was the end of our relationship. Anyway, 'alluring' is tough to achieve when your eyes are welling up.

Downstairs, Mother had prepared a tin of *Brunkager* for my once (and future?) fiancé. I also had a small present tucked into my matching martini-beaded bag.

And of course, I had to bring Sushi along . . . otherwise, when I returned smelling of Rocky, the purse and shoes would suffer more damage than a few lost embellishments.

Besides, I had sprayed my neck with the perfume Tony had given me last Christmas, a dead giveaway to the dog. (OK, maybe I *was* trying to be a little alluring.)

We went out to the car, Sushi and me, where the night was clear, stars strung across the sky like the ceiling of the darkened Bijou, only real and not the demented nostalgic pretense of a late theater owner.

Sushi stood on the passenger seat, staring straight ahead, panting in anticipation of being with the love of her life once again. Why couldn't I be that way? (Not the panting.) I wanted to. Wanted to forgive and forget and not so much start over as pick up where we left off. The only thing stopping me was me.

As I drove the river road cautiously, watching for deer, I cleared my head. No preplanned allegations, or cross-examinations, nor closing arguments allowed. Not even prepared small talk. I have always said, prep all you want for a certain verbal outcome, but it is never – *I repeat never* – what happens.

About five miles out of town, I turned left on to the narrow dirt lane that led to Tony's cabin.

A tall yard light illuminated his property, a typical small farm homestead. On the left, a red barn with ubiquitous rooster weathervane; in the back, a windmill, blades still in the silent night; to the right, the cozy house – actually a cabin – with smoke curling out of its chimney.

After shutting off the engine, I wanted to take a moment in the car, but Sushi was beside herself, pawing at the passenger door, eager as a child anticipating Christmas morning gifts. I leaned over, opened it, and she took off like a furry ballistic missile.

Tony, seeing my arrival, had come out on to the porch, and let Sushi in. He was wearing navy slacks and a burgundy crew-neck sweater.

I left the car, crossed the yard, and went up the three wooden porch steps to meet him.

We stood facing each other.

'Merry Christmas,' he said.

'Merry Christmas,' I said.

'How are you?' he asked.

'All right,' I lied.

He gestured. 'Come in and get warm by the fire.'

He turned to open the door, but I held back.

'Tony?'

He faced me again.

'I don't want to talk about any of it.' Meaning the case, my involvement, and our disagreement.

He nodded. 'Neither do I. So let's not.'

Breath came out of me, unbidden.

'Thank you,' I said.

I couldn't hope for a better Christmas present.

Inside, a pleasant, woodsy aroma awaited, the cabin roomier than it appeared from without. To the left was a cozy area with fireplace, crackling with flames dancing like happy elves. Waiting patiently were that familiar overstuffed brown couch and, to the right, a four-chair round oak table and small china hutch, the kitchen just beyond. A short hallway led to a single bedroom, tiny bathroom with shower, and back door leading to a small porch.

At one time, the log walls had showcased Tony's collection of old snowshoes nailed on haphazardly. But he'd since replaced them with antique fishing gear we'd found on our various antiquing trips: rods, wicker creels, and flies (not the buzzing kind) displayed in glass cases.

He took my coat and hung it on a peg between a hunting jacket and the strap of his holster with gun. The weapon was oddly reassuring, a symbol not of violence but of an old-fashioned male protecting what – and who – he loved.

With the pressure off, I relaxed.

Sushi was shamelessly crawling all over Rocky, who'd sprawled by the fire, giving himself over to this friendly assault; he'd long since learned early to play dead while she had her way with him.

'Care to help me in the kitchen?' Tony asked.

'Sure. What are we having?' It had to be Italian, of course, my favorite kind of cuisine. And his last name was Cassato, after all.

'Bolognese. The way my grandmother made it.'

Grandmothers again.

Tony had set out the ingredients on the counter, and there were a lot of them. We were apparently going to spend some time in the kitchen due to the complexity of the recipe. A fortunate happenstance, or an ingenious strategy?

Either way, it worked. We fell back into a comfortable

rhythm, all the way through the preparation of a delicious meal with wine, coffee and *Brunkager*, and washing the dishes with me on drying duty.

It wasn't until we retired to the couch that I became apprehensive again. Tony must have been feeling the same way . . .

An exhausted Sushi slept next to Rocky in front of the dwindling fire. Outside, the starry night had been usurped by big falling flakes, indicating how fast the atmosphere could change.

My purse was on the floor, and I took out the small box wrapped in silver paper, which contained an assortment of fishermen's flies I'd ordered online.

Not knowing the difference between any of them, I had picked ones that sounded like drinks (pink squirrel, zonker, and tequeely), rather than others with more overt connotations (nymph, humpy, and threesome).

I said, 'Those are for your Canadian trip.'

Tony took a yearly summer excursion to the Haliburton Highlands for trout fishing.

'They'll be perfect,' he said, admiring them. 'Thank you, Brandy.'

He leaned forward, reached under the couch, and produced a box even smaller than mine.

And I knew exactly what it was.

The engagement ring I'd returned to him.

There was something vulnerable, yet endearing, about the way Tony had hidden it until – what? – I had given *him* something? Or that he felt confident enough that the first evening we'd spent together since the rupture had gone well enough to take the risk?

I removed the wrapping and opened the little satin case.

'It is a beautiful ring,' I said.

Tony took it from my hands, shut the box, and placed it on the end table.

'It's here, if and when you want it,' he said. 'If you do.'

'Thank you.'

The door was open, all I had to do was walk through it.

He put one arm around my shoulders, and I laid my head

against his chest. Moments later I fell asleep, and even later waking myself up with a snort.

'Sorry,' I muttered. 'Took some sleeping pills last night and they're still having an impact.'

'I was conked, too.'

'What time is it, anyway?' The fire had dwindled into glowing ashes.

'A little after midnight.'

That late?

I moved away. Raised fists to my shoulders and yawned. Blinked. 'I should go. Roger will be bringing Jake in the morning.'

Tony got to his feet, extending me a hand. 'Say hello to your son for me.'

'I will. I hope you'll be able to spend some time with him while he's here.'

'I will do my best.'

The conversation had turned stilted.

I stooped and picked up a snoozing Sushi. She was a snorer, too, and so loose in my grasp, she might not have had a single bone in that fuzzy body.

At the door, Tony helped me into my coat.

'Thank you for a lovely dinner,' I said.

Seriously? That's all I could come up with?

'You're welcome. Be careful driving home, the road could be slick.'

That's what *he* came up with?

I went out to the van.

Roger wasn't supposed to arrive with Jake until noon, but his black Mercedes pulled into the drive a little after ten.

I was on the couch having a second cup of coffee, still in my pjs, robe and slippers, hair tangled, eyes raccooned from mascara I hadn't washed off.

But that didn't matter. My son was here! And not just for a weekend, or short school break.

I watched from the foyer as Roger and Jake unloaded suitcases and duffel bags from the trunk. And, since there was too much for them to carry, I threw on a coat and went out into the cold to help.

Although it hadn't been that long since I'd seen Jake, he seemed older, taller. His face, which had once mirrored only mine, now bore hints of his father.

Roger looked the same, but tired.

Jake gave me the fish-eye. 'Rough night?'

'I'll say.' I joked, 'The fleet was in.'

He laughed.

Roger didn't think that was funny, but then, he never did have much of a sense of humor.

Mother, alerted by Sushi's barking, had come to the door, holding it open while we struggled to bring everything inside in one trip.

Sushi was excited to see Jake – Roger not so much, just putting up with his presence – and flung herself at the boy until he dropped his bags and picked her up.

Mother took charge. 'Leave everything for now. I want my grandson to see his room so we can discuss changes to be made.' She waved a dismissive hand. 'Brandy, take the boy's jacket.'

Which I did, adding it to the pile of luggage.

Then Mother, with an arm around Jake's waist, walked him up the stairs, as if they were ascending into heaven.

'My dear boy,' she said, 'we're going to have *such* adventures together.'

Holmes had a new Watson, Wolfe another Archie. But I wasn't worried. Jake was smarter than his mother, and knew better how to handle his grandmother. And while he had become tangentially involved in a few of her cases, it was mostly through cyberspace.

I turned to see Roger's reaction, but luckily he hadn't clocked Mother's comment. Still in his coat, he was heading to the library.

I followed.

Roger went straight to the stand-up piano, and pulled out Mother's blackboard.

I held my breath.

But she had wiped it clean – both sides (he checked).

Roger couldn't have heard about last night, yet. If so, he likely wouldn't have brought Jake. I needed to steer the conversation away from the topic hanging over everything.

'You look tired,' I said.

'I haven't been sleeping well,' he replied.

'Well, your business is very stressful.'

'It's not that,' he said.

'Your health?' I asked, concerned.

'No.' A sigh. A swallow. 'My marriage.'

Oh, dear.

'Brandy, can I . . . talk to you?'

I let out a wry laugh. 'You're coming to *me* for marital advice?'

He laughed himself. 'Yeah, funny, huh?'

I put Supergirl hands on my hips. 'Well, I *am* a good listener.'

I sat on the piano bench and patted the space next to me.

'How bad is it?' I asked.

'Bad enough. We're talking about separating. Neither Laura nor I are involved with anyone else. It's just . . . we seem to argue about *everything* these days.'

I let him unload. Roger's main complaint was nothing any other married (or not) couple with stressful, demanding jobs went through continually: not enough time for each other.

When he was finished, I said, 'Don't do anything for a while. Nothing rash. See if removing Jake from the equation will ease the tension. Laura is good for you, and you her. Fight for what you have, or lose it if you don't.'

He nodded.

We stood, and walked together to the front door, where he turned to me. 'Take good care of Jake.'

'You know I will.'

His smile was warm, the warmest he'd given me in a long time; but in a brotherly way. 'Thanks for the advice.'

I watched from the doorway until his car drove away.

What is it about someone who gives advice, then refuses to take it herself?

I found my phone and texted Tony: 'Forgot my ring.'

He texted right back: 'I'm home. Come and get it.'

Brandy's Trash 'n' Treasures Tip

After-Christmas sales are a good time to add to holiday collections – or begin new ones – taking advantage of discounted prices. But be selective. How many ceramic Santa gnomes does anyone need?

BARBARA ALLAN

Is a joint pseudonym of wife-and-husband mystery writers, Barbara and Max Allan Collins.

BARBARA COLLINS made her entrance into the mystery field as a highly respected short story writer with appearances in over a dozen top anthologies, including *Murder Most Delicious*, *Women on the Edge*, *Deadly Housewives* and the best-selling *Cat Crimes* series. She was the co-editor of (and a contributor to) the bestselling anthology *Lethal Ladies*, and her stories were selected for inclusion in the first three volumes of *The Year's 25 Finest Crime and Mystery Stories*.

Three acclaimed collections of her work have been published – *Too Many Tomcats* and (with her husband) *Murder – His and Hers* and *Suspense – His and Hers*. The couple's first novel together, the Baby Boomer thriller *Regeneration*, was a paperback bestseller; their second collaborative novel, *Bombshell* – in which Marilyn Monroe saves the world from World War III – was published in hardcover to excellent reviews. Recently they collaborated on the short suspense novel, *Cutout*.

Barbara also has been the production manager and/or line producer of several independent film projects.

MAX ALLAN COLLINS was named a Grand Master by the Mystery Writers of America in 2017. He has earned an unprecedented twenty-three Private Eye Writers of America 'Shamus' nominations, many for his Nathan Heller historical thrillers, winning for *True Detective* (1983), *Stolen Away* (1991), and the short story, 'So Long, Chief.'

His classic graphic novel *Road to Perdition* (with illustrator Richard Piers Rayner) is the basis of the Academy Award-winning film. Max's other comics credits include 'Dick Tracy';

'Batman'; and (with artist Terry Beatty) his own 'Ms Tree' and 'Wild Dog,' featured on the *Arrow* TV series.

Max's body of work includes film criticism, short fiction, songwriting, trading-card sets, and movie/TV tie-in novels, such as the *New York Times* bestseller *Saving Private Ryan*, numerous *USA Today* bestselling CSI novels, and the Scribe Award-winning *American Gangster*. His non-fiction includes *Scarface and the Untouchable: Al Capone*, and *Eliot Ness & the Mad Butcher* (both with A. Brad Schwartz).

An award-winning filmmaker, he wrote and directed the Lifetime movie *Mommy* (1996) and five other films, including the current *Blue Christmas*; his produced screenplays include the 1995 HBO World Premiere *The Expert* and *The Last Lullaby* (2008). His 1998 documentary *Mike Hammer's Mickey Spillane* recently appeared in an expanded, updated edition on Blu-ray and streaming services. The Cinemax TV series *Quarry* is based on his innovative book series.

Max has completed a dozen-plus works begun by his legendary mentor, Mickey Spillane, among them *Dig Two Graves* with Mike Hammer, and the Caleb York western novels.

'BARBARA ALLAN' live(s) in Muscatine, Iowa, their Serenity-esque hometown. Son Nathan works as a translator of Japanese to English, with credits that include video games, manga, and novels. Barb and Max have two grandchildren, Sam and Lucy, nine and five respectively.